BOG HAMMER

Larry Jeram-Croft

Copyright © 2014 Larry Jeram-Croft

All rights reserved.

Cover image: Lieutenant Bond; @ Crown Copyright 1991

Also by Larry Jeram-Croft:

Fiction:

The 'Jon Hunt' series about the modern Royal Navy:

Sea Skimmer
The Caspian Monster
Cocaine
Arapaho
Bog Hammer
Glasnost
Retribution
Formidable
Conspiracy
Swan Song

The 'John Hunt' books about the Royal Navy's Fleet Air Arm in the Second World War:

Better Lucky and Good
and the Pilot can't swim
Get bloody stuck in

The Winchester Chronicles:

Book one: The St Cross Mirror

The Caribbean: historical fiction and the 'Jacaranda' Trilogy.

Diamant

Jacaranda

The Guadeloupe Guillotine
Nautilus

Science Fiction:

Siren

Non Fiction:

The Royal Navy Lynx an Operational History
The Royal Navy Wasp an Operational and Retirement History
The Accidental Aviator

Chapter 1

Commander Jonathon Hunt, DSO and Bar, the Royal Navy's newest promoted Commander and veteran of several major military operations, stood at the bottom of the white marble steps of the Ministry of Defence Main Building in London, feeling lost. Awkwardly dressed in a new dark suit and carrying a briefcase, he felt like a fish out of water as he gazed up at the imposing doors at the top of the steps. Up until now, his service career had consisted of a protracted period of training, both to be a seaman officer and then a pilot, followed by an almost continual series of deployments to various ships and squadrons. The roar of London traffic was continuous. The day was grey. It was cold, sleeting and threatening to snow. Everything was in total contrast to what he knew.

It seemed like only yesterday that he was in command of his squadron and newly married to the wonderful Helen. His squadron's foray into the Mediterranean had culminated in the relief of the hijack of the Cruise ship Uganda and the aftermath had been chaotic to say the least. Then he and Helen had tied the knot. He couldn't have been happier. At the start, their return to the squadron had been a bit awkward for him. The powers that be had decided that Helen could stay on as his Staff Officer. There were several precedents. He soon realised that no one else had a problem with the relationship.

In retrospect, those few months had been the happiest he could remember. Helen moved into his little cottage in the local village and immediately started to tidy it up. He didn't mind. In retaliation, he introduced her to all the locals in the village pub and the delights of the local beer and their habit of locking everyone in on a Saturday night. She loved it.

Then everything changed. The first tumultuous event started with a phone call. Jon was sitting in his office in the squadron. It was from Admiral James Arthur. The Admiral had been in overall command the previous year in the Mediterranean as Commodore Amphibious Warfare and was now freshly promoted to Rear Admiral.

'Jon, this is Admiral Arthur, I wanted to be the first to let you know and congratulate you. You've been selected for promotion to

Commander. Very well done, first shot as well and I believe it's thoroughly deserved.'

Jon was completely speechless. The last thing he had been thinking about was promotion. Up until now, his promotions were based on time served but as a Lieutenant Commander, he moved into a selection zone after three years of service. Any further movement up the rank ladder was based purely on merit. The promotion zone lasted for five years, with selections every six months. To be selected at the 'first shot' was unusual and something of a compliment to say the least. It had never remotely crossed his mind that he would be a recipient.

'Jon, are you there?' The Admiral's voice sounded amused.

'Sorry Sir, you caught me more than a little by surprise there. Thank you for calling it's all a little overwhelming.'

'I'm sure it is but don't let me keep you, enjoy the day. We'll talk more later no doubt.' The line went dead and Jon put the phone down and sat back in his chair feeling numb and completely unsure about how he felt. His thoughts were interrupted by a loud cheer from outside. The door flew open and his old friend and Senior Observer, Brian Pearce along with Helen and what looked like the rest of the squadron attempted to crowd into the small office at the same time. There was the pop of a champagne cork from somewhere and a glass was thrust into his hand.

'Hang on a second, you bloody shower. How the hell did you all know about this before me? I've only just put the phone down.'

Helen answered. 'A little bird told us darling and just gave us enough time to get a few bottles ready. Oh well done.' And she gave him an enormous hug to everyone else's cheers.

That night as he lay in bed with Helen the whole thing started to sink in. Not only that but all the ramifications of what it really meant.

He rolled over and looked at Helen. 'Do you think I could turn it down?'

'What? Your promotion? Don't be silly Jon. Of course not and why on earth would you want to do that anyway?'

'Because there are no flying jobs for Commanders in the navy. Now, if I was in the RAF, their squadrons are commanded by Wing Commanders but we do things differently in the dark blue.'

Bog Hammer

'Ah, I see your problem. What do you think they have in store then?'

'I'm not sure but it will either be a staff course or behind a bloody desk somewhere or even worse, both. I'll talk to the appointer tomorrow but I've got six months before I actually get to wear my brass hat, so I will just have to enjoy them while I can.'

Helen turned and gave Jon a hug. 'Life moves on you know darling, think of all the other things you could do.'

'Like what?'

'Well if you've been promoted so early, surely they'll give you a ship to command at some time?'

'Hmmph, maybe, I hadn't really thought that far ahead. Not sure how good I would be at driving such a large lump of iron. I'd rather be blatting around in a Lynx.'

Helen knew Jon well enough by now to realise that the idea of a ship command had caught his imagination. She remembered a long ago conversation, when Brian had told her that Jon was the most un-ambitious person he knew. She realised that Brian was right. Jon lived for the moment. He gave every part of him to do the best he could but never, ever, had his eye on the main chance. She realised that the promotion had really come right out of the blue. Silly ass, it was one of the reasons she loved him so much.

She sighed and stroked his hair. She had some news of her own and it had to be discussed some time. 'Jon, while we're on the subject of good news. Now that they are allowing WRNS to transfer to the navy as regular officers, I heard from my appointer today but didn't want to ruin your surprise.'

Jon leant up on one elbow and looked at Helen enquiringly. 'About time too, I forwarded your application weeks ago.'

'Yes, well, I've been accepted. I go to Dartmouth in April. They're letting me keep my rank because of my degree and past service so I join as a Lieutenant.'

'That's fantastic. It'll be bloody hard work though, you realise that?'

'Of course but there's one more thing, I was a bit naughty last month. When I told you I had to go up to London, it wasn't to meet with my appointer. I actually went to Biggin Hill. I didn't want you to know in case I failed.'

'Go on,' Jon replied with a dawning realisation of what was about to come.

'I did my aircrew assessment board and passed.'

Jon said nothing.

'So I need your permission to take two weeks off in February to go to Roborough to do my flying grading assessment and if I pass that then I join Fifty Six Flight at Dartmouth.'

Jon groaned and rolled over on to his back. 'So, just as they kick me upstairs, you get to learn to fly. Jesus Helen, we'll never get to see one another. Why the hell did we get married?'

'Oh Jon, we'll still have weekends, it's not as if you're getting a sea appointment when we won't get to see each other for months on end. You know how much this means to me. Ever since the training officer took me flying in a Sea King last year, I've wanted to do this, you know that.'

'Helen I can't possibly complain, you're only doing exactly what I've done and given half a chance I'd do it all over again. But remember, it's a long and very difficult course. Not that many make it. I would hate to see you disappointed. You're going to be the first woman to attempt it and I suspect that many will be waiting for you to fail.'

'Just let them try.' There was a note of steely determination in her voice.

Jon looked down at his beautiful wife. 'You know, for a girl, you've got a pretty tough streak.'

'Only when I need to use it,' she replied with an impish grin. 'I can be all girl as well when I want to be.' She put her arm around his neck and pulled him down stopping any further conversation.

But that was months ago and here he was now about to start a new chapter in his career. It was only two weeks past that he had signed for his last flight as captain of a naval aircraft. His handover to his successor had gone by in a blur and suddenly he was no longer in command of anything. With an emotion that was half way between trepidation and anticipation he marched up the steps towards the massive open doors.

Chapter 2

'Lieutenant Helen Hunt OBE, Royal Navy, Bloody, Well, Stand, Still,' The parade ground Chief Petty Officer almost screamed into her face from a few inches away. Then he took a pace backwards. 'And the rest of you bloody shambles are no better. So let's start again. We stay here until you prove to me you know your bloody left from your bloody right.'

If she wasn't so tired and cold Helen might have smiled at the Chief but she knew that would have definitely not been a good idea. It was almost as if he had turned himself into a caricature of the archetypal parade ground sergeant you so often saw in the films. The problem here was that it was for real and if you gave him the slightest cheek, off you would go, running around the ramps that surrounded the parade ground at the front of the Britannia Royal Naval College until he told you to stop. It didn't matter that in this intake of new officers, there was probably a future Admiral and that everyone in her squad already outranked the man significantly. Here, he was the king and he knew it. Jon had warned her about Dartmouth but hearing about it and experiencing it were two different things. The day started at five thirty which was just enough time to get dressed for Early Morning Activities or EMAs for short. The first hour of the day was spent either in the Gym or on the parade ground, as it was this morning. A quick breakfast then preceded a morning split between classroom lectures or more parade ground fun. The afternoon was more of the same except that at least two hours were spent on the Dart River driving the various boats that belonged to the college or playing sport. Helen soon discovered a love of sailing and spent as much time as she could in the various dinghies and small yachts that were provided for them. The day didn't end until nine in the evening and then their cabins were inspected during evening rounds, to ensure that every sock was folded correctly, that every welt in their boots and shoes was spotless. By ten o'clock sleep was a mercy.

Helen was one of only three girls at the college and right from the start it had been made quite clear to them that they would be expected to meet the same standards as the men. Initially, there had been four of them but one girl had only lasted two weeks before the stress told and she disappeared. Helen was made of sterner stuff and the more pressure they put on her, the more she dug her toes in. To be fair there didn't seem to be any bias towards the girls but she knew damn well that there were plenty of people waiting to see her fail. She and the other two girls were the vanguard of a major change to the navy, a change that many didn't want. She snapped back to reality just as they were dismissed by the parade ground monster and were able to double march back into the college for a half hour of sanity and breakfast.

She realised that she was actually lucky. In order to be allowed to join as a potential pilot, she had signed up for a short service commission. This meant that she only spent three months here at the college before moving on to dedicated flying training. Her two compatriots were General List officers and would spend a whole year here. She didn't envy them at all.

The three months passed in a blur. On more than one occasion she felt like throwing in the towel. Then she remembered what this was all about that if she got through it one day she might be allowed to fly and the thought spurred her on. She knew Jon would understand if she folded but she would never be able to look him in the eye in the same way, which was another reason to succeed. She may have done well during her flying grading assessment at the little airfield in Plymouth flying the elderly Chipmunk aircraft but this was the first serious hurdle to overcome. The one thing that helped her beyond measure was her previous experience. Nearly all the rest of her class knew nothing about the real navy. Her service for almost two years in a naval squadron as well as having time at sea, albeit on an RFA, had stood her in good stead. She had been surprised that there didn't seem to be any resentment towards her for it and she did her best to say as little as she could. However, at the start of training, all of them were required to stand in front of their divisional officers and class members and introduce themselves. She had tried to minimise her past exploits but the questioning had been tough and in the end, she had told them all about her part in the Uganda hijack. She had even told them of her night locked up with the homicidal maniac, Karim. The last thing she wanted was to be looked on as someone who boasted about her exploits but she had no choice. The stunned silence that met her when she finished seemed to confirm her worries, right up until when everyone started to clap. The problem then was hiding her embarrassment.

That's not to say that she got on with everyone. She was by far the oldest on her course and also the most senior, so she was made course leader. Although none of the others came out and said anything overtly she could tell that several of the men resented her presence. That didn't stop a couple of them making passes at her at the same time. In this, she was in familiar territory and she fended them off with ease. Being married to a Commander did no harm either.

There was a lighter side as well. Towards the end of the term, they had a mess dinner. For most of the young midshipmen this was their first taste of formal wardroom life. However, like all things at the college, there was a lesson to be learnt. Helen took one look at the bar before the meal and realised what was going on. She did her best to warn her classmates but young lads who had been largely deprived of alcohol for weeks on end were in no mood to listen. She had to smile to herself when the after dinner speeches seemed to go on forever. It was a strict naval rule that no one excused themselves from the table until after the loyal toast and the Mess President had given permission, the usual fine being the cost of a round of port for everyone and at such a big dinner that would have cost a fortune. The pained look on the faces of those who had imbibed several pints of beer before the meal was a clear indication that the lesson had been learnt.

There were two occasions when the system almost got the better of her. For obvious reasons, she shared her cabin with the other two girls. One evening towards the end of their course, when things were meant to be a little more relaxed, the Duty Sub Lieutenant, a tall thin blonde lad called Hutchings, for some reason decided to blitz their cabin during evening rounds. He found fault with everything and ordered a rescrub in half an hour. Helen had had enough and flatly refused to do anything. It wasn't just the girls either, he had been as anal with the men's cabins as well and everyone felt the same. When the little Hitler returned to find what was effectively a mutiny on his hands he stormed off without another word. The next day they were all summoned to the Divisional meeting room and given the biggest bollocking they had ever received, from their Senior Divisional officer. However, no punishments were handed out. Helen scored that as a minor victory for the oppressed.

The final hurdle was the dreaded PLX. This stood for Practical Leadership Exercise and took place over several days on Dartmoor. The aim was to split the division into small teams of four and give each trainee twelve hours in charge. An officer would oversee them and assess their leadership skills. That was the overt reason. Everyone also knew it was designed to see how the trainees coped under stress.

Helen was teamed up with three of the men from her class and they all spent the first night sheltering in the lee of a stone wall, somewhere on a piece of the moor in a wet and very foggy night. They only had basic rations and no shelter, other than what they could contrive themselves. The next morning they were cold, wet and hungry when the supervising officer arrived. Helen groaned inwardly. It was the same Sub Lieutenant Hutchings who had given them a hard time the previous week. He handed one of the men a piece of paper. They had a five mile walk to a river. The task there was to get over it without getting wet. As it was fairly wide and swollen as the result of recent rain, there was fat chance of that. Having finally managed a crossing, the team leader was changed and off they went over the moor again to be confronted by a lake. On the shore were some oil barrels, rope and spars of wood. As expected, they had to make a raft and cross to the opposite shore. Two hours later they made it and set off again into a gathering mist. Navigation started to get difficult but after several more hours, they found their site which they would be staying in for the night. Some poles and sheets of canvas at least held out the prospect of better shelter than the previous night.

Hutchings, who had been remarkably quiet for most of the day, then spoke up in an annoyingly smug tone. 'Make yourselves comfy boys and girls. I'll be back in the morning for day two. Looks like everything's wet but feel free to try to start a fire if you can.' So saying, he headed off downhill into the fog that was now quite thick.

'Hope the silly bugger knows where he's going,' Jerry, the current team leader muttered to them all as his silhouette disappeared in the grey. 'I would really hate to think of him getting lost in this weather.'

His remark brought out several chuckles as they all set to making the best shelter they could. In one thing Hutchings had been right. All the wood they gathered was soaking and in the end, they had to give up on the idea of a roaring fire. However, their little hexamine stoves were good enough to heat an evening meal and huddling together for warmth seemed to be reasonably effective. But it was a long night and by the morning, despite their efforts, they were all starting to really feel the cold. They used almost the last of their fuel to make hot drinks and breakfast which warmed them a little and waited for their mentor. The fog was now extremely thick. No one came.

'Jesus, it's meant to be July,' Jerry muttered looking out of their little makeshift tent. 'I can barely see two yards and the bloody wind is getting up. Anyone got the time?'

Helen looked at her watch. 'It's gone nine. Surely someone should have arrived by now? They've got all the maps and the day's tasks.'

They all agreed that the weather was responsible for them not being found but no one could agree what to do about it.

After another hour of inaction, Jerry summed the situation up. 'Look guys, we seem to have two options. We can stay here and wait but who knows how long this weather will last or we can try and walk out. Any other ideas?'

Everyone agreed that the exercise was over. Even if someone turned up now, it would be too late to finish it. They needed to be back at the college by tomorrow at the latest for the final course exams.

Helen was strongly against moving. 'Look, if we leave here, we have no way knowing which is the right way to go and if they do come looking for us then they won't find us. We've a little food left and reasonable shelter.'

'All good points Helen but I've a good idea where we are and who knows how long this weather will last? We could be stuck here for days. It may be July but we were all bloody cold last night, especially as we can't light a fire. I really don't fancy another night out in this, do you? Come on let's have a show of hands.'

Helen found herself outvoted and reluctantly agreed to go with the others to attempt to find civilisation. Jerry suggested that heading downhill would be logical, the moor had to end somewhere and maybe they could find a stream and follow it out. Without either a map or compass it was about all they could do. At Helen's insistence, they folded up their meagre tent and poles and shared them out to carry along with the packs they already had. At first, all went well. The visibility was so bad that they had to use one of their ropes to hold on to, so that they didn't lose touch with each other. They walked for what seemed like hours, slowly getting colder and wetter. There was no sign of the sun, so they didn't even know which direction they were headed. At least by following the slope they should avoid going round in circles. Eventually, they found a brook and with a lightening of the mood started to follow it down. Their relief turned to despair when it ran into the ground in a large crack in the rocks and they realised they were in a blind valley with no idea of which direction to take out.

Suddenly the day got even worse. Mike, the youngest of the group had climbed up on one of the rocks to see if it would give him a better view. The granite was rain slick and as he came down, he slipped and with a yell of agony, he caught his leg in a crack in the rock. They all heard the sound as his leg snapped followed by his anguished cry.

Helen got to him first. 'I'm first aid trained, anyone else here done the course?'

No one had, so it fell to her to do what she could. Mike's lower leg was at an unnatural angle and she could see the bone pushing against the skin, which luckily was un-punctured. With the help of the others, they did their best to make him comfortable but he was clearly in agony even though she managed to immobilise the leg with a jury rigged splint.

Jerry was looking very worried. 'I think I should go on and try to get help.'

Helen knew their original decision to move had been wrong and wasn't going to compound it now.

'Right everyone, I'm pulling rank, I'm the only Lieutenant here, so I take responsibility for what happens. No one goes anywhere. What we do is get as much shelter set up as we can and then try to make some form of signal fire so that as soon as the fog lifts we can be found.' She could see that Jerry was about to disagree. She looked him hard in the eye. 'Jerry I may be female but I outrank you so don't even think of arguing.'

He subsided with a rueful grin. 'Whatever you say Maam.'

Two hours later the search party found them. The fog had been lifted by the wind and Helen had got one of their hexamine stoves with their last block of fuel, under a pile of wet leaves and grass. As soon as she judged the weather good enough, it was lit. The smoke was dense and did its job.

Mike was stretchered out ahead of them and they were surprised to see how close a road was. The sight of the RN minibus was a vast relief.

Their Divisional Officer who was with the search team told them that they were the last party to be found, all the others had managed to reach civilisation on their own.

'Why didn't you use your maps and compass?' he asked in a puzzled tone. 'There should have been plenty in your emergency pack.'

'What emergency pack Sir?' Helen responded warily.

'The one your supervising officer left with you.'

The three of them exchanged glances. For a second Helen wondered whether they had made a really stupid error but her comrade's faces confirmed her own thoughts.

'Sub Lieutenant Hutchings never gave us one Sir.'

The Divisional Officer said nothing for a few moments. 'Leave that with me but well done all of you, that can't have been a pleasant experience.'

Ten days later Jon stood proudly on the ramps around the parade ground, in his best uniform, as his wife marched her class smartly in front of the Admiral. Behind him was the massive stone facade of the college and before him the parade ground and then the hill dropping away to the river and the town itself. Was it really so long ago that he was down there, with his highly polished boots, whitened webbing and borrowed sword? It all felt a little surreal. His wife had successfully passed out of the Britannia Royal Naval College, the first female naval officer to do so.

When the ceremony was over he was amused to see her automatic reaction to salute, fight with her desire give him a hug. The hug won out.

'Well done darling,' he said into her ear. 'Did you enjoy it?'

'You know damn well how hard it was but yes, in a funny way, it was alright. Now I get to play with the aeroplanes,' she said with an impish grin.

'Hmm don't forget the trip to Seafield Park first. If you thought your little jaunt on Dartmoor was hard, the aircrew survival course will be something else altogether.'

Chapter 3

Time in the Ministry of Defence seemed to drag one minute and then proceed at breakneck speed the next. Jon got back to the office from Helen's passing out parade the next Monday morning courtesy of the Yeovil to Waterloo train. He was already getting good at falling asleep in it for the duration. A brisk walk along the south bank and over Westminster Bridge would have him awake enough to greet the day. He shared his office with three other Commanders and an inner office housed their boss, Captain Brian Desmonde. He still remembered his first day here. The first hurdle to overcome was simply getting into the building. A front desk rather like that of a large bank housed security staff who dealt with visitors and new joiners. He gave his name and after a little searching it was found on the requisite list. A telephone call then confirmed his veracity and he was issued with a temporary pass. He then had to use the swipe card on one of the glass airlock type entry doors. The first door hissed open and then shut behind him before the inner one opened and he was in the hallowed halls.

'Jonathon Hunt?' a portly individual asked as he exited the door system.

Jon nodded.

'Hello old chap, I'm Pete Scott the Admirals secretary. I'm a Commander too. One of the problems around here, you never know what rank the bloke you are talking to might be. So first lesson, be careful until you know. Anyway off we go, the Admiral has asked to see you as soon as you arrive.'

Jon was led up an escalator and then along various corridors and then a lift until he was thoroughly lost. All the time his guide kept up an amiable chatter, which Jon only half listened to. He guessed they were approaching the sanctum of the great and the good when carpet appeared and the decoration became less Spartan.

'Here we are then, the lair of the beast.' He was ushered through an imposing oak door into what was clearly the Admiral's outer office. 'Just hang on there a second and I'll check that the Boss is free.'

Within a few minutes, Jon was sitting in a large leather armchair opposite Admiral Arthur who was also dressed in a standard MOD business suit. His tall frame suited the clothing and it seemed to Jon that this was a man far more comfortable in his environment than when they had last met at sea.

'Coffee Jon?' The Admiral asked and before getting a reply he poured two cups from the jug already laid out on the table. 'So well done on the bar to your DSO and a wedding also I hear?'

'Thank you Sir, I feel pretty lucky I have to say and congratulations on your promotion as well.'

The Admiral smiled. 'Yes, we all came out of that little fracas intact, thank goodness. It could have gone so badly wrong. The fact that it didn't is down to you and that brave wife of yours. I hear she's at Dartmouth now? So when we meet next she won't be able to ignore my orders by claiming she isn't a real naval officer.' His words were softened by the amused tone and grin on his face.

'Yes Sir, but I have singularly failed to get her to call me Sir.'

They both laughed before the Admiral continued. 'Now look Jon, this is your first time in the MOD and away from the toys. No, don't get me wrong the front line is what the navy is all about but there is a lot more to it than flying helicopters and sailing ships. You've proved that you know how to fight but you have to understand that there is another, just as important element to what we have to do. Here in the MOD we don't face the bad guys out in the real world. Here we face the bad guys in the government and the other two services. I'm not being flippant when I say this. No government wants to spend money on defence when it doesn't have to. They would much rather spend it on schools or hospitals. Or maybe a bit more cynically on things that will get them re-elected. No government has a field of view beyond about five years. Meanwhile, we have to cope with terrorists in Northern Ireland and their bombs in London, five in the last year by the way. The Soviet Union is looking very unstable these days. Iran and Iraq have fought themselves into the mire. We only got the Falklands back by the skin of our teeth, as you know better than most. Who knows what will happen next? It's our job to do the best we can to convince the politicians to give us what we need to cope with all these things. Not only that but the other two services are competing with us for the same resources and the in-fighting can get quite bloody on occasions.'

'Like when the RAF moved Australia five hundred miles to increase their air cover and convince Dennis Healey that we didn't need our nuclear carrier?'

'That's apocryphal but yes that's the sort of thing. It really needs to stop. It makes us all look silly from the outside and is very inefficient. It's one of my aims to promote more joint service thinking but it's going to be an uphill struggle. Look, I'm not saying all this to try and teach you your job, that will be up to your boss, Captain Desmonde. I want you to realise that you will need to learn, not only a new set of skills but also a new mind-set. Our weapons here are all on paper. The wars we fight don't have clear outcomes, certainly not in the short term. It's a very different form of warfare but that's what it is. And you will need to master it all if you want to prosper. The navy needs people with all the skills. You need to be able to fight a ship and a desk with equal daring.'

They talked for a little more and then Jon was escorted away with his ears ringing, to meet his new immediate boss. As they walked more confusing corridors he reflected on the Admiral's words. He had never really liked the man and hadn't been impressed with his attitude when he commanded in the Mediterranean as Commodore Amphibious Warfare. However, he seemed totally in his element here and his words made a lot of sense. It was almost like joining a new navy and this was his first day. The difference here was that there would be no training courses, no lectures, it was sink or swim.

The Admiral' secretary took him to another office. There were people sitting at several desks inside, all with curious faces as they walked past and then he was in an inner office and another suited man rose to greet him. Captain Brian Desmonde was an aviator of the old school. Fixed wing jets such as Sea Vixens and Phantoms were his pedigree and he was well known throughout the Fleet Air Arm. Jon had served with him before when he had been Commander Air at the air station at Portland some years previously. A small active man with a neat beard, now turning grey, he rose at Jon's entrance and advanced smiling and extending his hand. He exuded energy and his handshake was dry and firm.

'Jon, nice to see you again, welcome to the madhouse. Has the Admiral been giving you all that guff about being at war?'

Jon smiled ruefully. 'Yes Sir but he seems to have a point.'

'Hmm, maybe but we have a simple job to do here. You are now in the wonderful Directorate of Operational Requirements DOR(Sea) and part of the aviation team. You will be looking after small ship's aviation and what we will need in the future so that our friends in the Procurement Executive go out and buy it for us. Well that's the theory at least. In fact, as I'm sure you know we are about to upgrade all the Lynx fleet to Mark Eight standard and that will be your prime concern for the moment. But I'll let your predecessor hand that over to you. Now, you're recently married I hear?'

'Yes Sir but she's at Dartmouth doing basic training so we don't see too much of each other at the moment.'

'Bloody hell Jon, I must have missed that one you sure do pick them. Last I remember you had a rather cute Norwegian girl in tow. Anyway, let's talk about the important stuff. I don't expect to see you at your desk before ten thirty on Monday and after two thirty on Friday. We both live near Yeovil so will no doubt be sharing the same train quite often. To make up, it is accepted that we work late. However, if your work is up to date I don't expect you to sit around. I am not impressed by people who work ridiculous hours. To me, it either means you're bloody inefficient or you've got too much work to do in which case you should be telling me so. I'm afraid there is a culture here that the more junior you are the earlier you get in and the later you leave. Not in my department there isn't. And you may be well impressed with your new shiny rank but Commanders are ten a penny around here, so I'm sorry but you're back at the bottom of the food chain again. Oh and if you want to arrange meetings at Westlands in Yeovil on a Monday or Friday feel free. We also have a social life here. Once a month, all the Fleet Air Arm officers in London have a run ashore somewhere disreputable. There are plenty of other reasons for a party on top of that. The Sherlock Holmes pub just up the road is our local. We get cheap theatre tickets and other deals, so make the most of being in the capital. Have you got accommodation?'

'Yes Sir, I've arranged to take over my predecessors digs near Regents Park.'

'Good and if you intend to cycle into work you need to be bloody careful. I do and I've already had a couple of near misses with taxis. Right, that's enough from me, off you go and enjoy the handover. We'll talk at the end of the week.'

Jon walked out with his head reeling and the rest of the week was no better, it passed in a blur.

Now several months later he was just beginning to know just how steep the learning curve he was on really was. Life was completely different. He shared his digs with Pete Crowe an old friend from his Sea King days who now had the Commando Helicopter desk. His other comrades in arms were Mike Clark and Dennis Osmond who looked after anti-submarine and fixed wing aviation respectively. They were a friendly crew and the atmosphere in the office was excellent. 'Bouncy' Brian kept them all in line during the day and regularly led them astray in the evenings.

As he pushed the office door open, he saw he was the last to arrive.

'On your own Jon?' Mike asked. 'Didn't you see the Captain on the train?'

'Nope, he's doing something at the air station at Yeovilton today, should be back tomorrow morning.'

'Ah yes, I remember now. Well at least we won't get dragged off to the pub tonight. How was Dartmouth?'

'Spooky, it seems like it was only yesterday I was there and seeing Helen marching about was weird but she's done well. I'm taking a week's leave next week to tie up with hers before she goes off to Seafield Park.'

'Was there any fall out about them all getting lost on the moor?'

'Ah yes, I asked about that and it seems the dickhead Sub Lieutenant won't be making a career out of her Majesty's navy any more. It seems he was under scrutiny anyway.'

'Oh well thank goodness. It only gave them a scare and one broken leg.'

'You're right Mike but it looks like some bastard has filled up my in-tray and I was only away for a few days, so I'd better get stuck in.'

Chapter 4

'You've lived in Somerset for how long? And you've never come here before?' Helen sounded incredulous as she looked out over the stunning view from the top of Glastonbury Tor. Looking to the west she could see the Bristol Channel and the square buildings of the Hinckley Point nuclear power station. Sweeping around, most of Somerset was laid out in a panorama of fields, hills and woods.

Jon lay back in the grass and looked at the clear blue sky. 'I'm going to have to confess to never having been to the Cheddar caves or Wookey Hole and definitely not the Glastonbury festival either.'

'Married to the mob that's his problem.' Brian's voice chipped in.

'Hey, why did I need to visit all these places when I was flying over them nearly every day? However, I will admit that this is a rather fine place, especially as I know of an even finer pub down in the town that does excellent Sunday lunches.'

'As long as we don't end up stoned before we get there.' Kathy, Brian's wife, added. 'Did you smell the odour of burning straw as we walked up the high street?'

'Nope,' Jon replied. 'I was too busy wondering which mystical crystals or Tarot cards to buy from all the bloody shops or for that matter dodging all the people dressed in Kaftans.'

Everyone laughed. Then Kathy broke in. 'Brian I'm sure we had two daughters when we arrived, do be a dear and go and see if they've fallen over a cliff or something.'

Brian lumbered to his feet with a sigh. 'A father's duties are never done, see you in a moment.'

'So Jon, how's London?' Kathy asked.

'Everyone asks me that,' he replied. 'I suppose I should say it's wonderful, a challenge, an expansion of my naval career.'

'For some reason, I don't think that's what you are going to say though, is it?'

'No. Look, it's so different as to be almost a different career. I can see why it's necessary and why some people thrive on it. My problem is that my service career to date has taken a rather different path and not only am I not prepared for it, I'm not even sure that I like it. But don't worry, I have a cunning plan to sneak into Helen's training Flight and learn to fly all over again.'

'Oh no you're bloody well not,' Helen immediately replied. 'The last thing I need is you bossing me about and telling me what to do.'

'You mean like I do at the moment, Lieutenant Hunt?'

The remark earned Jon a gentle kick. 'Sorry Sir, anyway you'd have to take a demotion and I can't see you giving up that nice shiny brass hat any time soon.'

Jon pretended not to notice Helen's comment. 'Anyway, to continue from when I was so rudely interrupted. Then there's London itself. It's noisy and dirty, the first thing I do when I get home on a Friday is have a shower to get the grime off.'

A grunt from Helen accompanied that remark. 'You mean the second thing if I've managed to get home before you.'

'That's enough of that you raving nympho. Anyway, going back to London, the people never make eye contact. In fact you need to make sure you don't, otherwise they seem to take that as acceptance that you will get out of their way. So there you are amongst thousands of people and you might just as well be in the desert. The tube is dirty smelly and crowded and if you use a bicycle then your life expectancy is measured in weeks.'

There was a thump next to Jon as Brian sat down. 'They're over there darling, playing with some poor chump's Labradors and having a great time. Is the war hero whingeing about being stuck in the MOD?'

'Not whingeing Brian,' Jon got in first. 'Well, maybe a little. I suppose its culture shock as much as anything else, both the job and the lifestyle.'

Brian looked over at Kathy. 'Should I tell him do you think?'

'Bit late now love, you've already got his interest.'

Jon leant up on one elbow. 'Spit it out sunshine.'

'Er, well, I've got a new appointment. Kathy's not too delighted but at least it's not London.'

'Come on.'

'I'm going back to sea. I've got to do the Principle Warfare Officers course first but then I join my ship as the senior PWO and Operations Officer.'

'Oh well done. Hang on, the way you said that, there's something more isn't there. Come on what ship?'

'Prometheus, she'll be just out of major refit.'

'Bastard,' but it was said with admiration. 'Who's the skipper?'

'Some chap called Paul Fulford, a Commander. Have you heard of him?'

'Nope, but that's not surprising, do you want me to ask around.'

'No thanks Jon. I'll let it be a surprise.'

'Any idea of your programme?'

'It's quite a few months before she's even out of refit, so not really. We'll have to do a full work up. After that, I'm not sure.'

'Well the work up will be fun that's for sure. Best of luck Brian.'

'Thanks mate, now how about that lunch you were talking about.'

An hour later they were all sitting in the sunshine around a wooden table in the beer garden of the Glastonbury arms. Brian's two little girls were running around happily in the children's play area and the adults were all studying the menus.

Brian looked across the table. 'So Helen, what's the split of pilots and observers on your course?'

'Oh about fifty fifty, there's thirty two of us in total.'

Jon looked up from his menu. 'That means about eight pilots and ten observers will actually make it.'

Kathy was amazed. 'That's a hell of a lot of drop outs Jon.'

'It's a tough course and I'm only talking about getting to the bit where you get your wings. After that, there's Operational Flying Training to get through and some find that hard. Getting your wings means you can fly an aeroplane, passing OFT means you can fight it.'

Helen looked at Brian. 'Brian, I hope this isn't tactless but did you start out wanting to be an Observer? There's quite a lot of banter with our guys that all Observers are failed pilots.'

Brian looked pained. 'And quite a lot of truth in it as well. But no, I never wanted to be the dick with the stick. I joined Dartmouth to be a seaman officer but as you all know we have to specialise in one of the warfare disciplines. Doing that from inside an aircraft seemed much more fun than a dark Operations Room.'

Jon grinned. 'Well, you've got your comeuppance now old chum, because that's exactly where you're headed next.'

Brian smiled back. 'Good point but at least I'm not stuck in some dingy office in smelly London.'

'Touché you bastard, you wait, I'll escape somehow.'

The waiter arrived with their drinks and took their orders which diverted the conversation for a while.

That evening Jon and Helen were cuddled up in the living room watching the television.

'Jon, is this course really going to be that bad?'

He pulled his head back to look at her. 'You've easily survived Dartmouth, so will it be physically harder? Then the answer is no. However, being able to fly, is something you've either got or you haven't. The problem is that there is only so much time to teach the skills. If you can't hack something you will get at least one or two more goes at it but after that, it's the chop. There just isn't the time in the course to keep repeating things. You'll find some of your friends will be there one day and off the course the next. Frankly, it can be a bit brutal but there's no way round it. But look, you did well on your assessment and grading and the other year, my training officer said you had a natural skill. Half the trick is to believe in yourself.'

'Thank you Jon,' she kissed him on the cheek. 'And this survival course? I've heard some horror stories about that.'

He laughed. 'Helen its tough but absolutely nothing to what we've both been through for real, remember that. Oh and I have an idea how to make it a little more bearable. You're quite skinny enough as it is.'

'So it's true, you get very little food?'

'Well I'm sure it's changed somewhat from when I did it but in my time we got a whole Oxo cube on day three and a live rabbit on the second to last day.'

'And if it's changed, I don't suppose they will have made it any easier.'

'Hah, no, but I've had a word with a few chums and they are still using the same real estate down in the New Forest so maybe we can do some contingency planning.'

Chapter 5

Helen realised that Jon had been right. Things had definitely changed on the aircrew survival course since his day. On day three, no one had given her a bloody Oxo cube and it wasn't a rabbit but a chicken. She was wearing the same clothes she had started out in, hadn't had the slightest chance to wash apart from the time she had fallen in a river and that really didn't count. Sleep had been almost as hard to come by as food. The boys were coping well and she knew the staff were keeping an extra eye on her. They would be disappointed. And now, towards the end of the course, her morale was high. Now their little bit of contingency might just pay off. She had been creeping through the wood for several minutes, having successfully escaped observation. They were now permanently camped up in the woods in pairs, having been on the run for over a week but she didn't want to give Jerry, her companion false hope. Where was that bloody tree? It had seemed so obvious when they had come here the other Sunday afternoon but now she was tired dirty and ravenously hungry and everything looked different.

The course had started off extremely well. The little naval establishment of Sea Field Park was an out-station of the main airfield at Lee-on-Solent near Fareham, otherwise known as HMS Daedalus. It was a small country house that had been taken over during the war and retained all the atmosphere of a sleepy private house rather than a military school. However, out the back were buildings with classrooms and even a special chamber for taking prospective aircrew up to twenty five thousand feet to demonstrate the effects of oxygen starvation. That had been hilarious. Each student had been given a simple task, like writing their name or playing draughts with a neighbour. They had then been told to take off their oxygen mask. It didn't take long before most motor functions simply disappeared, what was even funnier was that when the oxygen was restored the candidate had no recollection of losing the plot. Lectures on aviation medicine then led into a very intense first aid course. Classroom lectures were interspersed with practical exercises with some very realistic wounds to treat. They were even taught how to cope with the 'ABFN' which translated as the Able

Bodied Fucking Nuisance. He was the guy who, although not hurt, always seemed to get in the way. Jon had warned Helen about the final exercise and had stayed well clear of the 'crashed helicopter' whose crew they were ostensibly helping. Sure enough the student who climbed up the side to see to the pilot, who was half hanging out of the cockpit of the old Whirlwind, firstly got a faceful of vomit for his thanks and then when the pilot's arm had come off, he received a fresh spray of blood from the stump as the 'victim' operated a hidden pump. That's not to say that dealing with the casualty with an eye hanging out had been great but at least she didn't look like a refugee from an abattoir after it was all over.

After all the fun and gore they moved on to the survival stage. Lectures were interposed with more practical exercises. They spent a night blundering round part of the New Forest with compasses and maps as well watching films about how to resist the various interrogation techniques that the dastardly enemy would try on them. As Helen had some practical experience of what it was really like she was interested but far less concerned than some of her younger companions seemed to be. The course culminated in the infamous ten day exercise. The staff were old hands at what students might get up to and so before they were taken off in the bus they were all forced to change clothes in front of the staff and then had all the possessions they were allowed to take carefully searched. Helen was afforded her own private search and of course nothing was found. However, that wasn't the same with the men. Large quantities of contraband were confiscated much to their chagrin and the amusement of the staff. All the money found was 'donated' to the King George the Fifth fund for Sailors which was only fair, as everyone had been forewarned.

Once ready, they were taken out of a different door to the one they had come in through, to the waiting mini buses. Once again, prior knowledge came to the fore and on the excuse of kneeling down to tie a bootlace, Helen was able to retrieve the ordnance survey map she had secreted under a thin layer of soil in one of the flower beds. She had it on good authority that food was one thing but knowing where you were going was even more important.

Their first night had been spent on the water. Eleven of them in a ten man dinghy, floating in some gravel ponds near Ringwood. It actually hadn't been too bad unless you were the unlucky one with their feet at the bottom of the pile. After a few minutes, the loss of circulation would force the victim to kick his feet out rather than risk gangrene setting in. Helen had come up with a partial solution. She half opened one of the door covers and was able to roll into it rather like a hammock. It was comfortable and relieved some of the pressure inside but was bloody cold.

The rest of the week they were on the run, sometimes on their own, sometimes in teams. Various tasks were set them, like carrying one of their own on a stretcher for five miles and then crossing a river. It soon became apparent that even one body was a massive weight to carry over any distance. One morning they were given an escape and evasion exercise followed by some fairly realistic interrogation. By the end of seven days they were exhausted and even though most had managed to scrounge some food from unsuspecting tourists or knowing locals, they were half starving.

So now she was praying that her stash was still intact. Whether what she was doing was in the category of cheating or merely using her initiative was completely academic. She was bloody hungry and round here somewhere was a tree with a little birds nest on it and underneath it was her supper. Suddenly, she spotted the nest and immediately started to dig next to the roots. With her heart in her mouth, she felt metal and there it was, the old sweet tin that contained something more precious than gold. Clutching her treasure, she carefully made her way back to where they had built their bivouac. Having been run ragged over the past week, this phase of the exercise was all about pure survival. They had to learn to make shelter, provide a means of being found and then survive, so they were not being supervised by the staff anything like as much.

As she crept into their camp, Jerry called out. 'Where the hell have you been Helen? I was getting worried.'

She didn't answer immediately, merely wrenched the top of the large tin and displayed the contents.

Fifteen minutes later, she realised she had another potential problem. It was a still day and although the staff weren't around, the other course members were. The question was, could they eat the corn beef hash that was cooking over their fire before the wonderful smell alerted the others nearby and they all came to beg some?

Bog Hammer

Jon was walking through central London with a spring in his step. He had just attended a meeting at St Giles court where the procurement staff were based and being such a lovely day, had decided that a stroll down Shaftsbury Avenue and Whitehall was far in preference to being crushed in the sweaty tube. In fact, he was finding that walking was often faster than the tube and often far more pleasant, even though most of his compatriots seemed to disagree. It also gave him time to think, something that was far more difficult in their noisy, busy office. He was grateful for the weather, Helen was doing her survival course in the summer months, he had done his in February and the weather had been bloody.

He turned down Charing Cross road and headed towards Leicester square almost without thinking. Walking through the London crowds was becoming automatic and he now managed to avoid the throngs of other pedestrians without conscious effort. Afterwards, he realised that was why it took him so long to recognise the girl coming out of the shop on his left. She had actually turned and started walking away from him before his thought processes caught up with what he had just seen. For a second, he thought he must have been mistaken but that cute, swinging rear end and the glimpse he then got of her face in a shop window, confirmed it without a doubt. It was his ex-girlfriend, the Russian spy, the refugee from the Arctic, Inga. For a moment he considered speeding up and catching her attention but then the anger over the way she had treated him while he had been abroad in HMS Chester made him realise it would probably be a bad idea. He had Helen now and she knocked spots off any other girl he had ever known. However, he had never found out what it was that had been the root cause of their break up and wondered if by following her he might find a clue. He knew she was ambitious and had always expected that some poor unsuspecting millionaire would be the next victim of her undoubted charms. He wasn't required back in the office any time soon, so with an internal grin, he decided he would spy on the spy. It didn't take long for him to be disappointed. She headed directly for a bar with a number of tables set out in the sunshine. As she approached, a middle aged man stood up and they greeted like close friends and with what seemed to be a degree of passion. Jon didn't dare stop or stare too hard and continued to walk nonchalantly walk past. He was careful that Inga didn't catch a glimpse of his face but something bothered him about her companion. He was dressed in a conservative business suit and there was nothing particularly unusual about him but Jon was sure he had seen him somewhere before.

Putting the encounter out of his mind as none of his business any more, he headed back to his desk for another fun afternoon of reading files and writing letters. It was not long before the phone rang.

'Is that the illustrious Commander Jonathon Hunt Royal Navy, all round good egg and bon viveur?' the voice asked.

Jon immediately recognised who it was. 'It certainly is and would that be the world famous master spy and sometimes crap Royal Marine impersonator, Mister Rupert Thomas, by any chance?'

A chuckle met Jon's remark. 'It certainly is old chap, I'm back home now and a little bird told me you were incarcerated in the dungeons of Whitehall. Fancy meeting up for a beer some time?'

'Absolutely, are you over the river in that green mausoleum?'

'I'm afraid so. I'll tell you all about it when we meet up. How about tonight?'

'Yes why not? Do you know the wine bar on the opposite the Whitehall theatre, it's very originally called Whites.'

'No but I'm sure I can find it. Meet you there about eight?'

'Good for me.'

Jon put the phone down. It was really good to hear from Rupert again. They had been through quite a lot together in the past. The last time they had met was at Jon's wedding and then Rupert had had to head straight back to the Lebanon oversee the final closing of the British Embassy there. Presumably, he now had a new job. However, there was something in the way he spoke that gave Jon the distinct impression that there was more to the invitation than the desire to catch up on old times. All in all, it had been an interesting day.

Chapter 6

Whites was fairly quiet, caught in the time gap between the end of the working day drinkers and the seasoned evening party goers. Jon spotted Rupert immediately. He was seated at one of the small tables, in a partly partitioned booth near the small dance floor. Rupert saw him at the same time and waved him over. There was a bottle of red on the table and he leaned forward and filled an empty glass, handing it to Jon as he sat down opposite.

'Cheers old chap,' Jon acknowledged as he took a gulp. 'You've no idea how well that goes down after a day cooking the books.'

Rupert grinned back. 'I know the feeling, sometimes it's just nice to escape. So Jon, how's life treating you and that lovely wife of yours?'

'Oh you probably don't know. She's joined the real navy at last and is just about to go to RAF Leeming to do her Elementary Flying Training. She'll be there until Christmas. It'll be a bloody pain getting up there to see her at weekends but it's what she wants to do.'

'Bloody hell Jon, I hadn't heard, although I can't say I'm surprised. It was clear she was frustrated as a Wren and look how well she did in the Med. I hope she calls you Sir now.'

'Hah, you're not the first one to crack that joke. More to the point, I am now working for a certain Admiral who used to be COMAW. I'm really looking forward to when they meet again.'

'That will be interesting. I'd love to be a fly on the wall. What's he like these days? Has becoming an Admiral mellowed him at all?'

'Not really, although he's clearly well in his element in the MOD. I'm not sure he liked being at sea, he seems far more comfortable fighting his wars from a desk.'

'Unlike you old friend I suspect?'

Jon grimaced. 'They call it losing your virginity, once you work out what it's all about. I'm just about there but the jury is still out about whether it's for me. It's such a different environment and there are some seriously ambitious people about. Do you know there is one of the guys, an office down from mine, who apparently comes in every morning deliberately at a time when he will encounter the Admiral on the stairs. The day I start doing that I'll shoot myself.'

'I could tell you similar stories about my lot. I guess you just have to plough your own furrow. At least you have a pretty impressive record to fall back on. I suspect most of the people you are talking about have nothing like that.'

'I guess. You know Rupert, despite all the time we've spent together I know very little about your private life, you're not married are you?'

'No, although I do have a girlfriend, we should all get together some time. I'm probably back for good now. My last job was probably my last in the field. I was also promoted recently and I'm too senior to go shooting real bad guys any more.'

Jon spotted the attempt to steer the conversation away from Rupert's private life. He wasn't surprised. Rupert had always been very reticent about discussing it in the past. 'Congratulations, although I've absolutely no idea how the rank structure of MI6 works. Is it the same as the rest of the Civil Service?'

'Basically yes, I'm what you would call a Grade Seven which is equivalent to you as a Commander in the military.'

'Oh, I see, so you're stuck in the office trap as well. So what job have they given you or can't you tell me?'

'Well I could but....'

'You'd have to shoot me afterwards,' Jon finished for him and they both laughed.

'Something like,' that Rupert said. 'But what I can tell you is that whatever job I have now it's going to change radically over the next few years. The consensus is that the Cold War is about to enter a new phase but no one really knows what it will be.'

'Oh, what do you know? Or rather what can you tell me?'

'Well, the Soviets are really counting the costs of their military expansion now. They spend ridiculous amounts of their GDP on their military and most pundits reckon they won't be able to afford it for much longer. The West spends between three and five per cent. Current estimates are that they are spending almost forty five per cent. It can't continue for all sorts of reasons. For example, there are strong indications that they are planning to pull out of Afghanistan soon.'

Jon snorted in amusement. 'The British Empire tried to pacify the place not so many years ago and look how well that went. No one is ever going to keep that country.'

'I think you're right. It's cost the Soviets a fortune and they've achieved bugger all. But that's just one symptom. Basically, the West and that means the Yanks, are forcing their military spending to levels they can't sustain. It's rather like before the First World War when we and the Germans kept building more and more Dreadnoughts and look how that ended. This new chap Gorbachev seems to be a bit of a reformer, although no one knows which way he'll jump. The real worry is that if their empire does collapse then there is no way of predicting the outcome and of course that could be bad for us.'

'Thanks Rupert, you've just cheered me up no end.'

'Look on the bright side it could go well for us. Most of the satellite countries want to get out. Just imagine Germany in one piece again.'

'I'm not sure I actually want to do that, history repeating itself and all that.'

Rupert looked thoughtful for a moment as he refilled their glasses. 'I'm not sure whether I should be telling you this Jon but as you were rather intimately involved and have the security clearances I think you ought to be told about the fallout from your trip to the Arctic in Eighty Three.'

Jon looked intrigued. 'I thought that was all done and dusted, never to be spoken of again?'

'Yeah, we thought that too. But listen, six months ago the Yanks got a high level defector and they've finally shared some of his feedback with us. You remember the NATO exercise that was running at the time?'

'Good Bowman? Yes, I was part of it remember?'

'Well, the Soviets weren't sure it really was an exercise. Apparently, the defectors first words were along the lines of 'what the fucking hell were you lot doing? We almost went to war.' It seems the Politburo were really concerned that the exercise was cover for a first strike. There was all the hassle over deployment of Pershing, the announcement of Star Wars that year and don't forget that Maggie and the German Chancellor went to SHAPE and got involved in the nuclear release procedures. Thank Christ Reagan didn't go there or who knows what would have happened. Their little Arctic raid ramped the paranoia up a notch as well. The current assessment is that the Cuban Missile crisis was a walk in the park compared to this. Apparently, the whole Soviet nuclear arsenal was at launch stations. It was only when the exercise stopped and all the NATO staff went to the bar that they realised it really was an exercise. There are some seriously rattled politicians and senior military now looking at the whole thing very carefully. We don't want to get into a situation like that ever again.'

'Bloody hell Rupert, so if things had gone differently in the Arctic, I could have started World War Three?'

'You and half a dozen others. It really was a hair trigger situation for a while and the thing is we never even knew.'

Jon sat back in his seat and contemplated Rupert's words. He took a large swig of wine while he thought. 'So, with all this turmoil in the Evil Empire and this new knowledge I'm guessing there's a fair degree of paranoia being generated over here as well?'

'You could say that, we live in interesting times as they say.'

'And I know you Rupert. You wouldn't be telling me this without a reason, now would you?' Jon asked. 'I hope this isn't the start of another one of your nefarious schemes. Every time we get together the ordure seems to hit the rotating blades one way or another.'

Rupert chuckled. 'We have had the odd eventful trip I agree and yes there is something I would like some help with but its low key at the moment. You can turn it down and no one will know but I wouldn't ask if I didn't think you were the right man.'

'Go on.'

'As you know MI5 is responsible for internal security and my job in MI6 is meant to be international. However, the lines are often blurred and one of my jobs is working with Five in London. Some time ago, it was clear that the Soviets were getting more information than they should. We've traced some of it to the MOD. To me, it's clear that someone in Whitehall has sold out. We decided to approach you because you haven't been anywhere near the place until recently and with your track record we know we can trust you.'

'So you want me to spy on my own people Rupert? I'm sorry, I'm not sure that's something I want to get involved in.'

'I completely understand and if that's what I wanted then I wouldn't ask. At this stage, all I want is your agreement in principle. We are going to set a trap, we're not sure quite what or how yet but the basic idea will be to feed in some appropriately tailored information and see what happens to it. All I'll want you to do is act as my conduit and then if we get a bite, act as a sort of look out. Sorry, I can't be more specific at this moment but our plans are all a little vague. We're just scoping our approach at the moment.'

Jon knew he could trust Rupert but this all seemed a little ridiculous. 'And will anyone else know about my role in this?'

'Not in the MOD, that's the point. Look, I can only ask you to do this but I've explained how perilous things are currently. We can't have a leak at such a high level at the moment. We really need to catch this bastard. Your role will be simple and although crucial, we'll keep you well away from any fall out. We can keep in touch this way as we know each other, it will seem to be a purely social thing.'

'Rupert if it was anyone else than you I would say no but seeing it is you, alright I'm in. There's two things though.'

'Oh, what?'

'Firstly, MI bloody Six can pay for dinner tonight.'

'Fair enough and the second thing?'

'Remember what I told you the first time? When we went on that little trip to Argentina together?'

'Go on.'

'No plan survives the first shot of the enemy.'

Chapter 7

The runway beckoned in the distance, a long streak of concrete, cut into the Yorkshire plain. The white, threshold piano keys, were streaked with black rubber from the thousands of aircraft landings. Buildings and hangars clustered on its northern side. In the far distance, the higher ground of the Yorkshire moors could be seen. From six hundred feet the view was breathtaking but Helen saw none of it. Inside the cramped and vibrating machine she was strapped into, she only had one aim, to land the bloody thing without the instructor sitting next to her raising his voice yet again. Every time he criticised her flying in his patronising manner, she felt the pressure rise and that made her more nervous and so she made more mistakes. This time she would get it right. She finished the descending turn on to her final approach and noted that her height was spot on. She throttled back and lowered the flaps fully, feeling the nose drop as the extra drag was generated. She trimmed it back up with the little trim wheel by her right knee. As the airspeed crept down to sixty knots she increased the throttle a little to keep it there and concentrated on the threshold of the runway which was approaching fast.

'You're getting too low,' the voice was terse.

Stifling the urge to tell him she already knew that, she increased the throttle a little more and the aircraft responded. Soon they were over the white painted piano keys at the runway threshold and she raised the nose and slowly closed the throttle, holding the nose up with more rear stick as the speed bled off. There was a noncommittal grunt from beside her which immediately diverted her attention and the aircraft dropped harder onto the runway than she would have liked.

'Right Helen, that's enough for today, just taxy her in please and we'll debrief in the briefing room.' Her instructor's voice gave no indication of how he felt the trip had gone but there again it never did.

As soon as the propeller stopped, he jumped out leaving Helen to fully shut down the little red and white Bulldog light aircraft. She breathed a sigh of relief as she watched his green clad body stride across the tarmac towards the long low building alongside the hangar. Something would have to be done, she couldn't continue with this guy. Well, she could but not for much longer that was clear.

The debrief was as short and unhelpful as usual. Her instructor listed all the mistakes she had made, offered no praise or even mentioned all the things she had done correctly. He finished off by saying she would have to improve radically if she wanted to continue on the course. As he left and headed off for the instructors crewroom she sat for a while wondering what to do.

Later that afternoon she was called in to see the Boss. Lieutenant Commander John Bruce was an aviator of the old school as testimonied by all the photographs on his office walls of Sea Vixens and Phantoms. However, everyone liked and respected him. As the Commanding Officer of Royal Naval, Elementary Flying Training Squadron at RAF Leeming it was his last job before retirement and he seemed to really enjoy being responsible for teaching the new aircrew how to fly.

'Ah Helen, come in,' he said with a fatherly smile as she tentatively opened the door. 'Take a seat, I won't bite.'

'Thank you Sir but a summons to the Boss's office is quite intimidating.'

'Hmm, well let's get straight down to it then. I've just had Mike Howard your instructor in and he has been less than complimentary. Says that you panic too much and are having trouble in the circuit and with landing. Now is that a fair assessment?'

Helen though carefully. 'Sir, when I did flying grading in the Chipmunk, which is much harder to land as it has a tail wheel, I had no trouble at all. In fact, they said I could have gone solo early had it not been that they don't allow that during grading. The Bulldog is a much easier aircraft in many ways.'

'You haven't actually answered my question you know.'

'Sorry Sir. Yes Lieutenant Howard is right I am having trouble with landing but I'll be quite honest, it's not the aircraft that is causing me the trouble.'

'Spit it out girl. You clearly have something to say about your instructor.'

'Alright Sir, I'll speak plainly. He always criticises and never tells me when I've done something right. Its bloody hard to concentrate when all you get is instructions to do something differently and although he never loses his temper, I get the feeling he is always about to. Honestly Sir, I think he wants me to fail.'

The Boss sat back and looked thoughtfully at Helen. 'Of course, it doesn't help that you are a girl, the first to do this course and a very attractive one at that. Also we all know about what you and your husband got up to recently. I'm afraid that many men look on that as a bit of a threat, irrational as that may sound.'

'Oh no Sir, I understand. I always knew that things would be hard but I feel I'm not being given a fair chance.'

'There's only one way to find out. You and I are going flying right now. Go and get your gear and meet me in the briefing room in ten minutes. It's a bit late in the day but we should be able to get in an hour or so before the airfield shuts.'

To her surprise instead of flying round and round the airfield, practicing landing and take offs, the Boss took them out into the local area and proceeded to show Helen just what the little aircraft was really capable of. She had been given a small demonstration on her first familiarisation flight but this was different. For a while she thought they were spending more of their time upside down than upright. She almost blacked out with G forces several times and even started to feel the first stages of airsickness before he relented and they headed back to the airfield.'

'Nice little machine the Bulldog,' the Boss said nonchalantly as they settled into the cruise. 'It's a shame the oil system doesn't allow the engine to run upside down for any length of time but otherwise it's got loads of power and is very responsive.' He turned and grinned at her like a schoolboy. 'Think you can take her from here, find the airfield, fly into the circuit and land?'

Not trusting herself to speak she just nodded and took control. Ten minutes later, without the Boss saying a word, she pulled off a perfect landing and they taxied back to the flight line.

'Right Helen, there's nothing wrong with your flying. As of tomorrow you get a new instructor. Is that all right with you?'

'Er, of course Sir, thank you very much.'

'And don't get in the shit again young lady, you don't get too many chances you know that don't you?'

That night she poured her heart out to Jon over the phone. He listened patiently as she told the story. He knew she was upset but also that everyone went through something like this during the various courses needed to get to the front line.

When she had come to the end he responded. 'Helen, I never told you this but something very similar happened to me. Not during Elementary training but when I got to Basic training on helicopters. You are going to get to fly the new Gazelle but in my day we trained on the very basic Hiller. It was a bit of a pig and I had real trouble just flying the bloody thing. I ended up on warning and only scraped through. For a while it was touch and go, so I know exactly how you feel. I'm sure the new instructor will settle you down. It would seem that the last one was a bit of an idiot.' They talked some more and when Jon put the phone down he felt a wave of longing wash over him. He knew exactly how she felt and really wished he could be there for her but she was over two hundred miles away and would have to face it alone. For the first time, he really doubted the wisdom of them being separated so much. They had only been married for a year and he had hardly seen her for the last six months. He hated himself for thinking it but maybe if she was chopped from the course, it would actually be a good thing. He immediately berated himself for the thought. He knew how much she wanted to succeed.

Two hundred miles away, Helen was thinking much the same. She missed Jon terribly. Maybe she should just pack it in and become a simple housewife. As the thought crossed her mind she gave a little chuckle. Not only would she hate it but she knew Jon would too. Neither of them were that sort of person. There was only one thing to do, pass the bloody course.

And she did just that three months later. Seventy five hours flying the Bulldog, in a wide range of disciplines, had passed in a flash. Her new instructor was an old and bold Royal Air Force Flight Lieutenant. Nothing phased him and he encouraged rather than criticised. Helen recovered her self-confidence and suddenly everything started to make sense. Her final handling check at the end of the course went extremely well, although she was surprised to be called into the Boss's office soon after.

'Helen, come on in. Don't worry there's nothing wrong this time,' he smiled encouragingly at her.

She noticed her instructor was already sitting down next to the Boss.

'We just wanted to debrief you on the course and also ask you a rather personal question.'

Mystified, Helen sat down where indicated and nodded.

'Now Helen, how much do you weigh?' the Boss asked.

'Nine stone but why on earth do you want to know that?'

He grinned. 'I don't suppose you would want to put on a few pounds then, say another twenty?'

'Not really but why on earth are you asking?'

He chuckled. 'Helen, we try to assess the best future for all our students, in particular, whether they should be recommended for fast jet training. There are three of you on this course who we would like to recommend and you are one of them but for you there's a problem. For fixed wing students, the next phase is to go on to flying the Hawk trainer at RAF Valley and it has an ejection seat as I'm sure you know. To get it to work safely, it has to weigh the right amount and if you are fairly light they can add ballast but there's only so much that can be fitted. So there is a minimum weight and you just aren't heavy enough. It's not only you, the RAF have several female students they would like to train but they all have the same problem. They are looking at a fix but it will require modification to the seats and will take at least a year.'

To the Boss's surprise, Helen looked relieved. 'It's not a problem, Sir, even if you could have offered me the option I wouldn't have wanted it. Jon and I have talked this over and as you know I already have some Fleet Air Arm experience. I want to fly helicopters. There is far more variety and scope for doing different things.' She saw a look of disappointment flash across the Boss's face. He was an old school, fixed wing, aviator after all. 'Sorry Sir but there is only one type of jet to fly in the navy and only one sort of ship to fly it off, I don't want to spend all my time flying Harriers off a CVS.'

The Boss nodded. 'A fair point and a moot one at that of course. Anyway, well done Helen, you did very well on the course and I wish you luck at Culdrose after Christmas. Oh and I'll be looking forward to the leaving lunch on Friday and anything you lot come up with to say goodbye to our Air Force cousins as well.'

'Point taken,' Helen replied with a grin. 'We might have a few ideas on that score.'

Two days later, Helen was sitting next to Jon at the top table of the Officer's Mess of RAF Leeming for their leaving lunch. Jon had only just made it in time as the train up from London that morning had been delayed.

'Helen, was that a white ensign, I saw flying from the flag staff at the main gate of an RAF air station as I came through in the taxi?' he asked with a big grin.

'Er yes, we decided to have naval morning colours today. It's our last day after all. The whole course marched up to the main gate fifteen minutes before the RAF normally hoist their flag and did the full naval ceremony. The staff on the gate didn't know what to do so just let us get on with it. Oh and unfortunately there was a funny knot in the halliard and they don't seem to be able to get it down again. Apparently, they are waiting for a cherry picker crane from Harrogate to arrive so that they can get to the top of the mast.' She said this all with a completely straight face.

Jon burst out laughing. 'Oh dear, has anyone said anything to you? You're the course leader after all.'

'The Station Commander, he's the Group Captain over there at the end of the table was quite cross and I got a ticking off. It was followed by a big chuck up from everyone else. It's not the only present we've left them either.'

'Oh God, what else have you done?'

'Not me. It was one of the others who had the idea. Well, we all helped just a little bit. They won't get the joke until well after we're gone so it's quite safe.'

'Why don't I like the sound of this?'

Helen giggled again. 'We drew the outline of a giant Crab in the grass, just short of the threshold of the main runway.'

'But they'll see that straight away.'

'Oh no they won't. You see we did it in weed killer, nothing will appear until the grass starts to grow in the spring.'

Jon almost choked on his glass of wine and had to force himself not to laugh out loud. 'Brilliant,' he choked out around guffaws. 'They'll not forget you lot in a hurry. Hey but let's look forward, we've got two weeks leave at home.'

'And then I get to fly a helicopter at last,' she responded with a wide smile.

Bog Hammer

Christmas was spent at Helen's parents rambling old farmhouse. Her father was as distant as ever, although two of her brothers, their wives and various children turned up and made the house a chaotic mess in no time. Helen was the image of her mother and Jon always remembered the anecdote that it was best to look at the mother to see how the daughter would turn out. In this case, he was heartily encouraged. Mary was still slim and elegant at the age of sixty five and that boded well for Helen. They all went for a long afternoon walk and that was followed by an even longer meal. Eventually, all the children were marched off to bed and things settled down a little. As the evening progressed, the grown ups also all slowly filtered away until Jon found himself alone with Helen's father. In his early seventies, he had also aged well, with a shock of silver hair and a remarkably unlined face.

They had never really spoken at any length, although Helen had told Jon about her father's antipathy against the military and how he had reacted when she had joined the WRNS years earlier. When she had announced that she was joining the real navy there hadn't been any of the previous fireworks but even so, Jon knew he disapproved. Now, with a reasonable amount of malt whiskey inside him, he decided to seize the opportunity and try to find out the reasons.

'James, you were in the navy during the war, I understand?'

'Yes but I don't talk about it.'

'No, Helen has told me that. You don't like the idea of her being in the navy either.'

'No I don't.'

'Can I ask why?'

James sighed and looked into the fire which was slowly burning down. 'Maybe you can, you've been in combat after all, although what you've been through and what I experienced are two completely different things.'

Jon nodded but said nothing. If the flood gates were going to open he didn't want to spoil the moment.

'I was a young Lieutenant at the time, in a small Frigate, a bridge watchkeeper. We were an anti-submarine escort. For several years we escorted Atlantic convoys. That was bad enough, especially in the early years, seeing ships torpedoed in front of you and not being able to do anything about it. Pulling half drowned survivors out of freezing water and seeing dozens more dead floating with them. But then we were put on the Arctic convoys, you know about them I expect?'

'Taking supplies to Russia over the Northern Cape into Murmansk, I've been up there as well. I know what it's like.'

'I wonder, living in a two thousand ton ship in winter was an endurance test like no other. We sometimes picked up so much ice it's amazing we didn't capsize. The weather was bad enough but we had to go close to Norway and so the German submarines were able to intercept much easier than in the wide Atlantic. Even heading out to Iceland didn't help because at some time we had to close in to get to Murmansk. To cut a long story short our luck ran out on our third convoy. Two in the morning we were torpedoed. I was lucky I suppose, I was on the bridge. The ship split in two in an instant and most died there and then. We had these useless Carly floats which kept you afloat and that's about all. Nine of us made it onto one of them but the sea temperature was close to freezing and the air was even colder. I found out later that our survival time should have been less than ten minutes. Every time one of us died we stripped them and put on their clothes. By the time there were four of us left we were actually quite well clothed. Wet clothes in layers can actually give good insulation, like a modern wet suit. But by this time the convoy was long gone and nobody knew we were there. We lasted almost a day. When I say we, I really mean me, as the other three died one by one. Do you know what it's like to slowly freeze to death and watch people die in front of you? I literally had no hope, none at all. Sometime that afternoon I fell unconscious not expecting to wake up. So when I did and found myself in a bunk in a small fishing boat and was told I was the only one left alive, I promised myself that I would never allow any of my children to suffer as I did. Sorry, that's rather a simplistic explanation but you, of anyone, should be able to understand.'

Jon didn't know what to say. He couldn't imagine what it must have been like despite all the survival training he had done over the years. Finally, he spoke. 'That's a terrible story and I really can understand why you feel as you do James. But the modern navy isn't like that anymore. We have far better survival equipment for a start.'

'No it's not that, it's the complete loss of hope that I'm talking about and I know Helen has already experienced some of that on that

Cruise ship, the other year. Anyway, there's nothing I can do about it now. I know you will look after her as much as you can but she's chosen her career and it's still bloody dangerous as you well know.'

Jon didn't know how to answer that so he didn't.

Chapter 8

HMS Prometheus looked a sorry sight. The three and half thousand ton Leander class Frigate was propped up clear of the water in number two dry dock in Devonport dockyard. Her sides were a mess and her upper deck was covered in crates, discarded rubbish and green clad dockyard mateys. Brian Pearce, her new senior warfare officer looked at her from the side of the dock with a mixture of pride and concern. This was the same ship that Jon and he had served in six years ago during the Falklands War. Known as a Batch Three converted Leander she was very heavily armed for a ship of her size. Unfortunately, at the moment no one looking at her would be able to see that. The racks for her four Exocet missiles just forward of the bridge were empty and the launcher for the Sea Wolf Anti-aircraft missiles, just further forward was also missing, although Brian could see it in a cradle on the dockside not far away. The main radar array was also absent, so all in all she looked a very sad sight. Looks could be deceiving, as Brian very well knew, or at least as he hoped because the ship was due to recommission in less than two months.

The weather was typical for the time of year with leaden grey skies and a vicious cold wind blasting the hard rain into his face. The ground around the dry dock was full of puddles and the detritus of a busy dockyard. Brian turned to the taxi driver who had delivered him from the station and paid him before helping him unload the large metal trunk from the boot of the car. They placed it carefully on a relatively dry piece of concrete and the taxi drove off while Brian picked his way across to the gangway that bridged the deep drop of the dry dock floor to the ship's flight deck. He stopped at the end of the gangway and saluted, although he suddenly realised he wasn't sure whether he should or not. The ship wasn't in commission and there was no white ensign flying from the stern, so maybe it wasn't appropriate. Anyway, it was too late and he made his way over the little wooden lectern that was almost hidden in the lee of the hangar door and looked for the Quartermaster. For a second he couldn't see anyone and then a face appeared from behind the desk.

'Morning, can I help you on this fine and blustery day?'

Brian couldn't help but smile at the cheeky faced seaman huddled in a greatcoat that looked almost too large for him but was clearly keeping the weather out.

'Yes you can, Lieutenant Commander Pearce joining the ship today,' he responded in a formal tone. He had to restrain a smile as the young seaman suddenly came upright realising that this was one of the ship's officers.

'Sorry Sir, we weren't expecting you till this afternoon.'

'That's fine, I got an earlier train and what's your name?'

'Jenkins Sir, leading Seaman Jenkins. I'm a radar operator so I expect I'll be in your division.'

'I expect you will. Now, could you arrange someone to collect my trunk and take it to my cabin. It's on the dock just there,' he said pointing towards the shore.

'No problem Sir, would you like me to get one of the lads to show you to your cabin and the wardroom?'

Brian grinned, 'Jenkins you won't know this but I've served in this ship before. Thank you for the offer but I suspect I know where to go.'

So saying, he headed down the port waist of the ship to the large metal door at the far end and entered the cabin flat. Almost automatically he made his way to his old cabin, waves of nostalgia crashing over him before he realised it would belong to someone else now. The smell and atmosphere of the ship made him feel that it was only yesterday he and Jon had been here. He turned back to where the Ops officer's cabin used to be and sure enough his name had been typed on a card and put in the little slot on the door. Opening it, he realised it was quite a deal bigger than his old one although the bunk was still on top of the combined desk and clothes dresser unit, so there would still be a long way to fall if he got flung out in rough seas. Realising there was nothing he could do until his trunk arrived, he made his way down the steep ladder at the rear of the cabin flat to the 'Burma Way', the long corridor that ran the length of the ship. Almost opposite the ladder was the sliding door that opened into the wardroom. As he entered, he heard the sound of voices and sitting in the lounge area over coffee, were two white boiler suited officers.

They looked up as he entered. 'Morning, can we help?'

Bog Hammer

Brian wasn't surprised they didn't know him. He was dressed in civilian clothes after all. They probably thought he was some dockyard official.

'I hope so, Brian Pearce, Ops officer, just arrived.'

The two men stood and offered their hands. 'Andy Cummings, I'm the Mechanical Engineering Office and this is my deputy, Charlie Brooks. I hope you don't mind us being here in overalls, until today we were the only ship's officers on board.'

'God no, I don't mind, it's a stupid rule in my opinion. I was on board this ship during the Falklands and we all wore overalls all the time then. I was the Flight Observer then by the way.'

'Yes, we had heard. Anyway, welcome on board. There should be the rest of the wardroom joining over the next week or so. The Jimmy, Des Slater, he arrives tomorrow. Do you know him?'

'Can't say we've met. What about the skipper?' Brian asked as he helped himself to a large mug of coffee from the pot on the bar and took a seat.

The two engineers exchanged glances before the MEO looked at Brian with an odd expression. 'Paul Fulford, have you met him?'

'No that's another thing to look forward too I suppose.' Then, seeing the look on the other two men's faces, 'is there something I should know?'

'Well, he comes with a certain reputation but I guess you'd better make up our own mind, he's joining in three weeks.'

'OK, well I guess there's going to be a great deal to do before the skipper arrives, just how is the old girl?'

They talked for several cups of coffee and Brian realised just how much work was going to be needed to get the ship back into an operational condition. Soon there was a knock on the door and he was told his trunk was in his cabin, so excusing himself he went to unpack musing as he did so on all he had been told.

The next few weeks passed in an exhausting blur. Everything was in a mess and had to be put in order and with the ship's company trickling in slowly, there was never enough manpower. The ship was moved out of dock and put in the covered yard for painting which at least made her look like a warship again but made life on board even more difficult while it happened. Brian took delivery of vast amounts of books and paperwork and then all the highly classified cryptographic material which had to be carefully managed and put under secure lock and key. It may have been the same Frigate that he served on previously but the job was so different, he soon found he was looking back to the time when all he had to do was fly with Jon, with envy. But out of the chaos, order was slowly restored. The radars and other sensors were set to work and the Sea Wolf Launcher refitted. Although the Lynx Flight wouldn't embark for some time yet, Brian took it on himself to ensure that the hangar was converted back from an engineer's store to something they might just squeeze a helicopter in to.

Then the great day finally dawned when the new Commanding Officer arrived. The wardroom was just about complete and only the Flight aircrew and the officers under training were still to join. By now the ship was in the water alongside the dockyard wall and the grey waters of the Tamar River slid slowly past, as just for once the sun peeked out around the clouds. With the ship still not commissioned the Captain would arrive in civilian clothes and would not be given the pomp and ceremony associated with normal service. However, at the appointed hour all the ships company were mustered on the flight deck and only a few minutes late, a taxi drew up alongside the gangway. The man that emerged was quite small and slightly built. He had also lost quite a great deal of his hair, the remainder of which was a mousy brown. His narrow face looked pinched and sour. As he got to the gangway he stopped and looked over the ship with a frown in his face. Taking careful strides up the greasy wood of the gangway which was quite steep with a high tide just turned, he stopped at the top and the First Lieutenant went to greet him.

'Welcome on board Prometheus Sir, I'm Des Slater you First Lieutenant,' and he held out his hand which the Captain briefly shook.

'I see you have the whole ship's company mustered Number One. Very well, I would like to have a few words with them if you please.'

'Certainly Sir, we anticipated as much, if you would come with me.' And he led the Captain to a small dais set in the entrance of the hangar.

The crowd of men were silent as they waited for their new Commanding Officer to speak to them for the first time. He stood looking over them for several minutes, clearly gathering his thoughts.

'Gentlemen, I am proud to have been given command of you all and this ship. However, from what I have already seen there is a great deal of work to be done and not too much time to complete it. I won't keep you, I'm sure we will all get to know each other in the weeks and months to come. We commission in a fortnight so let's get to it.'

He stood down, nodding to the First Lieutenant as he did so. 'All Heads of Departments in my cabin in half an hour please Number One.' He stated rather curtly.

As the Captain turned and walked forward down the port waist, the First Lieutenant turned to the men, calling out, 'Ship's Company, dismissed. You heard the Captain, there's work to be done.'

As the sailors dispersed to their various duties, Brian turned to Des Slater. 'Well Number One, that was short and to the point. It seems our new CO is a man of few words.'

Des looked worried for a moment. 'Strange, he has a rather different reputation from what I've heard. Still, time will tell.'

Chapter 9

Jon and Helen had moved house. With Helen now appointed to 705 Squadron at Culdrose to start flying the little Gazelle helicopter, they had decided to let Jon's house near Yeovilton and take a married quarter at the air station in Cornwall. Although they could now spend more time together at weekends, the journey from London was long and tiring.

'Getting to Cornwall is almost as difficult as travelling to a foreign country,' Jon joked the first time he got wearily off the train at Penzance.

It was also sometimes a little awkward with Helen's compatriots from her training Flight. Here she was married to a Commander, a rank only second to God in their eyes, yet she was one of them as well. Jon had soon sorted it out the first time they all met up in a pub when still in Yorkshire, by insisting that rank stopped at the air station gate. Even so, it sometimes took time for them both to be accepted, especially on social occasions. Today, they had just come back from a long pub lunch with the boys and it had been great fun. For Jon it was like going back in time to the camaraderie he had experience when he was training. Now they were cuddled up on the sofa idling watching a film and trying to stay awake. Jon would be catching the sleeper train back to London that evening and wanted to make as much of the time he had with Helen as he could.

'So how's the course going? We haven't really talked about it at all this weekend,' Jon asked the top of Helen's head.

She sighed and snuggled up a little more. 'Really great, my first trip was absolutely fantastic. The Gazelle cockpit is mainly glass so you get an amazing feeling of flying, especially when you're close to the ground. I've just about cracked the noble art of hovering. It's nothing like the Sea King I flew when I was with you on 844, far more sensitive.'

Jon grunted. 'Yes, the Sea King is a bit of a lumbering beast. The Boss of 705 has offered me a ride in a Gazelle some time. Hey, if I wait long enough maybe you can fly me. That would be an occasion. The first husband and wife military flight.'

'Are you sure you would trust me? You've rather got just a few more hours than me after all.'

'Why not? Once you've passed the course, you'll be qualified. I'll see if we can arrange it. Hey, changing the subject somewhat. You know I told you that Rupert got in touch a while ago?'

She turned her head. 'Yes, you told me. Why, is the devious sod cooking something up?

'Yes and he's asked me to get involved. What I didn't mention was that he said they were worried about some sort of intelligence leak from the MOD and he asked me to help out but only in principle at that stage.'

'Should you be telling me this?'

'Helen if I can't trust you then who can I? But not a word to anyone else of course. Yeah, he's asked for another meeting this week and I've got a feeling he's come up with something.'

'Jon, does your Boss know about it? Couldn't it get really awkward for you?'

'You've hit the nail on the head there love. I'm going to have to insist on some form of top cover. If it all went wrong I could be hung out to dry. Anyway, changing the subject, its three hours before I have to leave for the train and I want to check something out.'

'Oh, what's that?'

'Well someone in the office described married life, when you only see each other at weekends, as 'all sex and washing.''

'Yes?' she looked into his eyes.

'Well, you've done my laundry.'

Two days later and Jon was fully back in the London grind. The weather was awful but apart from travelling between his digs and the office, he barely saw it.

His desk was his refuge and he could hide behind piles of files and his computer. The computer was a new innovation for all of them and many still preferred to use old fashioned pen and paper. The typing pool would turn a handwritten scrawl into the polished article and the general level of typing skills amongst his compatriots were pretty pathetic. However, Jon was rather taken with the idea and had the use of a portable machine for when he was out of the office. There was talk of linking them all up at some stage and being able to use them to communicate but that was far in the future as far as he was concerned.

Bog Hammer

One of the important things in his in-tray was what was called an Urgent Operational Requirement or UOR for short. This was a process for getting equipment to the front line and short circuiting the normal procurement processes. He had dealt with several over the months but this one was a bit different. The situation in the Gulf had been precarious for several years with Iran and Iraq targeting oil exports as a tactic in their war. Several countries, including the UK, had ships in the area on what was known as the Armilla patrol. Recently a new threat had appeared, small high speed boats armed with hand held missiles or guns and were being used by both sides. The original ones were Iranian speed boats made by the Swedish company Bog Hammar but that seemed to have been subtly changed and most people used the generic term of Bog Hammer these days for any armed boat. They were hard to detect and even when they were, there was often no way of deciding whether they were a threat or merely a civilian vessel until it was too late. As such, their military effect was far in excess of their size. The UOR Jon was staffing was to put the old Heavy Machine Gun Pod that he had used on his Lynx during the Falklands, back into service to counter the threat. When Captain Desmonde had passed the task onto Jon, it had seemed quite ironic that the person managing the programme was the only person to have used the gun for real. Jon's past experience was proving invaluable and the first outfits were about to be deployed into theatre.

However, his main task was the programme to upgrade the Lynx helicopter which was well underway and the new version, the Mark Eight, was going to be a quantum leap in capability from the current Mark Three.

He was explaining this to some of his colleagues over a mid-morning coffee. 'Look guys, the Observer in the current aircraft, actually puts a bit of clear plastic over the radar screen and uses a chinagraph pencil to plot the contacts. He then literally joins the dots to work out the course and speed of a target. Its Stone Age stuff, plus firing a Sea Skua missile can be a real problem. You can't actually see the target to identify it at maximum firing range and if you get too close, especially to one of the new Soviet ships with SAN 4, they can take you out in the process.'

Dennis Osmond the resident Sea Harrier pilot nodded. 'We have the same issue with the Sea Eagle missile, target identification is a real problem.'

'The Mark Eight is going to get a Passive Identification Device which will hopefully help a great deal. My only worry is, that with a new computer tactical system, the PID and other modifications, whether the damned thing will be able to get off the ground.'

Captain Desmonde, who had been listening in from the inner office came out and joined in. 'Nothing new there Jon, all aircraft get heavier the longer they stay in service. Hopefully, the procurers and Westlands know what they're doing.'

A ripple of laughter ran around the office. There was always a tension between the Procurement Executive and rest of MOD and then a further degree of cynicism about the motives of industry.

'Actually, it seems to be going quite well,' Jon responded. 'I was down at Westlands last week and the programme seems to be on track.'

Suddenly his phone rang and the general chat subsided as he answered it. After a brief conversation, he put the receiver down but everyone was back at their desks again. The call had been the expected one from Rupert. They would meet in the usual place tonight.

Whites was busy this time but Rupert had managed to get a reasonably secluded table and the obligatory bottle of wine was there sitting on the table. He rose and shook Jon's hand and they settled down over their first glass.

'So where are you taking me to dinner this evening old chap?' Jon asked.

'Good question, how about that Chinese restaurant near Leicester square where they are all incredibly rude to you but the food is great?'

'You mean Won Kei's? Good idea, haven't been there for a while. But come on, tonight isn't just social is it? I reckon you've come up with something at last.'

Rupert grimaced a little. 'To the point, as usual Jon. Alright, let's get this out of the way. To answer your question, yes we have an idea. It's quite simple but let me just check a few things with you first. So, just to be clear, the MOD filing system treats Secret and Top Secret files in different ways, is that correct?'

Mystified Jon nodded. 'Yes, anything from Secret downwards is put into the internal distribution system and is moved around using the registry staff. Top Secret stuff is only managed by direct hand. It is all run out of a separate registry. All files have to be personally signed for in the registry and once you've done that you are personally responsible for keeping it in your custody until you hand it back to the registry. Files are never passed directly from one person to another.'

'Good, so if information in one of those files were to be found in the wrong place there would be a cast iron audit trail to who had seen it?'

'Yes of course but before we go any further, I'm going to have to put my foot down about something.'

Rupert cocked an eyebrow. 'Go on.'

'I need some form of top cover Rupert. I understand the reasons you are asking me to do this but if it all goes pear shaped then I need to be able to prove I was acting correctly. It seems to me that this operation, whatever it is, could be compromised if anyone in MOD knows I'm involved, is that right?'

'Well yes of course. We don't know where the leak is, so we don't want to warn anyone in advance, no matter how low risk that might be.'

'Fair enough but that leaves me totally bare arsed. I'm sorry but I am going to have to insist that someone in my chain of command can bail me out if needed.'

Rupert thought for a moment. 'That's not unreasonable Jon and actually we have thought about it but it will have to be at a very high level indeed.'

'Go on, I need to know who you are considering.'

'The Secretary of State is the obvious man.'

'And the First Sea Lord please.'

'Really, why him?'

'He's the head of my service and frankly, I don't trust politicians.' Seeing the look on Rupert's face he continued. 'No, not in that way, I'm sure he's no spy but if suddenly it was politic to throw me to the wolves can you guarantee he wouldn't do just that?

Bog Hammer

The First Sea Lord wouldn't and he would have immediate influence on my direct naval chain of command.'

'Fair enough, trust me I'll sort it out before we move forward.'

'Thanks, well on that basis what's the sneaky idea?'

Rupert told him.

Bog Hammer

Chapter 10

Prometheus made it out of dockyard hands late and with a list of defects that still needed rectification. However, none were critical so her programme wasn't changed. After initial sea trials she was declared fit to proceed even though there were misgivings amongst some of the ship's officers. She left Plymouth for the naval base at Portland to undergo Basic Operational Sea Training, the dreaded BOST.

Four weeks into the six week training period, the wardroom were taking a rare break from the almost continual serials thrown at them by the Flag Officer Sea Training staff. It was a late lunch and most of the officers were gathered in the wardroom. The morning had been spent providing 'Humanitarian Relief' to the small town of 'FOSTeria' which in reality was the old gun emplacements on the side of Portland Bill, just above where the ship was docked.

'Alright everyone, just shut up for a moment and listen to me.' Des Slater called over the general hubbub. 'I've just had feedback from the Disaster Exercise we conducted this morning. You will be glad to know that the civilian population of the village we went to help are suitably grateful for our aid to the civil power that we provided. The support teams did a good job and the overall assessment by FOST staff was satisfactory, so well done.'

There were some surprised looks around the assembled officers. 'Bloody hell Number One that makes a change,' an anonymous voice offered up.

'Thank you whoever that was,' Des replied drily. 'Anyway, let's keep it up now.'

Just then the door slid open and the Flight Commander, Jerry Thompson came in. 'Sorry I'm late, had to get out of my flying kit, Tom will be along shortly. OK, why are you lot all laughing at me?'

Indeed there were chuckles breaking out all round.

'Er Jerry, you really don't know?' Brian asked.

'Sorry not a clue, I thought it all went rather well.'

Brian continued. 'Jerry when you flew Fred the Lynx up to the relief landing ground, did you notice a small fire below where you were hovering?'

'Yes but there was nowhere else to go until the lads had cleared the landing site of the rioters.'

'So you hovered off to one side for a while, and unfortunately your downdraft turned the small fire into a raging inferno. The nurses from Osprey sickbay were in attendance, assessing the first aid work the shore party were doing and they were dressed in their clean white uniforms.'

'Oh shit, I think I know where this is going.'

'You've got it, by the time you moved away and landed, they had been engulfed in the smoke and when it cleared they looked like something from a Benny Hill sketch after a bomb has gone off.'

'Oh bugger, did it affect the overall exercise?'

Des responded. 'Luckily for you it didn't. Nearly everyone saw the funny side but you'd better go up to sick bay after lunch and apologise.'

A wide grin broke over Jerry's face. 'Never turn down an excuse to apologise to a bunch of cute nurses Number One. I'm on it.'

'Oh shit,' Brian muttered to the MEO, who was sitting next to him. 'The last thing we needed was to give that tomcat another excuse to go chasing the girls.'

'Spoken like a true married man,' came the reply. 'Anyway, now the First of all Lieutenants has finished, I'm for some lunch. I haven't eaten since six this morning.'

The officers all moved en masse into the dining area and a convivial lunch then followed. For the first time in the BOST period, they actually had the afternoon off to catch up on basic admin work and it almost felt like a holiday.

For Brian, however, it was different. An Operations officers work was never done and the next day they would be partaking in the weekly Thursday War, when all the ships currently training left Portland for a simulated war exercise. This would be Prometheus's last 'war' and they had been given the privilege of being in command. The exercise scenario signal had already arrived and Brian spent the afternoon going through it so he could brief the Captain and other staff on what would be expected of them.

At seventeen hundred, all the ships Heads of Department mustered in the Captain's cabin for the brief. After a nod from Captain, Brian stood with a clipboard of signals in his hand.

'Gentlemen, tomorrow's Thursday War is going to be interesting, even if it is our last one. We will be in command as OTG and we sail at seven in the morning in company with three other Frigates and two RFAs. One of the RFAs has been designated as a carrier and as the High Value Unit, it's our job to keep her safe. Unfortunately, we will not be able to call on any of her fixed wing air assets as, of course, she doesn't actually have any. However, both of the RFAs have a Sea King embarked, so we can use them to screen our transit once we are in the deeper water clear of Portland Bill. We will need them, as the Dutch submarine also doing work up will be out there waiting for us. We can also expect air attack at any time from when we've cleared the breakwater. It will be in the form of Hunters from Yeovilton. Some will be doing conventional bombing but after ten in the morning all fixed wing will be simulating sea skimming missiles, so let's hope the Sea Wolf is up to it. So far nothing particularly unusual. However, there's a sting in the tail of this one. There is intelligence that the Soviets have a Foxtrot class conventional submarine somewhere in the area. She was spotted, along with a support ship, out in the south west approaches a couple of days ago but contact was lost. It's possible they may want to have a look at us exercising, after all we do it to them quite often. Whatever the reason, if there is any chance of her interfering, we stop exercising and become the hunter with an aim to letting her know that we know what she's up to.'

General debate followed Brian's briefing. After a few minutes the Captains stood.

'Thank you everyone, we all know what to do, please let yourselves out,' and he walked through the curtain into his night cabin without a further word. Brian and Des were the last to leave.

When they were well clear and out of earshot, Brian turned to Des and muttered quietly. 'It's nice to see Father in one of his more decisive moods. I just pray it stays until tomorrow.'

Des looked pensive. 'Brian, normally I would not let a remark like that stand. If it was anyone other than you I would give them a bollocking.' Then he sighed, 'but you're right of course. Just between you and me you'd better be ready to step in if he clams up on us again.'

Bog Hammer

The next day, things actually started off quite well. Brian and the Captain managed the Ops room with the Navigating Officer as Officer of the Watch on the bridge. Sure enough within minutes of leaving the harbour, fixed wing aircraft were detected. There was a limited channel for the departure around Portland Bill because FOST had declared a minefield out to the east, so the little fleet were unable to manoeuvre, which was of course why the aircraft attacked when they did. However, a good fight was put up and the FOST staff declared a successful departure. As soon as they cleared land, the two Sea Kings launched and started an active sonar barrier ahead of the force by hovering and lowering their sonar transducers into the water and then continually jumping ahead to clear the way for the ships. Prometheus's Lynx was launched soon afterwards to conduct a surface search up threat of the force, no easy task in such a crowded waterway and the other two Lynx were kept on deck alert. For a while, it was all quiet.

Suddenly the radio on the anti-submarine warfare net woke into life and one of the Sea Kings called a contact. For an hour they chased it until a simulated attack by one of the Lynx bought it to the surface. Honours were declared even as the Dutch submarine had declared an attack on one of the Frigates just before the Sea King found it.

Fifty miles ahead, Prometheus's Lynx was trying to make sense of a very busy radar image. Tom Pinter, the aircrafts Observer had been plotting ships everywhere. Luckily most were in the designated shipping lanes but you could never assume that the 'enemy' wouldn't use that for cover before sneaking out to make an attack. There were also enough other contacts spread around elsewhere to make life difficult.

'Sounds like they're having fun back at the force.' Jerry said as he listened in to the radio traffic.

'Yeah, they seem to have nailed that Cloggy sub though. That's good work, they're bloody hard to detect.' Tom responded.

'When shall we give them the next problem?' Tom asked. 'I've got a nice target ahead of them at about forty miles and closing.'

'Well the FOST staff said anytime we had a real contact, after the ASW phase, so about now I guess. They will be in Exocet range in about twenty minutes so we can start targeting for them soon. We'd better go and have a quick look at what the target actually is first though.'

It didn't take long to identify the radar target as a large ferry. In fact, they soon realised it was the one that operated out of Weymouth.

'I wonder if they know how many times the navy have sunk them over the years?' Tom asked jokingly. 'Anyway let's head back to our patrol position and alert mother to the enemy.'

Jerry turned the aircraft and headed back to the force. While the aircraft was facing away from the target the radar was useless as it only scanned a one hundred and eighty degree arc ahead of the aircraft, so he accelerated up to one hundred and fifty knots, to minimise the time the contact was not being tracked.

Suddenly something caught his eye. 'Tom, what the fuck is that in the water?' As he said it, he flared the aircraft and banked hard so they could both look down.

Perfectly visible four hundred feet below were a row of six black buoys in a line and it was clear from the wake behind them that they were moving quite fast through the water. It could only be one thing.

'Are there any of our boats around Tom?' Jerry asked.

'Not that we've been briefed on but that is definitely a submarine High Frequency radio aerial and if it's not ours then there's only one thing it can be.'

'Right mate you call it.' Jerry said.

'Bravo Charlie Xray Three this is Echo Mike Delta Five. Probsub, high four, in my position based on visual identification of surface trailing aerial. Will continue to track, my endurance is one hour twenty minutes. Request active assets to join me.'

In the Ops room the radio call caught them all by surprise. Without thinking, Brian ordered the two Sea Kings to break dip and join the Lynx before turning to the Captain who seemed to be staring into space. Taking that as confirmation that he was doing the right thing, he ordered the force to suspend the exercise and proceed with them towards the datum position.

The air in the Operations Room was electric, no one apart from Brian had any actual experience of a real encounter with the Soviets and no one doubted for a moment that they had caught the Soviet Foxtrot unawares. They also knew that wouldn't last for long.

Brian turned to the Captain. 'Sir, do we order the Sea Kings into the dip and alert the submarine that we are on to him or hold off while the Lynx is tracking his aerial?'

There was no response.

'Sir, I need a decision.'

'Do what you think is best Ops,' was the only reply.

'Get the Sea Kings pinging as soon as you can,' Brian called to the ASW director. 'We don't want to lose him if he pulls that aerial in, which he will do as soon as he knows he's been rumbled.'

'Right, it's going to take twenty minutes to get there, I'm just going up to my cabin for a few minutes. Ops you keep things going.' And to everyone's astonishment, the Captain got up from his chair and left.

There was too much going on for Brian to worry and the Captain returned before they were within sonar range of the Soviet. He was a changed man. Crisply ordering the disposition of the force, they soon had the Russian evading them until he clearly decided to sit on the bottom and wait for all the Brits to go home. That afternoon they were called off. They had made their point as had the Soviet but it had been invaluable training for the whole ship and morale was high as they re-entered Portland harbour. It improved even more when the FOST staff actually gave them a 'well done' assessment for the whole day's work.

That evening, Brian was torn between satisfaction at how well the whole day had gone and despair about what to do about the Captain. When he had returned that morning, in the dark confines of the Ops room, he could immediately smell the sour taint of alcohol on the Captain's breath. The problem was that knowing about it and being able to do something about it were two totally different things.

Chapter 11

Jon looked around the strange conference room in amazement. It was completely out of character with the rest of the building. The walls were covered in old oil paintings, mainly of sea going warships and were richly papered with a gold and green embossed paper. The ceiling was ornate plasterwork and the crystal chandelier wouldn't be out of place in Buckingham Palace. Yet apparently it was one of the most secure rooms inside the Ministry of Defence, daily swept for bugs and used for the most classified of meetings. He had been summoned here by an anonymous phone call that morning. The caller didn't give his name and he had no idea who else would be attending, as the room was currently empty. With nothing else to do, he availed himself of a cup of coffee from the free standing flask and several chocolate Bourbons which he proceeded to dunk while he examined some of the paintings.

Suddenly the door opened and a tall thin man in an expensive looking suit entered. With a shock, Jon recognised the Secretary of State for Defence. Behind him and smiling slightly came Rupert and two other suited men.

The Minister held out his hand as he came over to Jon who was frantically trying to find somewhere to deposit his coffee cup and half a soggy biscuit.

'Commander Hunt I believe.' The Minister's handshake was firm and although his mouth smiled his eyes were flinty hard.

'Yes Sir,' Jon responded, having managed to put his cup down.

'I've heard a great deal about you Commander and hope that you will be able to help us in this rather delicate matter, is that so?'

Jon looked over to Rupert who nodded slightly. 'Yes Sir, although I don't have any details about what exactly is expected of me.'

'No I understand that but you do know it's a matter of serious national security?'

'Yes Sir, Mr Thomas has outlined the problem but not the potential solution.'

'That's what this meeting is about. I won't be staying. I will leave you in his tender care but quite rightly you have asked for assurance that this won't rebound on you.'

Before Jon could respond, he continued. 'No, I understand and if I were in your shoes I would want the same. Rest assured, that whatever the outcome of this exercise is, you will not be compromised. You act with my full backing and authority. Here is a letter signed by me stating exactly that. Given a fair wind that should never be necessary.'

He handed Jon an envelope. 'And take my personal thanks for your involvement. We really need to plug this leak urgently. With all that is going on in the Soviet Union these days, this is the last thing we need. Hopefully, we won't need to speak again. Good day.' So saying the Minister left the room.

The temperature in the room rose by several degrees. Rupert introduced his two companions. 'Jon, this is Derek Smith from the Directorate of Naval Security. He's representing MI5 and this is Doctor Michael Patrick from the Defence Research Establishment at Farnborough.'

They all shook hands and Jon retrieved his cup and soggy biscuit while the others availed themselves of the facilities. They all took a seat and Rupert then called the meeting to order.

'Gentlemen, we all know why we are here but to summarise, we have been aware for some months now that intelligence had been reaching the Russians that can only have come from this building. Please don't ask me how I know, as you will not get an answer. However, what I can tell you is that all of it is classified Top Secret and is related to aviation matters, which is one of the main reasons that Commander Hunt is involved. He has only joined the MOD recently and so cannot have been party to the information and also to be honest, we have worked together before and I trust him implicitly.'

The other two men nodded and Jon didn't know whether to smile or blush, so he remained impassive.

'So what are we going to do about it?' Rupert continued. 'The idea is quite simple. We are going to invent a new and fictitious technology which is why Doctor Patrick is involved as it has to appear credible. A proposal will come into the MOD at Top Secret classification and also code worded. The distribution will be

Bog Hammer

extremely limited to start with, comprising certain senior staff and Jon as the desk officer for the project. Another reason for Jon's involvement is that the first test vehicle will be a Lynx for which he has responsibility. We will know within two months whether our leak is one of the people with clearance and if it isn't we will widen the net until something gives. Clear so far?'

Everyone nodded. 'Right, I'll hand over to the good Doctor to tell us of his miraculous breakthrough.'

Doctor Patrick coughed and then started to speak. He was in his sixties, with a thin hawk nose and a rather nasal voice. 'What we have come up with is a project which is called 'High Eye'. The reason will be clear in a moment. It is based on some very theoretical research that certainly at the moment is a blind alley but which could appear totally credible to an outsider. As you know radar operates at high radio frequencies. 'High Eye' is a project to produce a radar system that operates at extremely high frequencies, X-rays to be exact. To make such a system work, the X-rays would have to be coherent like laser light and we know no way of doing that but if we could, we are talking about immensely long ranges and the ability to see through solid objects. It would be a military game changer in all senses of the phrase. The project is meant to be past the experimental stage and we are supposed to have a prototype that we want to install in an aircraft within the next two years. The plan will be to do all this at the Experimental Establishment at Boscombe Down in one of the D Squadron Lynx aircraft.'

'Thank you doctor,' Rupert said. 'In case you're wondering Jon, we need a fully credible audit trail, so we will be generating correspondence from Farnborough to the MOD on the subject. It was, in fact, a real MOD sponsored research package but is about to be wound up as the good doctor pointed out because it had been concluded that the technology can't work. However, by keeping it alive, so to speak, it will appear totally credible. Derek, could you please outline your involvement.'

Derek Smith looked less like a security spook than anyone Jon could imagine. He was middle aged, with thinning sandy hair and could have been anyone's favourite uncle. *'Which was probably why he was chosen for the job'*, Jon thought.

'Jon, my role is to be your contact for all this. Rupert's lot will be monitoring the end of the pipeline to see if anything turns up over the far side. I will be leading the subsequent hunt in this country. We actually have one more person on the team from within the MOD. He is in the internal security organisation but we want to keep things as simple as possible, so I will remain your only contact, at least for the moment. So, shortly the relevant correspondence will arrive in Main Building and a meeting will be called. You will be acting as secretary and will take all the minutes. For at least six months we need to do nothing more than exchange paperwork and consequently look for any leakage. After that, if nothing has happened, we will review the situation. The good doctor actually has some equipment faked up that should give us at least another year before we have to stop the whole project. Hopefully, we will have caught whoever it is long before then. Any questions?'

They talked detail for another half an hour and then the meeting broke up. Before he left Rupert took Jon aside.

'Bad news I'm afraid Jon, now that we're under way with this we'll have to stop the socials.'

'What no more meals on MI6 expenses? Damn, I was getting used to those. But yes of course, I understand let's just hope we catch this bastard whoever he is.'

Later that evening when his office was empty, Jon opened the letter the Minister had given him. Not only did it give him the guarantees he had asked for but it had also been countersigned by the First Sea Lord. However, despite the reassurance the words on the page gave him, he still wondered whether they would enough if things went badly wrong.

He put it in a very secure place in his personal safe.

Two weeks later he was back in the same meeting room sitting around the highly polished wooden table. The meeting was chaired by the three star Director, Air Marshall Johnson, who Jon had never actually met but who looked vaguely familiar. He was a surprisingly youthful looking man with a shock of jet black hair and the lean figure of someone who kept himself fit. Prior to the meeting, Jon had been called into his Admiral's office and he had outlined what was required of Jon, which was basically to write the minutes if required. As Jon already knew all about it, he spent most of the time trying to appear suitably surprised by the whole idea.

Seated around the table were the three service two star officers, and Jon's boss, Captain Desmonde as well as Doctor Patrick. Looking at the assembled throng Jon couldn't imagine for the life of him that anyone here would be a traitor. He strongly suspected that the net would have to be cast wider but the project had to start somewhere.

The Director stood and welcomed all the attendees and asked them to introduce themselves. When they had gone around the table, he continued. 'Gentlemen what you hear today is classified as Top Secret, it is also under the code word 'High Eye'. Only those cleared to that code word are allowed access to any of the material and that is those people in this room only, I hope that is clear. Also, these meetings will not be minuted. Only notes taken of any actions allocated.'

There were nods all around the table. Everyone in the room had been in similar situations in the past.

The Director continued. 'Now many of you will be aware of the first law of secrecy, that the more classified something is, often the more boring it is as well. Well, not this time. Doctor Patrick here from Farnborough is going to brief us on a new technology that they have developed that has the potential to be a world beater. To our knowledge, no one else in the world has been working in this area and I don't think I'm exaggerating when I say that this is a breakthrough as fundamental as the invention of milli-metric radar in the last war. I think it best to let Doctor Patrick explain. Doctor the floor is yours.'

For the next half an hour Doctor Patrick outlined the project. Jon was impressed, the man seemed a natural actor but he also realised that much of the work that was being explained had actually been undertaken. It was only the conclusions that had been changed, that and the need to conduct airborne trials in the future.

Once the doctor had finished, the Director stood again. 'Thank you Doctor Patrick, I think I can say how impressed we all are and that you have clearly come up with something so amazing. Now, it is still early days and there is much work to do before this is turned into a practical device. This is the inaugural project meeting and for now it will be kept limited to this group. Commander Hunt here from DOR (Sea) will be the lead desk officer as well as secretary to this steering group. Any questions?'

The meeting lasted another half an hour and then the Director wound it up. After it was over Captain Desmonde came over to Jon. 'Are you familiar with the procedure for writing minutes at this classification Jon?'

'Not really Sir but I assume it's similar to the normal process?'

'Sort of, you must use a typewriter though and the ribbon must be destroyed afterwards also copies are only to be made with special authorisation. Any notes you have are to be logged as separate items and that includes your note book there. Either that or it has to be destroyed after you've written up the actions. Look, go to the X registry on the fourth floor and get the secretary there to brief you on the full process, I suspect you are going to become very familiar with it over the next few months.'

Jon did as he was told and found the classified or 'X registry' as it was known down a quiet corridor. He knocked and after a few moments was let in by an incredibly pretty girl. Long dark hair and a slim figure was hardly what he was expecting.

'Commander Hunt?' She enquired.

Jon nodded.

'We've been expecting you. Can I confirm your identification first please?'

Jon held up the photo ID card everyone wore on a lanyard around their necks when inside the building.

'That's fine Sir. I'm Petty Officer Jones and I manage all the Top Secret files for the naval section along with Lieutenant Horridge and Mr Thomas our tame Civil Servant. I'm afraid they're both out today so you're stuck with me.'

Jon managed to keep a straight face. He could think of worse people to be stuck with. For the next half hour, he was briefed on all the detailed procedures he would have to follow. It was clear that security was kept very tight indeed.

A thought struck him. 'Do the staff here have access to the contents of these files?'

'No Sir, only authorised officers can read them. For this new High Eyes project, we have a separate locked filing cabinet over here. I will ask you to set the combination and only you and the other code word authorised officers can see the files. In fact, only you will have the combination. We will ask you to put a copy of the combination in another secure safe that only you and Lieutenant

Horridge have access to in case you are not available in an emergency. It goes inside a sealed envelope, inside two sheets of carbon paper, so it can't be seen by shining a light through it and with your signature over all the seams so it can't be tampered with, in. It's all standard procedure. All files have to be signed out in person and they are mustered every three months by yourself and one of us.'

'Wow, it looks like I'm going to be pretty busy then?'

'Actually in my experience, Sir, the files are not accessed that often but of course it depends on the project. So we won't be seeing that much of each other I'm afraid.' She smiled at him.

Jon suddenly realised he was being flirted with and almost automatically for a moment was tempted to respond. Then a vision of Helen floated in front of him and he discarded the thought.

'Thank you Petty Officer Jones,' he replied rather more curtly than he had intended, so he continued in a more consolatory tone. 'You've been very helpful, yes I'm sure we will be seeing each other fairly often over the next few months. Now you'd better show me where I can type up my notes for the new file.'

Jon spent fifteen minutes typing a brief set of action notes from the meeting onto a standard form and then logging those and the briefing notes provided by Doctor Patrick as the first documents in a new file. He then shredded his own notebook from the meeting. After that he set the combination of the filing cabinet on the Manifoil Mark Four combination lock and having checked it worked before shutting the door, he then secured everything inside. Petty Officer Jones provided him with an envelope and he wrote the combination down, secured it inside within the sheets of carbon paper and then sealed it by signing over all the seams and then covering them with Sellotape. This was then secured in another small safe which had been left open for him and the job was done.

Later that day, Jon returned to the registry and signed the file out. He placed it in a locked brief case and took it around to all the attendees of the meeting. The Air Marshall left him waiting in his outer office but only took a few minutes to read and sign off the file. The other attendees signed it off even faster. It seemed no one wanted to hang on to such sensitive material for any length of time. Once the file was secured back in its locked cabinet, Jon breathed a sigh of relief.

Bog Hammer

'*The trap is set,*' he thought with some trepidation.

Chapter 12

Jon felt slightly uncomfortable in his best Number Five Uniform. Not because he was embarrassed because he had more medals than anyone else, including the Admiral who was presenting the wings today but because he realised he must be putting on weight. Either that or the damned uniform had shrunk in the year it had been sitting quietly in his wardrobe. He shrugged off the discomfort and looked around. The hangar of 705 Squadron had been cleaned and the neat row of bright orange Gazelle helicopters had been lined up along one side. The crowd of parents and other well-wishers, including Jon, were behind a barrier by the hanger doors. A dais had been erected on the other side and the Admiral was standing expectantly as Helen's Flight marched past with her in front. He felt a swell of pride seeing her. They may have shared their bed all night and breakfast that morning but that didn't stop her looking adorable and thoroughly professional at the same time. Calling the Flight to a halt she turned them towards the Admiral and saluted with the drawn ceremonial sword in her right hand.

'Fifty Six Flight ready for your inspection Sir,' she shouted in her parade ground voice. The Admiral saluted back and came down and joined her as they walked along the double rank of successful helicopter students. He then went back to the dais and one by one the officers were called forward and presented with their wings, which the Admiral fastened to their left sleeve just above the gold rings of their rank with a patch of temporary Velcro. Jon couldn't help but remember the same ceremony, in this same hanger, all those years ago when he had been given his wings. He suddenly realised he was even prouder of Helen than he had been himself on that day.

It had been a great week. He had taken leave and put the whole hassle of London behind him. The squadron boss, an old friend had invited Jon up to the squadron and shown him around personally. It was a long way from his day when they flew the old piston engined Hillers and Whirlwinds. The Gazelle was a quantum leap in terms of technology, with its gas turbine engine and modern control systems. He was then surprised to be offered a trip in one of the smart new machines. Although he had been hoping for the offer he hadn't wanted to ask in case his rank made it hard to refuse. Because he was no longer current as aircrew, they gave him the safety briefing all passengers have to go through and he put up with it without complaint. What surprised him totally was that as he entered the briefing room for the pre-flight brief, there was Helen already dressed up in her flying gear. Nearly everyone kept a straight face as Jon twigged who his pilot was going to be. Although they had talked about the possibility of doing this sometime before, he hadn't really considered it as a practical reality. However, the CO was quite adamant that as Helen had passed the course even though her wings hadn't been officially awarded yet, she was qualified to fly another naval pilot, even if he was her husband.

The Gazelle was an amazing machine. He and Helen sat side by side in a little glass bubble with the instrument panel in the middle of the cockpit which meant the view dead ahead was uncluttered by anything. Not wanting to put her off, he kept quiet while she went through all the pre-flight checks. Just before they took off, he almost shouted that she was pushing the rudder pedals the wrong way but managed to stop himself when he remembered that the main rotors of the aircraft rotated in the opposite direction to other naval helicopters. You had to use the opposite rudder to counteract the torque. Helen hover taxied clear of the squadron and was given clearance to take off by air traffic. Jon was immediately impressed by her coordination and flying skill. The aircraft seemed to be a natural extension of her arms and feet. They flew north into the local area.

'What do you think so far Jon?' she asked and turned to look at him.

'Bloody marvellous,' he replied. 'I'd forgotten just how much I missed flying and this machine seems the business.'

'You don't get in it, you wear it,' she replied. 'Do you want a go?'

'Try and stop me.'

For almost an hour they flew around Cornwall, delighting in the shared experience of the lovely little machine. Helen demonstrated some of the manoeuvrability that it had which was almost as good as his old love the Lynx and Jon got to grips with flying it. All too soon it was time to return. As they approached the airfield, Jon asked Helen if he could use the radio.

She gave him an odd look but nodded.

'Tower this is four two, is the circuit clear, over?'

'Four two affirmative,' came the reply.

'In that case, request direct clearance to seven oh five pan over.'

There was a definite chuckle in the controller's voice as the reply came. 'Four two you are cleared to approach as you see fit over.'

Jon turned and grinned at Helen. 'You know you've wanted to do this or you wouldn't be a pilot. That's permission to beat up the squadron if ever I heard it. Go for it.'

Helen grinned. 'And if I get a bollocking, I will say my Commander husband told me to do it.'

'Absolutely correct.'

The airfield perimeter was coming up and Helen dumped the collective and dropped the little helicopter's nose so that it was pointing down at about thirty degrees, straight at the squadron building alongside the hangar. She lined up so that they would pass right in front of the office block and as they approached the ground at about one hundred and fifty miles an hour she pulled in the collective and levelled out just above the ground. In the little glass cockpit, the rush of the ground below their feet gave an incredible impression of speed.

In a flash, they shot past the squadron offices at a height that was lower than the upper windows. Jon briefly caught a glimpse of faces looking out and then they were past. Helen pulled the nose of the machine up to almost vertical and let the speed wash off before rolling almost onto their back before diving back down in a perfect wingover. They shot back past the squadron before she banked the aircraft hard to the left and let speed wash off in the turn before flaring hard and coming to a hover directly over their landing spot. They touched down with hardly a bump.

Jon was very impressed. 'Bloody hell girl, not only have I got a wonderful wife but she's a damned good pilot as well.'

Helen turned to him. 'Well, I've been set a hard example to follow.' She leaned forward to try to kiss him but their helmets bumped long before their lips could meet.

He laughed. 'Don't you think you should shut this thing down, it looks like they've arranged the photographic department to meet us.'

Walking towards them, the squadron boss was accompanied by a senior rate with a large camera in his hands. Helen shut the aircraft down and they unstrapped and climbed out.

'Nice arrival Helen,' the Boss commented drily. 'I've checked and there are no rotor blade marks down the side of the building. It seems your husband has been teaching you bad habits already.' The laughter in his eyes belied any censure in his words. 'And now we need some photos for Navy News, the first husband and wife sortie in a military aircraft will be a good PR exercise if nothing else.'

Jon came back to the present with a start. All the students were now back in their places with their new wings proudly in place and the Admiral was about to talk.

'Ladies and gentlemen, parents and families, you should all be very proud. Obtaining a set of naval wings is not an easy task. Of course, it's not the final step in training to go front line but these officers will be able to wear their wings for the rest of their careers, whatever happens next. Now, I have one pleasant duty left to me and that is to announce the award to the top student. This award is accompanied by the presentation of a sword donated by Westland Helicopters. Lieutenant Helen Hunt, please step forward.'

Even Jon hadn't been expecting this. As Helen walked towards the dais the Admiral stepped down with a sword and scabbard in his hands and handed it to her.

'Well done Helen,' he said in a voice that all could hear. 'Not only the best student but also the first female student. Very well done indeed.'

Later that afternoon in the wardroom bar, Jon finally got Helen to himself. 'You clever sod, did you know you were top student?'

'No honestly, it came as a surprise to me as well.'

'So what now? Has the CO told you what options you have? He wasn't keen to tell me before you had been given the option to think about it.'

A small frown crossed her face. 'Yes, we were all called in individually before the ceremony to have our horoscopes read and be told where we were going. He said he couldn't offer me a Lynx Flight even though I was felt to be good enough because no small ships had been converted for female officers yet. Apparently, the same goes for both of the carrier based Sea King squadrons. The

Junglies are out for the same reason. I'm not surprised. So that leaves 826 who operate in Flights off various RFA's which do have suitable accommodation or 771 Search and Rescue who have just re-equipped with Sea Kings. What do you think I should do Jon?'

'Hm, 826 will be operational flying but 771 will be far more fun. It's rare for a new pilot to be offered that option, so you should take that as a great compliment. Search and Rescue is for real, you will be doing something valuable rather than just practicing for World War Three which seems to be looking less and less likely.'

'And there is another, much better reason, for choosing 771.'

'Oh, what?'

'Being shore based from Culdrose means we will be able to see much more of each other.'

'Oh, I hadn't thought of that.'

Chapter 13

Jon had discovered a new love in his life. The week after the Wings parade he had surprised Helen with a two week holiday to Egypt. There was a new resort being developed at the village of Sharm el Sheik and the prices were excellent. However, after just one day sitting around the pool boredom had started setting in. Helen seemed quite happy to lie in the sun and read a book, Jon realised he needed something to occupy him. So when some staff from the local diving club offered a day out to try Scuba diving he dragged Helen along. He loved it, she wasn't so sure but agreed to do the one week course with him. Once she realised that she could still work on her tan she started to enjoy it as well. When the course was finished they had another three days to start exploring the local reefs.

They were both enchanted. The water was almost body temperature and crystal clear. On more than one occasion Jon completely forgot he was underwater at all, seemingly suspended as if by magic as a variety of colourful fish swam by, ignoring him. They both found that their rapport above water also worked for them below and diving together as buddy pair seemed as natural as breathing. All too soon their time ran out but Jon vowed to come back next year and even investigate diving at home, even though all the pundits in Egypt warned him it was cold and murky.

Then in what seemed almost no time at all he was back at his desk in London. This time the capital was hot and sweaty which only seemed to make the exhaust fumes even worse. The only consolation, as one of his colleagues pointed out, was that the girls were wearing far less clothing which made the daily commute something less of a chore.

'Hey guys come in here,' Captain Desmonde called around his inner office door. 'CNN have some interesting news.'

Jon and the rest of the team crammed into the Captain's small office and looked at the small television he kept on a shelf by his desk. The announcer was just finishing a piece. There was a photograph of an American warship and superimposed over it a shot of an Airbus A 300 civilian airliner.

Bog Hammer

'Sorry guys, the piece has just finished but it looks like our American friends have fucked up yet again. The airliner was Iranian and the Yank cruiser has just shot it down.'

There was a stunned silence for a second. Then Dennis Osmond spoke. 'How the hell could they do that? That ship has the Aegis radar system on board. Jesus, if it can't tell the difference between an airliner and a military target what chance has anyone got?'

'Christ, most people think that the war in the Gulf is almost over,' Jon observed. 'God knows what this will do to tension in the area. I bet our Armilla patrol ship will be on her toes now.'

'Talking of which, how's the machine gun UOR going now Jon?' Captain Desmonde asked.

'Its deployed now Sir, the only real problem is that its range is less than quite a lot of the missiles the Bog Hammers have so the Lynx has to intercept at a good distance from their ship but does seem to be acting as a deterrent if nothing else. Keeps the bad guy's heads down instead of giving them a clear shot.'

'Good, well, it looks like the news has moved on from that item. However, I'm sure we will be hearing more about this incident. Oh and don't forget it's the monthly brief this evening in the wine cellar, so see you all there.'

Taking the hint, they all filed out and went back to their desks.

At five that evening, they all made their way down to the basement level. Jon could never get over what was down there. There was a large open space at least three stories high but instead of being empty, it held an ancient building made of carved stone. Inside it was held up with a series of stone arches. A legacy of when the MOD building was built over the top of it. It really was a wine cellar from the time of Henry the Eighth. Out of place it might be but it was a great venue for social gatherings. A table and chairs had been set out and Captain Desmonde took charge. Speakers were invited on a rota basis to keep all the naval aviators in touch with what was going on around the MOD. They were only allowed five minutes and the Captain had a large hand bell which he would ring once when there was a minute to go and then continually if the miscreant didn't shut up when his time was up. It was a very effective way of keeping the more verbose officers in line. However, this evening there was a break in tradition as the issue of the downed Iranian airliner was the

Bog Hammer

sole topic of discussion. It was confirmed that the aircraft was actually climbing out of the airport in Iran when the US Cruiser fired on it. However, it seemed that the ship was claiming that it had identified the radar from the aircraft as that of an F14 Tomcat which the Iranians were still managing to operate as a legacy of the days of the Shah. The general consensus was that it was clearly a tragic mistake. The ship was being attacked by eight Iranian Bog Hammers at the time, so maybe there was some excuse but with one of the most sophisticated command systems in the world on board, it still seems very strange that such a simple error could have been made.

Eventually, the meeting wound up and everyone made their way over to the table that in the tradition of the building was covered in glasses, several cases of wine and a large keg of beer. The level of conversation rose as the level of wine and beer diminished and before Jon knew it he was being enticed once more into a run ashore with the rest of the team. Captain Desmonde was clearly firing on all cylinders and he realised that yet another sore head was in the offing.

Not much later and they were all ensconced around a table in Whites. The plan such as it was, was to make a start there and then move on, probably into the murky depths of Soho for dinner. Jon had been telling his colleagues about his Egyptian holiday and his discovery of the joys of diving. As the others had yet to take any summer leave, he was fined for being too cheerful and sent to the bar to get in the next round. As he stood at the bar waiting to catch the barman's eye a familiar voice made his head turn.

'Hello Jon, I hope you are not too unhappy to see me?'

Inga, he knew that voice anywhere. 'Hello Inga, fancy meeting you again. No, actually I should thank you. Look, I'm a married man now.' He held out his left hand for her to see the wedding band.

'Well, I would never have expected that. Do I know the lucky girl?'

'No, I don't think so, we only met after I returned from America.' He studied Inga as he spoke. She was still the stunningly lovely, golden haired girl that he remembered but there was something different about her. She was expensively dressed for a start and there was an air of confidence that wasn't there when he knew her in Norway and afterwards. Just for a moment, he had a fantasy what it would be like to get her and Helen into bed at the same time. He quickly clamped down on the thought and forced himself back to the conversation. 'Well I have to say that life seems to be treating you well, what are you up to these days?'

'Oh, just living my life, you know, having fun.'

'Let me guess, there's a rich boyfriend around somewhere.'

She smiled at him. 'Of course Jon, how did you guess?'

He was spared the need to answer as a man appeared at her side and gave her a peck on the cheek. She turned and returned the kiss. With a start, Jon recognised the man he had seen her meeting all those months ago and also the man he was working with on Rupert's little project, Air Marshall Johnson.

'Ah, hello there Commander Hunt,' he said. 'Inga told me that you two knew each other in another life. You'll have to excuse us but we have tickets for the theatre and unless we rush we will be late.'

Before he knew it, Inga was whisked away and the barman was ready for his order.

When he returned to the table with the tray of drinks, there was great interest in the blonde he had been apparently chatting up.

'Sorry guys, she's an ex-girlfriend' he explained. 'And anyway, she's just gone off to the theatre with our good Air Marshall.'

Captain Desmonde nodded. 'Doesn't surprise me, he's known to like expensive women. He has private means apparently. The Air Marshall comes from a very wealthy family.'

Jon laughed. 'He'll need it to keep Inga in the manner to which she's clearly become accustomed. I always said she would marry a millionaire. It's probably one of the reasons she gave me the old heave ho. But bloody hell isn't he a bit old for her?'

'Middle fifties and she's what, early thirties. No, pretty standard if you ask me.' The Captain replied.

The conversation moved on and so did they all once they had finished their drinks. The next morning Jon's head felt just like he had anticipated. He was the first into the office so he busied himself with the coffee maker, sure that everyone would want its services when they arrived. He was interrupted by the telephone. It was Rupert.

'Jon we need to meet, lunch time in St James Park please, the bench opposite the old cabinet War Rooms.'

'Fine...'

Rupert cut him off. 'Don't say anymore Jon, see you there at one.' And he hung up.

Mystified and not a little intrigued Jon made his excuses at lunchtime and headed out across Horse Guards Parade to the park on the other side. Rupert was already there and as Jon approached he got up and walked next to him.

'Just keep walking Jon, just the two of us having a stroll.'

'Bloody hell Rupert this all a bit Jon Le Carre isn't it?'

Rupert ignored the remark. 'Listen, things are moving. It would appear someone has taken our bait. I can't tell you how I know but the project code word has appeared in another country. I need you to check all the paperwork and see if there is anything irregular and then we need to meet this evening. We won't use the MOD, meet me at Thames House at seven tonight, they will have your name on the door.'

Before Jon could answer Rupert turned and walked away down a side path.

'*Bloody hell,*' thought Jon. '*It's getting really serious now.*'

Chapter 14

That evening Jon walked past the Houses of Parliament and Westminster Abbey, down the embankment to Thames House. Unlike the modern and garish green glass building on the south bank that housed MI6 these days, Thames House was made of traditional stone like all the other government buildings in the area. He entered through the imposing doors and gave his name to the receptionist. Within minutes Derek Smith appeared and whisked him into the bowels of the buildings which was very different to the external facade. It was ultra-modern in an antiseptic way. Within a minute Jon was lost as they made their way down a maze of corridors to end up in a bland modern looking room with a central table and several chairs. Rupert got up as he entered and offered Jon a coffee from the government standard coffee flask.

'Sorry about all the John le Carre stuff as you put it Jon but the operation is getting very sensitive and there's no reason not to take precautions.' Rupert looked tired and strained. 'Now did you find out anything this afternoon?'

Jon took a seat. 'No, I checked all the paperwork and everything was accounted for. I looked at all the logs. I even checked the sealed envelope with the safe combination in it and I'm certain it hasn't been tampered with. So sorry but whoever leaked the information has to be one of the core team. Now look, there's something I need to know.'

'Go on.'

'Alright I will but first, can you tell me what level of detail we think has been divulged?'

'Why do you ask that?'

'Simple really, whoever is passing on the information can easily just recite what he knows from memory. However, if there is detailed technical detail being passed over then parts of the file need to have been copied or photographed. Now, you've asked me to check all the access to the paperwork so I'm assuming you think the latter has happened.'

'We'll make a spook out of you yet Jon,' Rupert replied with a wry grin. 'You're right of course. It seems that some of the technical aspects of the good doctor's work has been provided. So what is it you don't understand?'

'Where your information is coming from but I understand if you can't tell me that in detail. Can you at least tell me whether it's from the Soviet area?'

Rupert nodded but didn't say anything.

'OK, then there's something I found out last night. It's to do with Pickwick. Does Derek here have the clearance for that?'

'Yes, you can speak freely.'

'Do you remember Inga, the girl we brought back from the Arctic? The one that had been a spy and got me into deep shit at one stage?'

'How could I forget? She ended up your girlfriend for a while didn't she?'

'Not for long.' Jon said with a grimace. 'Well, I met her again last night and she was with Air Marshall Johnson.'

Jon's statement stopped the conversation dead for a moment.

'Jesus, we cleared her when she defected,' Rupert eventually replied. 'I debriefed her myself, are you suggesting she is up to her old tricks?'

'I'm not suggesting anything Rupert. I had to tell you because it's obviously something that we can't ignore but look I know her really quite well and would be amazed if she was. The girl has her eye on the main chance and from what I can see that's why she's with Johnson.'

'You're probably right Jon. I also know her quite well don't forget but that's not to say that someone isn't putting pressure on her, especially if they know who she is seeing. There's something else isn't there? I can see it from the look on your face.'

'God, this makes me feel so disloyal Rupert but yes there is. I've only taken the file around the team on three occasions. All the members bar one read the file in my presence. The only one that makes me wait in his outer office is the Air Marshall.'

'Which could give him time to copy it?'

'You would know more about that than me. There's no photocopier in his inner office but I assume a camera could be used quite quickly.'

Rupert didn't say anything but got up and walked around the room for a few seconds clearly thinking furiously. Eventually, he sat back down and looked at Jon. 'Thanks old chap, that's really put the cat amongst the pigeons. I have to say that the Air Marshall would have been last on my list of suspects. Do you have anything more?'

'No sorry, I find it hard to believe as well Rupert and let's face it, its all rather circumstantial isn't it? I assume you can crawl all over Inga's recent past and see if there is anything there.'

'Yes of course, we can and we will. And you've not had any suspicions raised about any of the other team members?'

'No absolutely nothing, as I said, everything seems to be in order. But look this doesn't make sense. If the Air Marshall is our man, how stupid would he have to be to use Inga as a conduit? Even if he isn't using her and dealing directly with a handler, having a girlfriend who is a known defector is the last thing he would want.'

'Or he could be hoping that it was so blatant that we would think exactly that.' Derek said.

Jon sighed. 'Jesus, this is not my world guys, I'm just telling you the facts you can make of them what you will. And there's no way whoever is helping you at the other end can give an idea of his source?'

'Jon, it doesn't work like that.' Rupert added. 'And frankly, even if it did I would not want to compromise them in any way. No we have to work this from our end only. So I think we'll have to introduce something into the project for the eyes of the Air Marshall only and see if that leaks across. If it does I'm afraid we'll have our man.'

They talked for another half an hour but Rupert and Derek decided they both needed to go back to their respective head offices in light of the new information and called the meeting to a halt.

On the way back to his digs Jon felt torn. He really didn't believe Inga was working for her old masters again, at least not voluntarily. Nor did he think that such a senior officer could be risking his whole life and career in such a way. Dammit, the Cold War seemed to be grinding to a halt. There had to be another element to this.

A week later he was summoned. When he arrived at the Air Marshall's outer office he was immediately ushered into the inner sanctum where the great man and Doctor Patrick were waiting for him.

Bog Hammer

'Commander Hunt,' the Air Marshall pointed to a seat. 'I need you to take some notes. Doctor Patrick here has some rather startling news.'

Jon took the indicated seat and made a strenuous effort to maintain his composure. This was clearly Rupert's additional bait.

'Thank you,' responded Doctor Patrick. 'This will be fairly short but I didn't want to talk about it except face to face. We have had a development. A couple of weeks ago one of my team got his numbers wrong when he was transmitting on our prototype device. By a factor of ten to be exact. When he turned it on, it promptly burned a hole in the wall of the lab over fifteen feet away. All our earlier calculations showed that atmospheric attenuation would not allow the device to be used as a weapon merely a sensor. We are now having to completely revise our thinking. I'm afraid it has put the whole project on hold while we evaluate this new development. I have some briefing notes here in my brief case and if you could put them on file please Commander Hunt.'

He handed Jon a sheaf of papers. 'For the moment I suggest we keep this between the three of us,' he continued. 'Frankly, I don't really know where this will lead but the possibilities are quite staggering.'

The Air Marshall agreed. 'Yes, there's no reason to bother the full committee at this stage and from what I gather it may need to be put up the chain first once Doctor Patrick's team have confirmed their initial findings.'

As soon as the meeting finished, Jon took the papers down to the secure registry. His head was whirling. The new 'development' was really clever. If anything was designed to motivate a traitor it was the discovery of a major new weapons technology. The problem was that Jon just couldn't see the Air Marshall as that man.

He knocked on the door of the registry and it was opened by Lieutenant Horridge, the man who actually ran the section. It was only the second time Jon had met him as he normally dealt with the cute Petty Officer. Horridge had clearly come up from the ranks as he was only a Lieutenant and in middle age. A plump man he nevertheless always managed to look harassed. He let Jon in with a brief greeting and went back to his desk.

Still trying to work out what was going on, Jon made a mistake opening the safe, having finished dialling the number, the damn thing refused to open. Cursing under his breath, he reset the lock and concentrated once more on the fiddly process of getting the six digit combination right. As the door opened with a satisfying click and he pulled out the pink file to put the new papers in it, he suddenly had an idea. If it didn't work, it would do no harm and if it did it would mean there was more to this than anyone had thought.

Chapter 15

Brian was enjoying the afternoon watch on the bridge of Prometheus for a change. His normal place of duty was the gloomy Operations Room or his cabin, working through the sheaf of signals the day always seemed to throw up. However, today they were returning from Gibraltar and doing a fast transit home up the coast of Portugal and then Spain. Cape Finisterre was a hundred miles to the north and then the Bay of Biscay. They should be home in two days and he was really looking forward to some leave as were the rest of the ship's company. Exercising in the Mediterranean as part of NAOCVFORMED which translated as the Naval On Call Force in the Mediterranean had been hard work but fun. Five ships from five nations had made up the NATO force that got together once a year to exercise. In this case, the exercises had been enlivened by the presence of a Russian Kresta 2 destroyer who seemed keen to join in. Sometimes he even seemed a little too keen and had to be warned off. The Force Commander had been a Turkish ship and it had been quite amusing to see how he treated the Greek ship. They had never actually come to metaphorical blows but it had been close on a couple of occasions. A final run ashore in Gibraltar whose border was now open with mainland Spain had been a welcome break but everyone was getting tired and needed a rest.

The ship was cruising at eighteen knots and riding a long, low Atlantic swell with gentle ease. The occasional curtain of spray would be shouldered up from her bows and spatter the bridge windows with salt. The sun was out and the sea, a cross between grey and blue. Luckily there was no sign of the fog that had a habit of cloaking this part of the coast and Brian was glad of that because there were enough fishing boats to worry about without the added problem of low visibility.

'Bridge this, Ops room,' a voice called from the speaker above his head. 'New contact, track two five zero, bearing three five five, range twenty five. Closest position of approach is half a mile. Estimate it's probably Tidepool.'

Brian clicked the microphone which was hanging by a stalk over the Pelorus in the centre of the bridge and spoke into it. 'Bridge

Roger. Can you give them a call and confirm. Let me know when you have and I'll inform the Captain.'

Brian had been waiting for this. They were due to rendezvous with the RFA Tidepool for a Replenishment at Sea to ensure they had enough fuel to complete their voyage. Tidepool was heading to Gibraltar. They could probably make it to Devonport without the RAS but it was policy to keep ships topped up as much as possible at all times and as they were passing it was too good an opportunity to miss. It also offered a good training opportunity for the ship as well.

Five minutes later, the Ops room came back and confirmed that it was indeed their tanker and that they should be up with them in another twenty minutes.

Brian moved over to another microphone. 'Captain Sir, bridge, the Tidepool has been contacted we are twenty minutes from rendezvous, would you like me to pipe for special sea duty men to close up and get the ship ready.'

'Yes please,' was the prompt reply. 'I'll be up directly.'

Brian breathed a sigh of relief. He was now quite good at reading his Captain and his moods. It wasn't unknown for him to go to sleep after lunch and when woken up could be either extremely irritable or almost supine. Today it seemed like the decisive Captain would be in attendance. Brian just hoped it wasn't because he had been drinking too much.

He turned to his Bosun's Mate and told him to make the call on the ship's main broadcast to prepare the ship for the serial. Just as it broke into life, the Captain appeared from the starboard bridge ladder and as the ship gave a gentle lurch so did he. Luckily he tripped forward and grabbed the rear of his chair which was mounted on a pedestal on the starboard side of the bridge. Brian couldn't make out whether it was just a simple trip or something else.

The Captain clambered into the chair. 'Well Ops, it looks like a good day for a RAS. As we agreed you can con the ship, I will observe from here. When was the last time you did one?'

Brian grimaced. 'Not for some years Sir, so I hope you are ready to help me out.'

'Nonsense old chap, I'm sure you'll be fine but let me know if you need help.'

Just then the First Lieutenant and the ship's Master at Arms appeared. The Master relieved the helmsman at the ships steering position, while the First Lieutenant reported to the Captain. 'Ship closed up and Specials are all at their stations. We're ready to go Sir.'

'Very good,' the Captain responded. 'Lieutenant Commander Pearce has the ship for the RAS but I will be here if needed.'

Jon and Des exchanged a glance before Des headed off to the foredeck, to check the RAS team were mustered and ready.

Just then the ship's Navigating Officer, Paul Brown appeared. Brian turned to him. 'Paul, can you call Tidepool and suggest a course of due north at twelve knots. I will use his starboard side.'

As the Navigating Officer turned to the bridge VHF radio, the Captain broke in. 'No, use his port side please, I always find it easier to con the ship from our starboard bridge wing.'

For a second Brian thought to argue but maybe the Captain was testing him. With the swell coming in from the west it would make it harder to control the ship without the lee of the bigger tanker offering some protection. Brian just nodded at Paul.

He was manoeuvring Prometheus astern of the big grey tanker, which had now taken up a northerly heading, as the First Lieutenant reappeared on the bridge. They both went out onto the bridge wing. Des would control the RAS team from there and Brian would con the ship using a remote microphone.

'All set old chap?' Des asked.

Brian grinned. 'As I'll ever be, I just hope father steps in when I cock it up, I haven't done one of these for ages.'

'He looks pretty relaxed.' Des responded as they both looked in through one of the bridge windows at the Captain, who was sitting in his chair and seemed to be staring ahead with a glassy look on his face.

They were approaching the stern of the RFA at speed now and Brian had no further time to worry. Prometheus was also heading north, parallel to the wake of tanker and closing with over ten knots of relative speed. The range and bearing of the tanker was being called out by the Second Officer of the Watch using a visual range finder and Brian made small corrections to the ships head to ensure they came up about one hundred and twenty feet clear of the other ship's port side. As they closed, the tanker looked terribly close but Brian remained confident they were in position. As Prometheus's bow wave intersected the wake of the tanker there was a moment's

Bog Hammer

hesitation before the Frigate forged through the underwater turmoil and drew smoothly alongside.

As they reached the correct position Brian ordered, 'stop both engines.' He knew it would take time for the ships steam turbines to spool down but he wanted the ship to hold her position. After a few seconds, he ordered, 'revolutions one two zero,' and then a few seconds later as Prometheus's speed bled off, 'half ahead both engines.'

The engine revolutions should allow the two ships to match speed. He waited with bated breath but they were still dropping back slightly so he ordered a small increase in revolutions until he was sure they were matched. He let things settle for a minute ordering very small changes to the ships head to keep the distance roughly correct. When he was happy he nodded to Des. 'When you're ready old chap.'

Des looked over the bridge wing and gave a thumbs up to the Chief Bosun's Mate or Buffer as he was universally known in the navy and one of the sailors pointed a rifle at the tanker. On the end of the rifle was a yellow plastic tube, which when the gun fired its blank cartridge, soared across the deck of the tanker trailing a light nylon line. The crew of the tanker, who had taken cover in case the Frigate's aim was off, then appeared and grabbed the line. For a second they seemed to struggle with it but then an officer on the tanker raised a flag and the Buffer on Prometheus ordered the deck party to haul the line back. Attached to it were two lines. One was a light one with coloured flags along its length and when it reached the Frigate it was taken to the bow, where it was kept taut by a party of sailors. Brian breathed a sigh of relief as he could now use the flags to accurately measure his distance from the tanker. The other line was an intermediate. When the deck party had that in hand they hauled away and dragged a heavy wire across. When the end of the wire was on deck it was hauled up and attached, via a quick release, to a small jib welded onto the front of Prometheus's bridge screen. Tension came on the wire and was then controlled by a self-tensioning winch on the tanker.

Des looked at Brian again, who realised he had now relaxed a bit and was actually starting to enjoy himself. He answered the unasked question. 'Clear to connect Des.'

Bog Hammer

The First Lieutenant picked up his flags and signalled to the tanker. Along with the heavy wire was another light line and this was connected to the end of the fuel hose that was hanging in loops under the tanker's derrick which had now been extended towards the Frigate. With more muscle power from the deck crew, the hose end was hauled across to the deck below the bridge wing and plugged into the ship's refuelling point.

Des turned to Brian again. 'Hose connected, permission to start pumping?'

Brian looked around carefully. Once fuel started to flow, it would be far more dangerous to disconnect in an emergency. All looked good. He glanced into the Captain but once again the man seemed to be feigning indifference. Hopefully, that meant he was content. He turned back to Des. 'Commence pumping.'

Another exchange of flags meant that fuel was flowing. Des leant over the bridge wing and the ships MEO looked up and gave a thumbs up which meant that all was proceeding normally.

Brian turned and concentrated on keeping the two ships in position with small heading and speed changes. It was dangerous to get too close, as the suction between the two ships could literally suck them together but he mustn't get too far out or the strain on the refuelling rig could get too high and something could break. It didn't help that being on the unprotected side of the tanker, Prometheus was doing her standard trick of rolling heavily. With six tons of radar installation on the top of her main mast, it was a problem with all this class of ship but even so things seemed good. All he had to do was keep this up for another half an hour or so and then they could be on their way.

Suddenly Brian's calm was shattered. Over the intercom came the panicked words, 'Full Ahead both engines, port twenty five.'

Completely nonplussed for a second, Brian looked into the bridge and saw the Captain waving violently at something. Immediately the ship began to heel and draw forward. With sick fascination, he knew what was about to happen and knew there was nothing he could do about it. Des had also realised the danger and screamed down at the deck party to take cover before pushing Brian down to the deck to shelter behind the screen. Brian landed on his back and looked up as the jib of the tanker's derrick made contact with something above them as the ship rolled hard. There were two enormous crashes.

Something seemed to hit the ship behind somewhere. He was pretty sure it was the stern crashing into the tanker as they turned away from her. The second crash came from somewhere above and was followed by two more smaller thuds. He was about to lift his head when a mist of choking diesel fuel filled the air. Grabbing Des, he pulled them both to the bridge door, wrenched it open and pulled them both inside to comparative safety.

The Master at Arms on the wheel was looking completely shocked. 'Sir, the Captain ordered the breakaway.'

Brian looked around. The Captain was staring out to starboard with a look of horror on his face. He suddenly straightened up, turned around and faced Brian. 'I'll be in my cabin if I'm needed,' and to everyone's astonishment, calmly walked off the bridge.

Brian didn't have time to work out what the hell the man was doing. 'Half ahead both engines wheel amidships,' he ordered. They were clear of the tanker and damage control was what was needed now.

Des called over to Brian. 'Brian you still have the ship, I'll get down on deck and assess the damage.'

Brian nodded and went forward to look out of the bridge windows, several of which were cracked he noted. 'Oh sweet Jesus,' he muttered. At first, he couldn't work out what he was seeing. The foredeck just ahead of the bridge held the corrugated canisters of four Exocet missiles but the starboard one was broken open and he could clearly see the white shape of the missile inside. Lying next to it where it had fallen was a large grey tube. He suddenly realised what it was. The aerial of their 967/968 radar must have been swiped by the tankers derrick as the pulled clear and the ship rolled. The aerial was only held on by its own weight and must have been catapulted off. There was no time to consider the situation. That was a live warshot missile, it was badly damaged and right next to three others.

Bosun's mate, pipe the ship to emergency stations and then pipe for the Weapons Engineer Officer to come to the bridge.'

Slowly, order was restored. Once the ship was at emergency stations all non-essential personnel were sent to the rear of the ship. The Weapons Engineering Officer, Eric Norman, inspected the damaged Exocet and then a council of war was held on the bridge.

Bog Hammer

'First things first,' the First Lieutenant said. 'How is the Captain? Anyone know what the hell happened?'

Brian spoke first. 'He's in his cabin and I've got the Petty Officer Medical Assistant in with him now. The Master at Arms says one minute he seemed to be almost dozing in his chair and then all hell broke loose. He assumed the Captain had seen something that required emergency action and so didn't query his order. Dammit, you wouldn't would you? If you ask me, he nodded off and then when he woke he saw the tanker and panicked. I can't see any other reason for his actions.'

Just then the POMA came up the bridge ladder.

'How's the Captain, Doc?' Des asked.

'Blind drunk Sir, passed out and comatose.'

'Oh for fuck sake. He didn't seem that bad when he was on the bridge.'

'No Sir he may not have been but he is now. There's an empty bottle of vodka by the chair he's asleep in. I've got his steward keeping an eye on him.'

Des looked at them all in the eye. 'I want this in the ship's log please. I consider that the Captain is no longer fit to command this ship and that means even when or if he ever sobers up. I therefore want it logged that I am taking over command. How say you lot?'

Brian spoke first. 'You have my total support Number One.'

The others all quickly agreed.

'Well Brian as the next most senior officer in the ship, if I'm acting Captain, you are now acting First Lieutenant.'

'Fair enough Sir, what do you want me to do?'

'I need WEO's input first. What the hell are we going to do with that damaged weapon container?'

WEO had no doubt. 'It's got to go over the side Des. If we leave it on deck it's a serious explosive risk. Not the warhead, that's actually quite safe but the rocket motor casing has been damaged. If it goes off, the others will probably go off with it and then we won't have a ship.'

'Right Brian, take charge and see what needs to be done. Doc, the Buffer tells me that no one was badly hurt but there are a couple of walking wounded that need to be looked at. They're been taken to sick bay as we speak.'

Three hours later the situation was improving. The radar aerial had been dragged clear and secured to the deck. Privately Brian thought it was probably just scrap but the consensus was that it should be retained not given the float test he wanted to give it. The Exocet was a different matter. The missile weighed fifteen hundred pounds on its own and in its container topped over two thousand. Normally a dockyard crane was required to move it. Off the coast of Portugal heavy cranes were in short supply. In the end, they slid it down from its angled launch rack using old fashioned block and tackles. Once flat on the deck the ship's engineers cut the guard rails adjacent to it down with angle grinders. A large shock mat was draped over the side of the ship. More block and tackles were tied to the missile casing and it was carefully pushed over the side and lowered to the water. There were several heart stopping moments when it banged against the ship's side as she rolled in the swell but the shock mat absorbed most of the impact. Then just before it reached the surface, the ship was stopped and all the tackles let go. With a gentle splash, the container hit the water and the ship then steamed slowly away.

Brian went up to the bridge where Des was watching the container through a pair of binoculars. 'Fucking thing won't sink Brian. We should have drilled some more holes in it.'

'Yeah right and who would have volunteered to operate the drill?'

'Good point, oh well we can't leave it on the surface we'd better get one of the starboard twenty mills manned up. Let's see if Leading Seaman Jeffries can actually hit anything with that peashooter of his.'

As the ship steamed to what they all hoped was a safe distance and the rest of the upper deck was cleared of personnel, the starboard twenty millimetre Oerlikon gun was made ready. As the only gun of any calibre on the ship, it was all they had to try and sink the weapon container. It was either that or rifles and they didn't want to be that close if anything went wrong.

With Tidepool already back on her way to Gibraltar and no other vessels close by, they steamed slowly past the floating box at a range of fifteen hundred yards.

'Clear to open fire,' Des ordered.

The machine gun started its rapid banging and spurts of white spray burst around the target. For a moment nothing happened and then there was a gout of fire. For a second Brian was worried that the missile might take flight rather like one had done during the raid he and Jon had conducted during the Falklands. But suddenly there was a large explosion and a massive blast of spray and when it settled there was nothing left to see.

Sighs of relief on the bridge were short lived. The sound of a door banging below the bridge, were followed by angry shouts. The Captain had come out of the door by his cabin onto the starboard waist. There was no one to stop him because everyone else was below taking cover. He clearly hadn't seen that the guard rails were no longer along that part of the ship and before anyone could do anything he stepped almost smartly over the side.

'Shit, man overboard.' Des shouted and the ship slipped into what was a well rehearsed routine. Within minutes the ship's sea boat was searching in the water. The Lynx was subsequently scrambled as well but despite searching until darkness, no sign of Commander Paul Fulford was ever found. In the end, they were forced to call off the search and resume their passage home.

On the bridge, there was an air of despondency. Des turned to Brian. 'Have all the relevant signals been sent Brian?'

'All that I can think of. As you know our suggestion that searching any further is a waste of time has been approved but the shit is really going to hit the fan when we get back.'

'Tell me about it. Why do I really wish I was in some simple cushy shore job right now?'

Chapter 16

'Hell, why can't I have simple sea job?' Jon thought angrily as he strode down Whitehall to the MOD Main Building. His head was still whirling with the information that Rupert had given him yesterday evening. Within a fortnight the new information they had planted had found its way into Soviet hands. Rupert was in no doubt that the Air Marshall was the guilty party and today there was going to be a confrontation and almost certainly an arrest. In an almost uncanny coincidence two days previously, Inga had disappeared off everyone's radar and now there was a nationwide hunt going on for her.

Against all his protestations Jon had been effectively ordered to attend the arraignment of the Air Marshall. Rupert, Derek and the Special Branch officers who would also be in attendance had insisted on it as he was a key part of the sting. When Jon got to the office Captain Desmonde was already there. He gave Jon an odd look as he arrived but told him not to stay but go directly up to Air Marshall Johnson's office. Jon hung up his coat and left.

When he arrived, the outer office was full. Rupert and Derek were accompanied by two severe looking men in suits who weren't introduced but it was clear to Jon they were police.

Derek acknowledged Jon's arrival with a simple nod and turned to the Air Marshall's secretary. 'And when does he normally get in?'

Before he could answer the door opened and the man himself entered. He took one look around with a puzzled frown, clearly recognising Jon but no one else.

'Good morning gentlemen, what can I do for all of you?' he queried in a mildly puzzled tone.

Derek stepped forward. 'Sir my name is Derek Smith and I represent MI5 although I normally work for naval security. This is Mr Rupert Thomas from MI6 and the other two gentlemen are Special Branch. You already know Commander Hunt. May we take some of your time in private please?'

His face looking even more puzzled, the Air Marshall directed them all into his inner office. It was a large room and he indicated the chairs around the small conference table. Rupert, Derek and Jon took a seat but the two policemen stood stolidly by the door.

'Anyone like a coffee before we start gentlemen?'

'No thank you.' Derek replied making it clear it meant for all of them.

'Well bugger that, my day never starts until the second cup.' And he put his head around the office door and told his secretary to get him a coffee. With the cup in hand he, returned, closed the door and sat at the table.

'Now gentlemen what on earth is this all about?'

Derek looked him in the eye and came directly to the point. 'Project High Eye is a fake, Air Marshall. The technology is a failure but we revived it. The reason we did so was to trap a spy. For some time we have been aware of extremely sensitive information making its way from this building to the Kremlin but have been unable to track the source. High Eye was the cheese in the mousetrap.'

'Go on.' The Air Marshall said. 'I fail to see what this has to do with me.'

Derek continued. 'The only people who knew about the project in the MOD were the high level steering group and Commander Hunt here. The Commander has been in on the trap from the start because we needed someone on the inside and he hadn't been in the MOD long enough to be part of any conspiracy. He is also well known to MI6 and has sufficient security clearance.'

Jon got a fierce look from the Air Marshall but nothing was said.

Derek continued. 'Within two months of the project being initiated in the MOD, detailed technical information was known to have been passed to Moscow. So as a test we added another element but limited its distribution. Only you and the Commander knew about it yet within two weeks this time the information had leaked.'

The Air Marshall was looking angry now. 'Are you suggesting for one moment that I am a bloody Russian spy? Have you completely lost your minds?'

Derek wasn't put off by his anger in the slightest. 'With respect Air Marshall, you are the only team member to have seen that information and you are the only team member whose girlfriend was a spy for the Soviets until only a few years ago. On top of that, you are the only team member who insists on reading correspondence about the project in his office without witnesses.'

Jon got an even steelier glance. 'Now look, I know all about Inga and her past, she told me dammit and I even checked with you lot once I found out.'

'So where is she now?' Derek asked. 'She disappeared two days ago.'

'No she bloody well didn't you idiots I know exactly where she is.'

When his statement was met by silence he continued. 'My family have an estate in Scotland I'm sure you know that. I also have a sixteen year old daughter by my last marriage. She and Inga are at our lodge up there. It's out in the sticks and has no telephone but if you check with the railways I'm sure you will find that they both bought tickets last week. Inga used my surname as it's well known and ensures they are given a good seat on the train. It should be easy enough to check.'

Rupert turned to one of the policemen. 'See if you can confirm that Saunders.'

The man left the room.

'And what's this crap about not having witnesses. I'm not required by any rules that I'm aware of to have someone watch over me while I'm reading, especially not some bloody junior officer. No gentlemen you'll have to do better than that.'

Jon winced at the words. This was not going well.

Rupert spoke for the first time. 'How do you explain that information that only you are party to is now in Soviet hands?'

'I can't, of course I can't. But there must be other people in this building who have access to the file.'

Rupert looked over at Jon. 'Jon, could you go down to the registry and retrieve the file please. Then when you come back, explain to us all how it is controlled?'

Jon nodded and left, glad to be out of the toxic atmosphere even if it was only for a few minutes.

He made his way down two storeys. As he approached the door to the registry in the distance he saw the familiar plump outline of Lieutenant Horridge hurrying away. Not thinking anything of it, he knocked at the door and Petty Officer Jones let him in with her normal beaming smile. He went over to his locked cabinet and spun the dials. When he opened the door his blood ran cold. Carefully looking at everything to make sure he wasn't mistaken, he removed

Bog Hammer

the file and locked it in his brief case. Then taking great care not to give away his emotions he casually asked Petty Officer Jones if she knew where Lieutenant Horridge was going.

'Sorry Sir,' she replied. 'He just got a phone call and said he needed to go to a meeting. He didn't look that well if you ask me.'

Jon made a snap decision. There wasn't time to put the file back, he would have to hang on to it but there should be time to catch Horridge before he left the building. He turned to Jones. 'You're to stay here Petty Officer, no one enters and no one leaves, understand? Ring the office of Air Marshall Johnson. Give a message for a Mr Thomas who is there now. Tell him from me that it's not the Air Marshall and that I think I know who it is. Understand?'

Looking frightened now, the girl nodded. 'Air Marshall Johnson, Mr Thomas, you know who it is.'

'Good girl, now I've got to go.' And he sprinted out of the door trying desperately to work out how to get to the main entrance as fast as he could. He ran down the corridor to the cross passage that housed the lifts. As soon as he got there he gave up the idea of using one. The stairs would be much quicker. He flung open the door next to the lift and started down the stairwell as fast as he could, taking two steps at a time when he could and almost talking a fall several times. He stopped at the first floor, remembering that the access to the main lobby was from there. The lobby wasn't too crowded. He could see from the top of the small escalator that led down to it. Continuing to run down the moving steps, he looked frantically ahead for his quarry. He was nowhere to be seen. For a second, Jon wondered whether he had been mistaken but no the evidence in the locked cabinet was too strong. Then he cursed remembering there was the smaller rear exit to the building but Horridge had been heading this way when he saw him. Then he spotted the man. He had clearly moved faster than expected. He was outside the main doors and leaving the building. Jon realised he had a decision to make. He could stop the pursuit and call Rupert but that would almost certainly mean his quarry getting away. No, the only thing to do was keep going.

Entering the little airlock he cursed the time it took for the doors to close and then open. Then he was free, as he ran outside, there was a shout from behind him but he ignored it. Where the hell was his man? He looked frantically both ways and spotted him to the left, about to enter Whitehall. Calming himself fractionally, he slowed down to a brisk walking pace and headed the same way. Another shout came from behind him but he continued to ignore it.

Suddenly Horridge held out his hand and with dismay, Jon realised he was hailing a taxi. Sure enough, one stopped on the far side by the Old Admiralty building and the man jogged across to it and got in. Cursing all the more Jon once again broke into a run and started looking frantically for another cab. This wasn't like the bloody films. There was plenty of traffic stopping Jon from crossing the wide street but bugger all sign of another taxi with its yellow roof light on. Taking his life in his hands, he ran across the road almost being run over in the process and attracting some rude gestures and horn toots from several drivers. Because the traffic was heavy and slow Jon was able to keep up with the cab which was about a hundred yards ahead but as soon as it reached Trafalgar Square Jon knew he would lose it. Then, up ahead by the Whitehall theatre, he saw a taxi stop and people start to get out. He redoubled his efforts and managed to reach it just before it drove off.

As he jumped in the driver turned to him. 'Sorry, I'm off shift now, you'll have to get another cab.'

Jon was having trouble breathing but wasn't going to be put off. 'Listen my name is Hunt, I'm a Commander in the Royal Navy and that taxi up there, the one by the lights has got a person in it who is almost certainly a criminal. I've got to catch up with him.'

The driver turned and gave Jon a quizzical look and then the expression on his face changed. 'Hey, don't I know you? You were the guy who stopped that ship hijack the other year.'

Still wheezing but seeing that the lights were about to change Jon was getting frantic. 'Yes that's me but look please, that cab, can we please follow it? I know it sounds corny but it's really important.'

The driver turned and pulled straight out to the annoyance of the car behind. 'You got it, my cousin's daughter was on the Uganda, whatever you say.'

He managed to get to within several car lengths of their quarry but had to jump the lights to keep it in sight. They turned left down the Mall, with Buckingham Palace in the distance and Jon sat back for a second trying to get his breath back.

'So, what's this all about then, some sort of spy is he?'

Bog Hammer

Jon really didn't know how to answer that but knew he needed the man on his side. 'Yes actually I think he is. Any idea where he might be heading?'

'Not yet, could be anywhere, let's just see where he goes.'

Jon wondered whether there was time to stop by a phone box but immediately discarded the idea. He realised he didn't actually know the number of MOD from a civilian phone anyway and even if he did he would almost certainly lose the chase if he did so. He wondered what they were doing back in the Air Marshall's office. Hopefully, Jones would have alerted them. Then he wondered about the shouts he heard when he left the building. With a start, he realised he was still clutching his briefcase. No one was meant to leave without either proving it was empty or showing signed authorisation that it could be removed with whatever contents it had. No wonder they were trying to get him back.

The cabs reached the roundabout by the Palace and turned north up Park Lane.

'Well he's headed towards Marble Arch now,' the driver observed. 'Don't suppose he's going shopping in Oxford Street is he?'

'No definitely not but what else is up this way?'

'Let's see, if he turns left down Bayswater Road then I might just have an idea.'

Sure enough, at Marble Arch they turned left down the Bayswater Road with the greenery of Hyde Park to their left.

'Listen mate, at the end of the park is Kensington Palace Gardens.'

'Sorry, I don't follow.'

'Well, number six is the Soviet Embassy.'

The penny dropped. 'Any chance of getting past and stopping him before we get there?' Jon asked desperately.

The driver clearly loving every minute didn't answer. He simply pulled out into the outside carriageway and accelerated. 'No one is going to believe me when I tell them about this,' he laughed as they drew alongside and then past the other taxi.

Jon caught a glimpse of his quarry as they shot past. He seemed oblivious to the fact that he was being followed. The driver then pulled in ahead of the other taxi and slammed on the brakes. Jon was thrown forward but was able to look behind and see the other cab also slam to a halt and the other drive gesticulate angrily. Jon didn't wait to see the result. He wrenched open the door and ran back. Horridge must have worked it out because he also flung open his door and started running. Unfortunately for Jon, he got out of the opposite side, straight into the flow of traffic which somehow missed him with a shriek of tyres and horns. Suddenly, it was like one of those childish games where you are on opposite sides of a table and neither of them could reach the other. Then with a look of desperation, Horridge made a break for it and started running down the road and then the pavement towards the Embassy. If Jon had any doubts about the man's guilt they had all disappeared now.

Horridge was an overweight middle aged man but he ran with the desperation of the damned and for a moment Jon was amazed at his turn of speed. Redoubling his efforts he realised it was going to be a close run thing. The gates of the Embassy were only yards ahead now. With the strength of his own desperation, Jon swung his briefcase at the head of the running man. It made contact with a satisfying crunch and flew out of his hand. But its job was done and Horridge came crashing down onto the pavement with Jon landing on top of him only seconds later. He was prepared for a struggle but clearly all the fight had been knocked out of the man, either that or he was unconscious. Before he was able to even think about what to do next strong hands started to pull him to his feet.

'That's enough of that Sir, you've got some explaining to do.'

Jon twisted his head and with relief and saw the face of a British policeman. 'It's alright officer, I'm a naval officer and this man is a spy who was trying to get asylum in the Embassy. I assume you were on watch here?'

'You may be right Sir but he isn't the man with Top Secret documents in his briefcase.'

With dismay, Jon looked back and saw that the briefcase had broken open and several sheets of paper were blowing around. What was worse was that their fracas had already attracted quite a crowd. Several tourists were already taking photographs. Jon suddenly realised that despite apprehending Horridge, explaining this all away was going to be bloody difficult.

Chapter 17

The large room in HMS Drake the shore establishment serving the dockyard in Plymouth was crowded. It was normally used for Courts Martial. Today it was being used to finish the Board of Enquiry into the incident involving the damage to HMS Prometheus and the loss of its Commanding Officer. A separate Coroner's inquest would also be held into the death of Commander Fulford. Brian was praying that the room wouldn't have to revert to its normal use as a result of the Board of Enquiry. He and Des Slater stood as the main people to take the criticism for what had happened.

He cast his mind back to when he had been called to explain his recollections of that day. The questions had started off enquiring about the Captain's mental state. The President of the Board was a four ring Captain called Henderson who Brian had never met but had a reputation of being something of a bulldog.

His first question was direct and to the point. 'So Lieutenant Commander Pearce, you probably worked as close to Commander Fulford as anyone in the ship. What was your opinion of him as a Captain?'

Brian realised you couldn't get more of an open ended question than that but had decided that total honesty was all he could afford. 'Sir, my Captain was often brilliant but the problem was that he was inconsistent and his mood seemed to be liable to change in an instant.'

'And what exactly does that mean?'

'Well sometimes he was extrovert and completely on top of the situation but sometimes it was almost impossible to get a word out of him or alternatively he would snap at you for absolutely no reason.'

'Did you have any suspicions about why he behaved like this?'

This was the question Brian had been dreading. 'Yes Sir I did.'

'Well don't keep us in the dark.'

'He drank Sir. It was quite clear to me that when he was in his extrovert mood he had been drinking.'

'How on earth would you know that?'

'Sir, on many occasions, it was while we were conducting operations and so we would be in very close proximity in the Ops room. He would be quiet and it was almost impossible to get him to make a decision. He would go back to his cabin usually saying he had to use the head and come back a different person. Being in such close proximity I could smell the alcohol on his breath.' There it was said, Brian felt better for coming clean even if it meant being disloyal to his dead Commanding Officer.

Captain Henderson exchanged looks with the two other members of his board before continuing. 'So, did you think that this behaviour was a danger to the ship?'

Brian winced inwardly at yet another question he was expecting but knew would be hard to answer. 'Up until the incident, no Sir, I did not. He never seemed incapacitated and at no point was the ship put in danger.'

'Yet you suspected your Captain was a drunk. So why didn't you do anything about it?'

'Your words not mine Sir. I suspected the Captain was a heavy drinker but who in the navy hasn't been brought up on that ethos? How many other heavy drinkers are there in the navy as we speak? And all doing a satisfactory job. I'm not a doctor Sir, my loyalty was to my Commanding Officer and that is what he got.'

'Very well and what do you think was the role of alcohol on the day Commander Fulford died?'

'When he came on the bridge that afternoon he seemed quite normal.'

'Sorry what does that mean?'

'Er, he was in what I called a decisive mood.'

'So, by your definitions, you knew he had been drinking?'

Brian saw the trap. 'No, I couldn't know that but I had my suspicions.'

'Very well go on.'

'Well after the emergency break away, he simply walked off the bridge. We were all stunned. It was hardly the normal action of a ship's Captain who has just caused a major accident.'

'We'll come to that later, let's stay on the topic of alcohol please.'

'The POMA came up later and was adamant that he had consumed a large amount of spirits and was comatose because of that.'

'But that was after he went down to his cabin?'

'I honestly don't know but if you want my opinion, he had probably been drinking before he came on to the bridge and drank a lot more afterwards.'

'And what about when he went overboard?'

'Well obviously he had woken up but what state of mind he was in I have absolutely no idea. For what it's worth I think the sound of the exploding Exocet was what woke him and he went outside to see what was going on before anyone realised he was awake. He didn't know the guardrails had been removed of course. In hindsight, we should have put some rope across but frankly there were more important things on our mind at the time. The upper deck was out of bounds after all.'

'Thank you Lieutenant Commander we will cover those topics later.'

The questioning continued relentlessly for several more hours. Brian was taken bit by bit through the whole day. He answered as honestly as he could but even after such a short time some things had already become blurred. That and the fact that the day had been traumatic to say the least. One more question was asked. It was the one he had been expecting at the start.

'Lieutenant Commander Pearce, do you have any knowledge or understanding as to why the Captain of HMS Prometheus ordered an emergency break away from the RAS which you were conducting?'

Brian was strongly tempted to answer with a simple 'no' but he knew that would not be accepted. 'Sir, up until that point the RAS had been routine. The Captain had entrusted me with the serial and at no point did he interfere or order any changes with the exception of insisting that we approach the tanker's port side. I thought this might have been to make it more difficult for me but he never really explained why. Up until the point of the breakaway, I was totally confident that we were refuelling safely and correctly.'

'Would you care to offer an opinion on the matter?'

Again he was tempted to say no. 'Sir, I can't, what I can say is that on several occasions I briefly glanced into the bridge and saw the Captain sitting in his seat. On each occasion, he seemed to be either staring ahead or down at his lap.'

'So you couldn't say if he was asleep?'

'No not definitely but if he was then his body position was correct.'

'Thank you Lieutenant Commander Pearce. That will be all.'

Brian left the room and realised he was shaking. He felt like he had run a marathon and been in a sauna at the same time.

He came back to the present, as the President of the Enquiry cleared his throat.

'Gentlemen the findings of the board are thus. Firstly, the damage to HMS Prometheus and the injuries caused to some of her crew were the sole responsibility of her Captain, Commander Paul Fulford. We find that the cause of the accident was the decision by Commander Fulford to order an emergency break away from the RAS the ship was conducting with RFA Tidepool. We cannot determine why Commander Fulford ordered such a manoeuvre and note that at no time did he offer an explanation for his actions. We would further like to commend the officers and ship's company of HMS Prometheus on their handling of what then became a perilous situation with damaged ordnance on board. We support the decision that was taken to jettison the damaged missile and then sink it with gunfire. We also support the efforts to try and recover Commander Fulford when he fell into the sea and the decision to stop searching at sunset.'

A ripple of what could only be relief swept around the room. Several people exchanged smiles.

'On the second issue of the death of Commander Fulford, it is not within our jurisdiction to rule on the matter. That said, we will be forwarding the following conclusions to the Coroner. Firstly, that all our evidence points to the fact that Commander Fulford was heavily intoxicated at the time. Secondly, that the missing guard rails almost certainly contributed to him falling overboard but that in the circumstances the ship's company were not, I repeat not, negligent in ensuring that temporary measures were taken. It is the view of this board that, with the other problems besetting the ship, all reasonable precautions had been taken at that time. Although he does not need to take our findings into account, nevertheless we will recommend to the Coroner that Commander Paul Fulford's death is classified as an accident. This enquiry is now complete, thank you.'

The three board members stood and left the room to a general hubbub from the ship's officers and other attendees.

Des Slater turned to Brian and shook his hand. 'At no point was I worried that that would go against us.' His relieved expression belied his words. 'We'd better get back on board and tell the crew. Afterwards, I strongly suggest that all officers repair to the wardroom where we will have a wake for our departed Captain.'

Chapter 18

Praa sands in Cornwall is a long, glorious stretch of shelving golden sand backed by dunes. At the western end is a car park and café. The eastern end, half a mile away, is served by a very small lane which only the locals know about. Consequently, while the western end is thronged by tourists, with shrieking kids and surf boarders the other end is an oasis of calm.

The late summer day was gloriously hot with barely a cloud in the sky. Helen and Jon seemed to have the beach to themselves, which was why Helen was taking the opportunity to sunbathe topless and get a more overall tan, much to Jon's approval.

He had arrived home the previous evening. Helen was glad to see him, not just because she missed him but she had been really worried over the reports in the papers.

Jon laughed it off. 'Don't worry darling, it's all been sorted out. But yes, the press getting hold of those pictures wasn't good.'

'Wasn't good? Come on Jon, the papers had a field day. It really didn't help that you had all that publicity when we got back from the Mediterranean. What did the Sun say? Oh yes 'Helicopter hero turned spy' that was it.'

'Yes but they printed a retraction the next day.'

'Come on Jon I want the whole story. You don't seem too upset and I thought you would have been devastated. I assume this is all to do with the thing you and Rupert were cooking up?'

Jon sighed. 'Look, just let me get a beer from the fridge and I'll tell you the whole gory truth, alright?'

Then having returned from the kitchen he made himself comfortable and started in on his story. Helen was amazed by his taxi cab chase across central London. 'If I didn't know it was you Jon, I would have thought it was part of a film script.'

'Do you know that's just what I thought a couple of times but it wasn't, it was deadly serious.'

'So come on, how did you know the culprit was in the registry and not the Air Marshall?'

'Oh that bit's easy, you see I never really thought such a senior officer could be a traitor and I was certain Inga wouldn't have wanted anything to do with her old lords and masters. I was honour bound to tell Rupert about the liaison when I discovered it but never really believed it meant they were involved. So I decided I needed a way of finding out if someone else was accessing the file, impossible though that was meant to have been.'

'Come on spill it.'

'Oh, I put the file in backwards.'

'Eh, how on earth can you put a file in backwards?'

Jon chuckled. 'You can't of course but most people, when putting a file on a shelf, put the top in away from them, so I did the opposite. It wasn't all I did. I had arranged the papers in such a way that any movement of the file would have moved them as well and there would be no hope of getting them back exactly as they were. But in fact, it didn't matter because as soon as I opened the safe that morning I saw the file was the other way around. No one else in the building had access to that locked cabinet except me. The only other person with access to the safe that held the combination in the envelope was the Lieutenant. When I set the combination and put it in the envelope, I put it in a small safe that was open and PO Jones closed and locked it but I checked later and only the Secretary had the combination to re-open that safe. So he had to be the culprit, that and me seeing him sneaking away as I arrived. Apparently, the Air Marshall's secretary inadvertently tipped him off that something was wrong. He rang him and warned Horridge that I would be coming down soon for the file and that there was a big security alert going on. He must have put two and two together and panicked.'

'Alright but how did the Lieutenant read your combination. I thought you said it was sealed in an envelope inside carbon paper. Had it been tampered with?'

'Nope, it was perfect and that had us all really worried for a while but as soon as our man was interrogated he, to quote a corny line, 'sang like a canary.' The answer was simple. His handler had provided him with doctored carbon paper. It worked almost as well as the normal stuff and certainly looked the part but was transparent to Infra-Red. Our man simply held a torch to the envelope and let it warm up a bit and he could read the combination through the paper. Rather like when you hold a torch against your hand and you can see through it a little.'

'Wow, I bet that's worried the security people.'

'You can say that again. They're going to have to rethink the whole procedure now. And of course it meant the bloody man had access to just about everything in the section. They're still trying to assess exactly how much damage he did.'

'OK, so what happened after the policeman grabbed you?'

'Well, my first priority was to stop him letting Horridge go. We were only a few yards from the Embassy gates and I was really worried about him making a dash for it. We ended up with this comic situation, where I was holding onto his trouser belt for dear life, while the copper was trying to prize me off. All the while I was trying to get the silly sod to listen to me and the tourists were taking happy snaps. I convinced him in the end by showing him my MOD ID card which was still around my neck. I wasn't worried for myself. If I was arrested it wouldn't matter but he had to understand that Horridge was the bad guy. In the end, he held on to both of us until help arrived. We were taken to Scotland Yard but only after I retrieved all the paperwork. Luckily, none had blown through the railings. Asking the Soviets for our Top Secret documents back would have been a little embarrassing to say the least, even if they were all fakes. Then once Special Branch was called in and Rupert and Derek were contacted, things settled down fast. It's just a shame the press moved so bloody quickly. Elements of the true story have been released now and as you know the press have all printed retractions. The only real problem is that we have to keep most of it secret, so the conspiracy theorists will no doubt have a field day.'

'So why the hell did he do it? Why betray your country like that?'

'I haven't got the full story but it seems to have been some form of blackmail. Our Mr Horridge was happily married but also had a succession of boyfriends. That and a reasonable sum of money changing hands.'

'Aren't these people supposed to be carefully vetted?'

'Yes and that's another bit of gristle for the security guys to chew on.'

'So what happened when you went back to work?'

'Ah yes well, that bit was awkward, to say the least. I was expecting a one way conversation with the Air Marshall but he never called for me. Initially, Admiral Arthur was really pissed off. It was quite funny in some ways. He was clearly really annoyed that he was one of the suspects and even more annoyed that one of his subordinates was in on the sting. On the other hand, the self-same subordinate had been quite clever and solved the problem. It was quite amusing when I let him know that I had direct authorisation from the Secretary of State and the First Sea Lord. Immediately the politician in him appeared and he was all smiles and congratulations. Even so, I don't think I've made a friend for life there. Captain Desmonde and the boys in the office were very curious and even more so when I told them I couldn't really say what I'd been up to. I was fending off questions for a while but it soon settled down. Then the First Sea Lord sent for me.'

'What? The great man himself?'

'Yup, the meeting was in his flat over Admiralty Arch, in the evening and I even got a couple of drinks out the guy. Actually, he's really nice. We even got a little pissed. Well, at least I did.'

'Hang on a second, let me get this right. Commander Jonathon Hunt Royal Navy, spy catcher extraordinaire, who got arrested in the public eye outside the Soviet Embassy with a briefcase full of Top Secret papers went and got pissed with the Fist Sea Lord the next day?'

'No.'

'What do you mean, no?'

'It wasn't the next day. It was two days later.'

Helen launched herself at Jon and the events of the previous weeks were forgotten.

His reminisces of the night were brought back in to focus as Helen rolled over to toast her back. She really did have a magnificent pair of tits. An idea formed in his mind.

'Come on Mrs Hunt, we can't just lie here all afternoon and anyway there's something else I haven't told you.'

'Oh what?' Helen asked suspiciously.

'Not telling you until we've been for a swim. There's a little sheltered cove just around the headland. I'll race you.'

'Hang on a second then while I put my top back on.'

'You know it's almost as sexy watching a girl put her clothes on as taking them off.' Jon said with a leer.

'I thought you wanted a race, come on then.' Helen jumped to her feet and ran into the surf a few yards away with Jon close behind. He held back as the sight of her buttocks in the skimpy light cloth was so enticing.

It might have been the end of the summer but the water was still cold. However, that gave them both the incentive to swim hard around the rock outcrop. When they were in the surf on the other side, Helen stood up with a whoop of triumph. The water was still up to her waist. Jon caught up a few seconds later and grabbed her. As he expected, the little cove was completely deserted. In fact, it was only a cove a few hours either side of low water.

Helen looked into his eyes. 'Right, I won, what is it you haven't told me?'

'In a minute. There's something I've always wanted to do.' He slid his hands under the top hem of her bikini bottoms and grabbed her buttocks.

She looked into his eyes. 'Jon is that a submarine in your trunks or are you just glad to see me?'

'Ah, the old ones are always the best but yes you can take it that whatever it is, its very glad to see you.'

She put her arms around his neck, lifted her legs and clasped them around his waist. 'We'd better hope no one is walking along the cliff path Mr Hunt.'

Sometime later, they were lying on the hard wet sand languorously drying out in the warm sun. Helen leaned over Jon and poked him in the chest. 'Right mister, I've won a swimming race and risked a charge of lewd behaviour in a public place, so cough up, what's this news? I was sure there was something you were holding back, you've just been too damned smug ever since you got home.'

Jon lay back and looked up at Helen, with what he hoped was the smug expression she had been seeing. 'I told you about my little session with the First Sea Lord. What I didn't tell you was what he also said to me.'

'So bloody well tell me, you infuriating man. I am going to bloody strangle you if you don't come clean, right now.'

'Alright, I don't want to be strangled. He told me that I had made myself unemployable in the MOD for a while. Despite the necessity of what we did it would make it very difficult for me to continue with the present incumbents in place.'

'But that's not good news. Why the hell are you so happy?'

'He offered me an alternative.'

'Go on.'

'You know all those exams I was doing while I was on the squadron?'

'The ship command ones?'

'Yes.'

'And do you know what the acronym SASB stands for?'

'Nope.'

'Sea Appointments Selection Board.' He looked at Helen to see if she would work it out.

A frown crossed her face for a moment then the penny dropped. 'But you're too junior. You've only been a Commander a little while.'

'Who says? Anyway, you can command a ship as a Lieutenant depending on the ship. I start my Commanding Officers Designated course in two weeks. So instead of being stuck in that bloody mausoleum in London, I'm going to get a ship.'

Helen laughed. 'You lucky bastard, why do you always land on your feet?'

He grinned back in unashamed happiness, leant up and kissed her hard. 'Because I'm just a lucky bastard I guess. Oh and that's got nothing to do with ships.'

Chapter 19

The autumn passed in a blur for Jon. His course covered all sorts of the subjects from warfare training to the basic seamanship that frankly Jon had forgotten since his days at Dartmouth. Then there was ship handling. Controlling four thousand tons of steel was a very different matter to nine thousand pounds of aluminium. He knew he was going to a steam powered ship so any order he gave had to be relayed to someone else, who then operated the relevant machinery and the ship then took its own sweet time to respond. Anticipation was key. Jon loved it and found he had the knack right from the start. That's not to say that it all went smoothly but you learn from your mistakes and Jon's were all small ones. Half way through the course he was called in to see his appointer as there were several options available as to which ship he might be appointed to. The discussion was brief and although he realised he was taking a risk, there was absolutely no doubt in his mind that he had taken the right decision.

They decided to have Christmas at home that year and invited Brian, Kathy and the kids down to share it with them. With Helen staying on at Culdrose once she finished training, they had decided to keep the married quarter for the moment. Although Helen had plans to look for somewhere to buy once the new year had started. It would give her a project as it looked highly likely that Jon would be away for much of the year. The married quarter was large and designed for a big family and for once it was full.

Christmas Day had been great fun but hard work, especially with two hyper young girls to keep under control but they had eventually collapsed and were sent off to bed. The adults regrouped around the television and a massive plate of turkey sandwiches.

'So Helen, are you a fully qualified Sea King pilot yet?' Brian queried through a mouthful of turkey.

'Sort of Brian,' she replied. 'I finished training last week and join 771 after New Year. But I'm on what you might call probation for about six months and can only fly as the second pilot. At some, point they will decide I have enough experience and hours to allow me to fly as aircraft captain.'

'Presumably, you didn't do too much Search and Rescue training on 706 because they're teaching anti-submarine pilots in the main?'

'You're right but they tweaked the syllabus a little for me and I even got in one rescue for real.'

'Oh, what was that all about?'

'We were down at the satellite airfield at Predannack practicing winching and a report came in of a diver with the bends in a cove near the Lizard. We were the nearest, so off we went. Luckily, we were able to land on the beach to pick the guy up and then we took him to Truro. They've got a decompression chamber there.'

Jon broke in. 'What she's not telling you Brian, is that with a bent diver, you need to minimise your altitude, as you know. Truro is up the Fal River so you have carte blanche to fly as fast as you can, as low as you can until you get there. I did it once years ago and lot of fun it is too.'

Jon and Helen exchanged knowing glances.

'You two are like little kids sometimes.' Brian observed with a grin. 'And before you deny it, remember how many hours I've had sitting next to you in various aircraft.'

'And what about Prometheus Brian, what sort of shape is she in now?' Jon asked.

'Ah well, it's taken a little longer than we thought to get her fixed. The radar aerial and the dents in the bridge roof were easily sorted although I'm not convinced that putting that damned aerial back was the right thing to do. Apparently, they're in very short supply.'

'Sounds like it could have been worse. The 910 Sea Wolf, fire control radar was lucky not to have been hit. That would have been a bugger to fix.'

'Yeah, we've still not quite worked out how the aerial got flung forward. It must have been some combination of ship movement and the RFA's derrick swinging. But the real problem was one that we didn't realise at the time. As we pulled clear, the stern hit the tanker. Luckily Tidespring was almost undamaged and we thought we had got away with it as well but when we got back to Devonport they found all sorts of secondary damage, including a misaligned propeller shaft and a twist in the hull.'

'But is it all repaired now?'

'So the engineers claim. We have sea trials after leave and then we'll know for real. That is if we ever get a new Commanding Officer. It's been very quiet on that front.'

'Surely your First Lieutenant is acting Captain and can take her out?' Jon asked innocently.

'I guess so but it's a bit unusual to be kept in the dark for so long.'

'Maybe Fleet have been waiting to get confirmation that she will be fully operational.'

'That's what we've all been thinking but a decision will have to be made soon.'

Helen leant over and punched Jon. 'Stop it Jon, for goodness sake tell him or I will.'

Brian looked at the two of them with dawning understanding. 'It's you, you bastard isn't it? When were you going to tell me?'

Jon laughed. 'About now actually but my dear wife got in first and less of the bastard and more of the yes Sir, no Sir, three bags full Sir please.'

'You forget Jon that I've worked with you as my Boss before, as well as serving with you for years. I know where all your skeletons are hidden.'

'Oh well I'm sure we can work something out. I join straight after leave and you're right, Fleet didn't want to announce the decision until the dockyard said she was good to go. When I was offered several ships I made it clear that there was only one I wanted. Don't tell anyone else yet but if all works out we're going to the Gulf on Armilla patrol in the spring. But you know, it's going to be weird being on board that ship again and as the Commanding Officer this time, really weird.'

'Well I've had time to get used to it and still seems odd at times,' Brian replied. 'But we need a skipper and I have to say I'm really glad it's going to be you. All that fuss in the summer in London seems to have paid off.'

'Maybe, I'm not sure I would want to repeat all that again though, exciting though it was. Anyway, it's sad about my predecessor. Was he really that bad?'

'No he wasn't actually, just bloody unpredictable on occasions, which made life interesting. The inquest came up with a verdict of accidental death by the way. They found his body a week later apparently there was very little blood in it, mainly vodka.'

'Let's start afresh when I get there.'

'Couldn't agree more.'

Bog Hammer

Brian couldn't shake the feeling of déjà vu as he stood on the flight deck of HMS Prometheus. She was alongside the same bit of dockyard wall as she had been when then last Commanding Officer joined and the weather was just as bloody awful. The difference this time was that the ship was operational, so when Jon arrived in full uniform he was piped on board with full naval ceremony. The ship's company were gathered on the flight deck behind the officers and once again the new Captain was offered a podium to stand on to say a few words.

Jon had never felt so alive in his life. The combination of rejoining a ship that had meant so much to him in the past and this time as her Captain was almost overwhelming. He was having to try really hard not to grin inanely at everyone around him. As he stood on the podium and looked at all the expectant faces looking up at him, all his pre-prepared words fled his mind and for a moment he couldn't think of a word to say.

Then it came to him. 'Good morning gentlemen. My name is Jonathon Hunt and many of you will know that I served in HMS Prometheus during the Falklands War as the Flight Commander. Consequently, I feel I know this ship extremely well. It's like coming home. However, what I don't know is any of you, bar a few individuals. So it will be my first task to remedy that. A ship may have a soul but that soul is only made up of the cumulative actions of her crew. One major lesson that the Falklands taught me is that it's not the quality of the ship or how well equipped she is with modern weapons but the quality of her people that makes her successful. So I hope we can make this ship a happy and extremely effective one. I will only mention the events of the recent past once and that is to say that as far as I'm concerned that is what they are, past events. Now, a previous Captain of Prometheus once called this ship a pocket battleship and he was right. We've got a busy year ahead so let's make this battleship work. Thank you.'

He stepped down to the silence he expected. The First Lieutenant saluted and Jon turned up the port waist and walked to the familiar door that opened into the cabin flat below and behind the bridge. It was really odd to walk into the day cabin he had been in so often before and realise it was now his own. But there was little time to think. His steward was there waiting for him and then the First

Lieutenant and Brian knocked and came in. His steward had already made some coffee and so the three of them sat and the work really started.

Two weeks later, Jon conned the ship through the channel past the western end of Plymouth breakwater. Sea trials were complete and despite a few problems, he was satisfied that the ship was in as good a condition as ever. The engineers were happy with the repairs. Four Exocet were once again in their containers below the bridge and all the radars were working. He and the ship's operation team had briefings to attend for their forthcoming deployment once they were alongside. There was even time for leave for everyone.

With a moment to spare as they continued down the channel, Jon picked up the main broadcast microphone.

'D'you hear there? This is the Captain speaking. Sea trials are complete and the ship is now operational again. Well done to all of you and thank you for all the hard work you have put in over recent months. As you all know, we will be sailing for Armilla patrol in three weeks. We now have the opportunity for everyone to get some leave. Please enjoy it. The rest of the year is going to be busy. Once again thank you all.'

As he put the microphone down, Jon reflected on what he had already found out. The ship was in as good condition as he could hope. Everything he had seen of his ship's company encouraged him enormously. When they sailed for the Gulf there would be plenty of time to get to know them properly and to work them up into an effective team. He suddenly realised he couldn't wait.

Chapter 20

Saying goodbye to Helen had really hurt. Partly because Jon knew he was going to miss her like anything but also because he was so looking forward to taking his ship to the Gulf that it made him feel guilty. Helen knew the dilemma he was in and did her best to make sure he knew that she understood. After all, she had quite a new and exciting challenge to look forward to herself in the coming months. They said their final farewells at Truro station.

'You look after yourself, Jon Hunt,' Helen said through tears as she hugged him hard.

'And you do the same Helen Hunt,' Jon replied hugging her back just as hard.

She managed a smile. 'Look, I'm not one for prolonged goodbyes. We get to see too little of each other as it is. You just go and do a bloody good job and come back to me in one piece.'

Jon looked into her eyes trying to get a final picture of her face. He knew from experience how hard it was to hold a mental photograph of someone when you were away for any length of time. Yes, he had plenty of real photographs but it was never quite the same.

'I could say the same to you.' There was a slamming noise behind them. The platform guard was coming towards them closing the carriage doors.

'Oh God it's just like that old black and white film, can't remember the name, anyway I've got to go.' He gave Helen one last lingering kiss and then jumped onto the carriage seconds before the guard closed the door on him. He was still staring out of the small window as the train pulled out.

As soon as he arrived in Devonport he was able to throw himself into the task of getting HMS Prometheus ready for a protracted and possibly dangerous deployment. The ache of leaving Helen behind was smothered in the worries of getting his charge into a condition to leave in a matter of days. It all seemed to happen in a rush and then they were off. The lines were cast off from the jetty. The ship's company were all fallen in on the upper deck wearing their best uniforms in 'Procedure Alpha' for leaving harbour. Salutes were piped to other ships as they passed their way down the Hamoaze. For the first part of the exit, Jon was standing on the roof of the bridge to get a better view of the ship's behaviour as they cleared the dockyard. Then he was down inside the bridge sitting on his chair, as the Navigating Officer passed him the various bearings of landmarks to allow him to give the necessary wheel orders to ensure the ship cruised safely down the marked channel. They glided past Plymouth Hoe and turned right past the bulk of Drakes Island into the wider area of the Sound. Then the lighthouse at the end of Plymouth breakwater was slipping by and they were clear of the clutches of Flag Officer Devonport and out into the wide waters of the Channel. The western tip of France beckoned ahead before Biscay, the Mediterranean and the Suez Canal. Suddenly it seemed an incredibly long way to go.

Before Jon could start brooding about the mountain they all still had to climb, the bridge VHF radio burst into life. 'Prometheus this is Rescue Five Zero, am I clear to close you, over?'

Jon immediately recognised the voice. He called over to the Yeoman to confirm the request, before jumping out of his chair and heading out onto the starboard bridge wing.

He scanned the sea and coast out to the west but there was nothing in sight. They were just clearing Ramehead and he could see clearly all the way across Whitsand Bay to St George's Island off Looe. Where was she?

Suddenly, there was an incredibly loud roar and a grey and red Sea King shot across the front of the ship at almost the same height as the deck. It pulled steeply up and executed a perfect wingover before returning and pulling hard into a hover alongside the bridge. Jon could see Helen sitting in the left hand seat waving at him. He could even see her smile. He waved back. Then in what seemed far too little time, its nose dipped and it accelerated away back towards the west and Culdrose. Jon stood for a little while before returning to the bridge. It wouldn't do for the sailors to see their Captain with a tear in his eyes.

Des Slater was taking an early mid-morning break in the wardroom when Brian came in. As Des was already pouring coffee he also poured one for Brian. They had been at sea long enough now to know a great deal about each other, including how they liked their coffee.

'Is the skipper keeping you busy Brian?' Des asked. 'Because I've hardly had a moment to spare since we left Guz.'

'Yup, that's Jon Hunt for you, he was the same when he commanded 844. It's all to the good though, you know that.'

'Of course, I suppose so. It's just that he's such a change from his predecessor. He's certainly making his presence felt throughout the ship. Half my job these days is finding out where the bloody hell he is. Do you know he spent a whole watch in the machinery control room last night? I wouldn't put it past him to be serving breakfast to the Junior Rates tomorrow morning.'

'You'd better get used to it Des. That's Jon to a tee. He likes to get to know his people as fast as he can and getting stuck in with them seems to be how he likes to do it. I'll bet you anything he already knows the names of every person in the ship and probably most of their life history. How are the sailors taking it?'

'At first, I think they were surprised to see him around so much. Most of them never got see Fulford at all. But they seem to be getting used to him appearing out of nowhere these days. Actually, I think they quite like it. Mind you I'm surprised he's left the Flight alone so much. You would think he would take a special interest there.'

'Ah, no I'm pretty sure that's exactly what he doesn't want to do. The one thing he really misses, apart from his wife, is being able to fly and I suspect he doesn't want to become a burden on them. Mind you, it's lucky the Lynx doesn't have a set of dual controls or he might not be able to resist the temptation. He did find it hilarious however, when he found out that the aircrew's Christian names were Tom and Jerry but he got the joke about calling the helicopter Fred straight away.'

'Actually, I suppose I should admit it but I never did quite understand that.'

'Oh that's simple. All the good Tom and Jerry cartoons were produced by a chap called Fred Quimby. His name appears in big letters at the start of each one.'

Des was about to reply when more officers started to pile in for the morning stand easy and the conversation broadened.

Later that morning, Brian knocked on Jon's cabin door with a sheaf of signals he needed to go through with him.

'Come in Brian,' Jon called. 'Oh bloody hell, that's a big stack, is there anything important in there?'

'No, not really. It's all mainly all routine stuff. There's a request for Leading Seaman Jeffries to go home from Cyprus for compassionate leave. His wife is having complications with a birth.'

'He must go as long as we can get him back once we're in the Gulf. After all he's the only gunner on the ship who's actually fired at anything and hit it.'

Brian was surprised once again by Jon's knowledge of the crew. 'You knew he was the Oerlikon gunner who took out the Exocet?'

Jon just smiled. 'What else Brian?'

'In the signals? Not a lot but the Flight Commander seems to feel a bit neglected. You've been sussing out most departments but left them alone so far.'

'Fuck it Brian, you know why of course. Yes, I'll go and see them soon. They're flying this evening aren't they?'

'Yes weapon loads and deck landings, then a surface search.'

'Right, I'll surprise them then.'

There was a knock on the door and the Chief Yeoman put his head around the curtain. 'Sorry to bother you Sirs but a priority Secret signal had just come in from Fleet.' He handed the sheaf of paper to Brian and discreetly left. Brian handed it to Jon who started to read. As soon as he had finished one page he handed it to Brian without a word. It took several minutes for them both to digest the contents.

When they had both finished, Jon looked over at Brian. 'Well, the Iran Iraq War may be officially over but as we were briefed before we left, there is still a great deal of tension in the area. This thing about the ownership of the Shatt al Arab waterway has never been cleared up. It was one of the reasons they went to war in the first place and as its Iraq's only access to the sea maybe I can understand why.'

'Playing Devil's Advocate, you do have to wonder about the American position in all of this. They've provided enormous help to Iraq, even turned a blind eye to the crazy amount of chemical weapons that they've been using and not always on the enemy. What was that operation last year? Oh yes, 'Earnest Will', they convoyed up all ships taking Iraqi and Kuwaiti oil but offered no protection to ships with Iranian oil. If I was Iranian I would be totally paranoid by now.'

'Most people think that's the reason Iran finally went to the negotiating table last year. I suspect they felt that the US was about to come in with both left feet. With the losses they've suffered over the years, one US carrier could probably have tipped the balance. Doesn't mean they've completely given up though if this signal is anything to go by.'

'So we can expect just a bit more than routine ship protection then?'

'Looks that way of this signal is correct, we'll get a full brief once we arrive.'

Chapter 21

That afternoon, Jon took a stroll down the Burma Way and slipped into the hangar via the rear internal door. The hangar and little Flight office at the rear were empty. All around him, carefully stowed, was the equipment to keep the Lynx flying. Along one wall were four spare rotor blades in their racks and below them the green fibreglass box of the spare engine he had to fight tooth and nail to be allocated before their deployment. Above him, the red painted firemain pipe snaked around the various ceiling fittings. Laid out in trolleys at the rear of the hangar ready for the forthcoming practices were the various torpedoes and missiles that the aircraft could carry. The air smelled of oil, grease and aviation fuel. He stopped for a second, all the memories of this place rushing back. This used to be his domain. It was from here that they had briefed for their mission into Argentina. It was from this hangar and deck behind it that they had flown all those sorties to destroy Exocets and rescue his friends, Marcel and Maria.

His reverie was rudely interrupted by the smiling face of Jerry Thompson. 'Good afternoon Sir, we didn't think you could stay away forever.'

Jon looked at the young Lieutenant and saw himself ten years earlier. 'Jerry you're right, now come on introduce me to your crew and you can show me what you're up to at the same time.'

Jon was led aft to where Fred was tied down on deck with nylon lashings. The Flight team of seven maintainers and Tom the Observer clustered around. Tom introduced them all and then continued, 'we were about to do some static weapon loads, in preparation for some real ones this evening Sir. Do you want to watch?'

'Delighted, I'll just stand to one side while you get on with it.'

Both aircrew jumped into the cockpit and the Flight team trundled out various weapons one after the other. They started with two Stingray torpedoes which were pulled up out of their trolleys with detachable weapon hoists onto their launchers on both sides of the helicopter. Once secure, all the safety pins were removed and handed to the aircrew who carried out various checks before returning the pins so the weapons could be safely removed. Two Sea Skua anti-surface missiles were then loaded and then finally the Heavy Machine Gun Pod which was loaded to the starboard weapon station. It was clear to Jon that this was a well-practiced team who all knew exactly what they were doing.

When the HMP was secure, he went forward and looked at the skin of the helicopter ahead of the muzzle of the gun. He could see it had been reinforced and that the little navigation light was also much stronger. He grinned as he looked up at Jerry who was sitting in the cockpit above him. 'When we had the first one of these the muzzle blast did a shed load of damage, we had to resort to masking tape.'

'Yes Sir, it's been heavily reinforced now as you can see. Its bloody good fun to play with though.'

They exchanged grins like schoolboys.

'Sir, we've all heard bits of the story. Is it really true you took out an Argie Pucara with one of these?'

Jon realised that the whole Flight had gathered around and that there was no way he could escape telling the story. 'I'll tell you as long as you agree to something.'

'Of course Sir.'

'In exchange for me telling salty Falkland's dits, you let me sit in the left hand seat for the first part of your trip this evening. You don't need an Observer for deck landings and I know what to do with the weapon pins.'

Jerry realised that the Captain had no need to make such a request. He could just have ordered it so was flattered that he had made the effort to do so. 'Of course Sir, as long as you can put up with my flying. We'll get your kit and briefings sorted out in a second. Now come on Sir, how did you get the only helicopter air to air kill in the world?'

Jon thought for a second, he hated shooting a line but these guys would understand. 'Well, we had the gun fitted almost as an afterthought. There were all sorts of odd modifications around and I guess we got lucky with this one. Earlier on in the war we had been bounced by a couple of jets and I think that the fact that what they thought was easy prey was able to fire back at them gave them such a fright they buggered off. But the Pucara was different. We were picking some people up from shore towards the end of the war. As we transitioned away this guy bounced us. I've no idea how he knew we were there. I guess some keen eyed Argie had spotted us from the hills. Anyway, we had a bit of a set to. He was only armed with two machine guns, pop guns really and probably had no idea that I had a cannon. He made a couple of passes at me and did some damage. I couldn't get the damned gun to fire initially. We had to reset all the switches. When he came at me around one of the mountains above Stanley it was all getting a bit desperate so I pulled up and barrel rolled. This slowed me down a lot and it was probably the last thing he expected. He just flew by. I just dropped the nose as we came upright and there he was. I couldn't miss.'

Jon's statement was met with stunned silence for a second. Then Jerry spoke. 'Jesus Sir, you rolled it? How close to the ground were you?'

'Oh several hundred feet at that stage, the ground was dropping away fast. Look, I know you guys are taught fighter evasion. I did some in Sea Kings as well. The thing is the Pucara was a lot more like a helicopter in terms of performance than a jet so the standard tactic of turning towards and then hard away at the last moment wasn't going to work. He could turn almost as fast as me. I had to do something unexpected. It certainly caught him off guard. He did manage to bang out though, which I'm glad about because he was pretty brave.' He could see other questions form on people's faces. 'Right, that's enough war stories from me. Haven't you lot got work to do and who is going to get me some flying gear?'

Later that evening, Jon climbed up into Fred's cockpit and strapped in. Jerry started in on his prestart checks and Jon realised he could still remember them all. It was like going back in time. When the rotors were engaged Jerry called for the question and answer pre-take off checks. Although Jon got out his borrowed set of flip cards, he realised he didn't really need them. He reeled off the list almost without thought. The next hour and half were wonderful. Jerry was clearly a very competent pilot and even though the ship manoeuvred to give some very difficult winds for landing, he coped with ease.

After each landing when the aircraft was secure the Flight would run in under the rotors and load the various weapons and then Jerry would launch and fly a circuit before returning to unload them. On one occasion Jerry informed the Flight that one of the torpedoes should have dropped but was stuck on its launcher. On return to the deck, the Flight went into the more careful 'hang up' procedure.

While they were waiting Jerry turned to Jon. 'So Sir, how do you roll one of these things? It's not exactly something they teach during training.'

'No it's not and of course its way outside the approved flight envelope but I thought it was general folklore amongst the Lynx community?'

'Not any more Sir, they've got very anal these days about abusing the airframe. They don't even like people beating up ships after one of our guys took out some aerials on a US Coast Guard cutter last year.'

'I suppose they've got a point Jerry. These machines are going to have to last quite a long time. The Mark Eight programme I was working on in the MOD has most of the airframes going on for years and they'll be far heavier with all the new kit we're going to squeeze in.'

Just then the ground crew signalled that they had safely removed the weapons and that the aircraft was cleared to launch. Jon breathed a mental sigh of relief as Jerry was now too busy to pursue his Captain to tell him how to break the rules.

All too soon it was time for Jon to jump out and hand over to Tom. It was getting dark now and having refuelled, they were going to head out in front of the ship and conduct a surface search looking for contacts for the ship to acquire as potential Exocet targets. Jon would be needed in the Ops room for that.

Later that evening while Jon was unwinding in his cabin Brian knocked on the door.

'Come in Brian, want to do a quick washup?'

'If you don't mind Sir. There are a couple of issues that I would like to go over with you.'

'Fine, fancy a small drink?'

They talked about the last couple of hours and how it had all gone before moving on to more general topics.

'Did you enjoy your trip this afternoon then? Jerry was telling us in the wardroom that you seemed to have fun. He also recounted a certain story about an Argie Pucara.'

'Ah, well, he blackmailed me into telling that one. Yes, I did enjoy it but I'll tell you something else. I keep telling myself how much I miss flying and I still do to a degree but while we were flying around the ship I kept looking at her and realising that she meant even more to me, does that make sense?'

'Yes it does, we all have to move on. I used to live in an ergonomic slum called a cockpit with a tiny radar and a few other things. Now I've got three radars, two sonars, a full ESM suite and a load of weapons. I guess we all have to grow up sometime. So tell me, how do you like being the skipper now that you've had time to settle in a bit?'

'I guess it's like most things, the issues I was worried about don't seem to really be a problem. I thought that as I'm not a member of the wardroom then I would get lonely here in splendid isolation but frankly I'm far too busy. Don't think for a moment that I won't want to be included in the odd run ashore when the time comes. No, the biggest thing for me and I would only say this to you Brian because we're friends, is that I worry about making a cock up. I'm still very new to all this and there are over two hundred people relying on me. Maybe with a bit more experience I will relax but not yet. Oh and one other thing, when we're alone together how about dropping the 'Sir', I have to say I find it rather disconcerting. We've known each other for so long after all.'

Brian looked at his friend and considered his response. 'Sorry Sir, but I can't agree. It's partly simple tradition but of course it's more than that. When we are on board you are the Captain and I strongly feel we should formally maintain our relationship.' He continued with a grin. 'And who knows, if I don't maybe I'll say something embarrassing in front of one of the other officers or crew.'

Jon sighed. 'Fair enough I suppose.'

Chapter 22

Helen was enjoying every minute of her time on 771 and at the same time hating every minute she was separated from Jon. She wrote to him every day and he wrote back just as often. As he knew when mail was leaving the ship he wrote daily in one letter that just grew until it was time to post it. She didn't want to bombard him with individual letters so posted once a week. She knew he was worrying about his new level of responsibility but reading between the lines, she also knew that he was having the time of his life. If she was honest so was she.

When she arrived on the squadron, she had been worried about being accepted. It was one thing to go through training as a girl but now she had to stand on her own two feet. In her joining interview, the CO made this abundantly clear but also pointed out that he expected the same from all his pilots. She left his office quite optimistic.

The squadron operated in crews and she was teamed up with a Royal Australian Navy exchange pilot, who to her surprise was actually called Bruce. It had caused endless amusement in the crewroom when he joined. In the back was Dick the Observer and Leading Aircrewman Owen who everyone called 'Tiny' because he was six foot six tall and built like a Sumo wrestler.

They operated a duty crew system but on busy days there might be the need for several aircraft and so quite often they were called out at short notice even if off duty. When not on actual rescues there was plenty to do. Helen was given a fairly intensive period of specific SAR training that included how to hover really close to cliffs as well as the specifics of how to get a winch wire down to a small boat in a big sea. She realised very quickly that Jon had been right about choosing the squadron. It was quite clear that everyone was motivated to do a good job because the job was really worth doing. The squadron had only changed over to Sea Kings in the last year. Previously, they had flown the older Wessex Mark Five which although a good machine, lacked the capability to operate at night. That task had been given to the Sea King training squadron on the other side of the runway and had been a burden to a busy unit with an important primary role. It made far more sense now that 771 was day and night capable with their own Sea Kings.

Today the crewroom was crowded, there was very little going on as the airfield was suffering under that well known meteorological phenomena known as the 'Culdrose Clamp'. Wet air blowing in from the Atlantic and hitting the Lizard peninsular, was forced upwards and cooled. The result was thick fog that had been known in some cases to last for weeks. Helen was on duty today but looking out of the window she doubted that there would be any flying. She couldn't even see the control tower on the far side of the runway. Instead, she was letting Bruce try to teach her the finer points of Uckers, the particularly vicious naval version of the children's game Ludo. She was struggling to maintain a straight face because Jon had already taught her how to play, if that was the right word. She knew the main rule was to convince your opponent that your version of the rules was the right one. It was a bit like poker in that respect and Bruce didn't know it but he was about to get a big surprise.

Suddenly the duty officer put his head around the door. 'Duty crew, briefing room, we've got a shout.'

Taking a last look at the weather, Helen followed Bruce out to the briefing room. This was going to be interesting.

As soon as the whole crew were present, the duty officer pointed to a map of the Channel. 'Right guys, we've had a Mayday from a yacht called Jennie May in this position here.' He pointed to a spot in Mounts Bay, about ten miles to the west of the Lizard. 'There are only two people on board, a husband and wife. The husband has slipped down the companionway hatch and is out cold. The wife can use the radio but that's about it. She doesn't know how to start the engine or even how to get the sails down so if one of you has to go down be bloody careful. The lifeboat is on its way as well but the tide is set strongly to the east for the next four hours, that and a south westerly Force Seven are both sending her towards the rocks. If you can sort them out or get them off if necessary and the weather is still crap here, St Mawgan are open so divert there. Any questions?'

The Boss put his head around the door and wished them good luck just as they stood to leave. Helen went straight out to the aircraft. It was already prepared with its blades spread for a quick launch. She jumped into the left hand seat and started making switches. Bruce wasn't far behind her and soon they had both engines and the rotors running. With both rear seat crew on board, they were ready to go.

'Listen up everyone,' Bruce called over the intercom. 'To save time we'll hover taxy over the perimeter and see if we can get down by Looe Bar. However, if the visibility is too bad we'll ask air traffic for an instrument take off and then Dick you can let us down once we're clear of the coast.'

After clearing his intentions with the control tower, Bruce lifted the big machine into the hover and carefully made their way across the airfield at a fast walking pace. As they approached the perimeter at the north western part of the airfield they looked for the valley that led down to the sea and the beach at Looe Bar near the little fishing village of Porthleven. Visibility looked better further down the valley so they continued. It was almost surreal sliding down the hill only ten feet above the ground. When they were almost at the large pool of water that gave the beach that separated it from the sea its name, the visibility cleared, although the cloud base was well below a hundred feet. Bruce lowered the aircraft's nose and accelerated out to sea.

In the rear Dick was looking at his radar. The victim should show up at this range especially if it had a radar reflector fitted, which yachts these days normally did. Meanwhile Tiny was preparing their equipment. There was far more room in the back of this machine than a normal anti-submarine Sea King. Although the radar had been retained, all the sonar gear had been removed which included the massive 'pit head gear' ahead of the rear crew station that housed the dipping sonar and its large winch. Consequently, there was plenty of space for him to move around and get the stretcher and other bits and pieces ready.

'I've got a contact in about the right place guys,' Dick called. 'Head one eight five, range is about eight miles. There's no one else around there, although I've got what looks like the lifeboat closing, about seven miles away.'

'Roger,' Bruce acknowledged as he altered their heading to intercept. 'Eyes out everyone it looks bloody rough so this could be fun.'

Helen was the first to spot the scrap of white that quickly turned out to be the yacht's sails. It wasn't easy to see against the whitecaps of the sea.

'Shit, why are they on port tack,' Tiny asked from the back. 'If they tacked on to starboard they might clear the land.'

Helen immediately saw what he meant. With the cliffs of the Lizard visible to port and only a few miles away, if the yacht could tack then they might be able to head out to sea enough for the tide to sweep them safely past the danger.

Helen called on the Marine VHF radio. 'Jennie May, Jennie May this is Rescue Five Zero, a helicopter approaching from the north do you read over?'

There was silence for a moment and then a woman's voice responded. It was quite clear that she was scared from the tone of her voice. 'Hello helicopter, yes this is the Jennie May, have you come to help? Er, over.'

'Yes we're here to help, can you update us on your situation please?'

'My husband is lying on the saloon floor. He's unconscious and I don't know what to do.'

'It's alright Jennie May, can I ask you your name please?'

'Oh, its Fiona, what are you going to do?'

'OK Fiona, well the first thing we will do is fly over you to assess the situation. Now is the boat sailing on an autopilot?'

'Yes it is but I don't know how to operate it.'

'That's fine just let us get to you. I'm going to call the lifeboat now if you wonder who I'm talking to.'

Helen then managed to make contact with the lifeboat. They should be with the yacht in about fifteen minutes, the only problem was that it looked like it would be very close to the cliffs by then. They flew over the yacht to assess the situation in detail and then Bruce summed up it up for the whole crew.

'OK, we've got a fifty foot yacht on a lee shore with not long before they are wrecked on the cliffs. Our priority is to save life and that means getting the two of them off the yacht. If the lifeboat gets to them in time they can do the job but I don't think we can gamble on that. The big problem is that there is only one terrified woman on the boat and the chances of her doing a hi-line transfer are very small. That yacht has a very tall mast so there's no way I can hover over it. I'm not going to risk the aircraft and more lives. So any ideas anyone?'

Tiny was the first to speak. 'Put me down on the winch Boss, you can swing me in if you have to.'

'Yeah right and end up with another casualty, sorry too dangerous mate.'

Helen had an idea. 'Let me talk to the woman again Bruce. Fiona this is Rescue Five Zero. You have a dinghy on your stern, can you release it and let it trail behind you on a long line?'

'I don't know, do you want me to try? I've done it in harbour.'

Helen looked at Bruce. 'Go for it girl,' he answered, immediately realising what Helen was thinking.

'Fiona, yes please as quickly as you can. We will hold well clear while you do it.'

They hovered clear of the yacht while a red foul weather clad person emerged from the hatch into the cockpit and stumbled to the stern where a dinghy was secured on davits. They seemed to take forever to release the dinghy but suddenly it hit the water with a splash and then to a groan of dismay in the helicopter immediately turned upside down. It started to stream behind the yacht but was brought up standing about twenty yards off the stern.

As Bruce manoeuvred the Sea King into position the woman went back into the yacht and the radio came back to life. 'This is Fiona, sorry that's the best I can do.'

'That's alright Fiona, now does the dinghy have a fibreglass floor or a soft one over?'

'Oh, it's not fibreglass, it's soft, does that matter?'

'Yes that's good, now we will try to put our winchman down onto the dinghy. He will then be able to pull himself into you.'

Bruce moved forward to get directly over the dinghy and immediately realised the small boat was lost to sight. Even though he had the yacht visual ahead of him it wasn't going to be enough to hold an accurate hover over such a small target.

'Dick, when we're roughly there, you will have to take control OK? And Tiny will have to go down without the stretcher at first. Get him to take the hi-line so we can get it down to him if needs be.'

Dick acknowledged with a curt 'Roger,' and then after a few seconds he called 'engaging Aux Hover Trim.' He could now fly the aircraft from the cabin door with a small joystick. It only had limited authority but was enough for him to be able to keep directly above the dinghy.

Bog Hammer

With the Sea King now hovering over the upturned dinghy, the winch was lowered with the green clad form of the winchman on it. With the wind gusting over thirty knots, it was impossible to stop him swinging but Dick judged it to perfection and just as Tiny was above the dinghy he lowered the winch quickly and the crewman ended up spread-eagled on the upturned hull.

Dick immediately called over the intercom. 'You have control Bruce, move back and left ten yards.'

Suddenly Bruce could see the dinghy and Tiny who was now pulling on the painter to approach the stern of the yacht. Dick was keeping the winch wire slack but only enough to stop it getting tangled. Within a few minutes, Tiny was clambering onto the stern and into the cockpit.

'What's he doing?' Bruce asked, as it was clear something next to the yacht's wheel had got Tiny's attention. Suddenly there was a small puff of white smoke from the stern and the yacht slowly turned more to the west. The sails started to flap wildly but the yacht was now clearly making progress directly away from the land and into the wind. 'Clever bastard got the engine going and has worked out how to make the autopilot change heading. Dick, I think we can get him off the winch wire now and Helen, call the lifeboat, they should be able to finish this off.'

They hung around while the lifeboat managed to get alongside the yacht. It was soon established that the man had started to recover so there was no need for any more winching. The lifeboat would accompany the yacht which Tiny seemed more than competent to manage, around the Lizard into the shelter of Falmouth Bay before heading to Falmouth itself.

It was four hours later before they managed to get back to Culdrose. Because of the fog, they had to divert to St Mawgan on the northern coast and wait until a weather window opened in order to get home. Tiny had arrived back at base long before them.

Helen was surprised by their reception back on the squadron. The Boss heard the debrief and issued a simple well done to them before going back to his office. In the crewroom, which was about to empty for the day there was only a certain amount of interest in what they had achieved. Helen realised that what to her had seemed an amazing experience resulting in the almost certain saving of two lives, was basically just another day in the office.

Chapter 23

HMS Prometheus lay snugly alongside the jetty in the bleak commercial port area of Jebel Ali in the United Arab Emirates. The temperature was sweltering but below decks it was relatively cool due to the chilled air system used to keep her computers at a safe working temperature. The Junior Rate's Dining Hall was full with the ship's Officer and Senior Rates all present so that they could be given the overall briefing on their role for the next four months. Captain Merryweather, the Senior Naval Officer Middle East, known as SNOME was sitting to one side of a large map of the Gulf while Jon introduced him.

Jon looked at his assembled people. 'As you know, Gentlemen the ship is here for Operation Armilla. Despite the fact that the Iran Iraq War is now officially over, there is still work for us to do. Captain Merryweather has come down from Dubai to give us the detail of the current situation.' Jon turned to SNOME. 'The floor is yours Sir.'

The Captain stood. At well over six feet, his head wasn't far from the deckhead but he didn't seem to notice. A thin man with sparse, thinning, sandy hair, he clearly didn't stay out in the sun much if his pale complexion was any indicator. He smiled at his audience.

'Thank you Commander Hunt. Yes, you're right, there is still a great deal of tension in the area. But first some background. This whole mess really started with the deposing of the Shah of Iran all those years ago. Iraq has always felt that it had some territorial claims on parts of Iran and they decided that in the turmoil following the revolution there was an opportunity to gain that territory. They are an almost landlocked country and need somewhere to export their oil from by sea in case their pipelines are compromised. What they hadn't gambled on was the resistance that the Iranians put up. I won't go into detail but the war was the biggest conflict on the planet with the exception of the two World Wars. During the fighting, Iraq had the tacit backing of the west and by that, I primarily mean the Americans. Many feel that the only reason that the Iranians went to the negotiating table in Geneva last year was because they feared that the Americans would finally become actively involved. You will be aware of the incidents of recent years, like the shooting down of the Iranian airliner by the US and attacks on American warships like the Stark. And of course, both sides have attacked commercial shipping. Almost one hundred and fifty vessels have been sunk or damaged. That is why you are here. Although the war is technically over there are still Silkworm missile batteries on the Iranian shore, especially around the Straits of Hormuz. They have a range of over sixty miles and a very large warhead. That makes that bit of water quite dangerous. However, there are other areas that are also considered precarious, like the waters around Iran's offshore oil refinery at Kharg Island towards the top of the Gulf. So the purpose of Armilla is to escort convoys from the north of the Gulf out past the straits and into the Indian Ocean. Any questions so far?'

A hand went up at the back. 'Sir, do we operate with the Americans or only with British ships?'

'Good question. Armilla is a British operation but that said we cooperate with the US forces here as much as is practical. However, as far as command and control go, you answer to Fleet through me and no one else.'

Another hand went up. 'Sir, wasn't the Stark fired on by an Iraqi aircraft?'

'Yes you're right, two Exocet in fact. There's never really been a satisfactory explanation but it serves to illustrate the dangers of the area rather well. I'm afraid the command and control exercised by both Iran and Iraq is somewhat lacking by our standards.'

The talk went on for another half an hour then broke up for lunch. Jon invited the Captain to his cabin for lunch after a few drinks in the wardroom. He knew there was more to discuss. As soon as the food had been laid out by his steward they were left alone to talk.

'So Jon, how was the trip out here?'

'Fine Sir, Suez was interesting but otherwise it was a straightforward transit. The First Lieutenant kept the crew on their toes with exercises. It didn't help that I told him that we regularly managed to get closed up to Action Stations in this ship during the Falklands, in under ten minutes. He was quite upset when we never managed better than twelve. I'm happy though because I know that adrenalin will provide the two minutes when needed.'

'Good, now as you know Battleaxe had to leave slightly early so you won't get a handover from her but frankly she had a pretty quiet time so you won't have missed much. However, now we come to the part of the brief that is for limited distribution only.'

Jon wasn't surprised to hear that there was more to come.

The Captain continued. 'A bit more background first. Before the war, Iraq was heavily allied to the Soviets and was considered by the Americans to be a state that sponsored terrorism. So it was a bit of a quandary when it looked possible that Iran might actually win. That was why the US provided the support it did. But now the war is over they are not so keen. Saddam Hussein is a monster and so are his children by all accounts. Also, the country is heavily in debt to the Saudis and Kuwait and neither country are prepared to write off that debt. It hasn't helped that the UAE and Kuwait are selling more oil than they should and the price has dropped which is really hurting the Iraqi economy as it tries to recover from the war. I have a detailed briefing document for you and please feel free to share it with your command team but no further please. Now, what does this all mean to you? Well, on the one hand, we have a deeply paranoid and well armed Islamic state that owns the whole north shore of the Gulf, on the other we have Iraq which is in internal turmoil and the US who don't seem to know what they want to do about either of them. Need I remind you what the Argentinian government did in 1982 to shore up their unpopularity? Well, Iraq actually has a claim that Kuwait belongs to them. It was part of the Ottoman Empire until 1922 when us clever British drew some arbitrary lines on a map and made Iraq virtually landlocked. So the jury is out at the moment I'm afraid. But now we come to the big 'however'. Current intelligence indicates that both countries are still jockeying to try to gain an advantage. Iran isn't in much of a position to get international help. They've upset everyone in the west and the Soviets are in no position to offer any real aid. This Gorbachev chap seems to have really upset the apple cart there. Iraq, on the other hand, seems hell bent on upsetting everyone as well. They've had a go at the Arab League about the oil issue but no one's listening. Their biggest problem is sorting out internal issues and getting their hands on money. The US are distancing themselves from them mainly because of Iraq's attitude towards Israel. So what worries us is that one country or the other will do something stupid to draw international attention to the other side, then even get some sort of punitive action in train.'

'What about the Chinese surely they have an interest as well?' Jon asked.

'At the moment they seem content to sit back and just make money by selling weapons. But even that's reducing. Iran for example is now making its own version of the Silkworm missile.'

'So is there any clear intelligence of a real threat?'

'Maybe and this is for you and your Ops team's ears only at this stage. We get limited intelligence from inside Iran. As you can imagine it's a difficult place for intelligence people to operate. However, there is every indication that they are planning something and it's something that they are spending a great deal of money on. We know for instance that they have expanded their military base on Kharg Island.'

'Hang on Sir, I thought that was an oil terminal?'

'It is but it came under so much air attack during the war it was heavily reinforced by the military and they never withdrew. There's a sizeable garrison on the north side by the airfield and satellite imagery shows continued building going on. In addition, there seems to have been a great deal of liaison with Pakistan recently but again we're not sure why. The general consensus is that Iran didn't want to end the war and are now about to try something. Your job will be to keep your eyes out. Convoy duty is the overt reason you're here but you will also be going places where it might be possible to pick up hints about what's going on.'

'Hmm, it all seems rather vague Sir but I can understand why. Rest assured we will be vigilant.'

'Good now here is your detailed briefing pack, as I said, just you and your Operations people to see it please and that's about it, so good luck. Your first convoy sails from Kuwait in four days.'

Later that afternoon Jon called his Heads of Department into his cabin for a final briefing. They discussed the readiness of the ship and her material state, all of which was satisfactory. Then Ops gave an outline of the forthcoming convoy they were due to escort from Kuwait into the Gulf of Oman. Brian also outlined the specific threats which were mainly the shore based Silkworm missile batteries and the small Bog Hammer fast attack craft. Aircraft and larger warships were also an issue but ones that the ship was designed to cope with. Finally, Jon called a halt but asked Brian to stay behind.

When everyone was gone he handed Brian a large scotch. 'Might as well drink up Brian, there's no real run ashore available around here, as I'm sure the ship's company will soon find out.'

Brian laughed. 'Don't worry, Des has already read them the riot act about how to behave in a Muslim country. I'm sure there'll be no trouble.'

Jon handed the dossier that SNOME had given him. 'Have a read through that in your own time Brian. There's actually not much more in it than we already knew. Except for the sting in the tail, have a look at the last paragraphs of the conclusions.'

Brian flicked to the end of the document and frowned as he read the sparse paragraphs. 'So they think Iran might be planning something but have no idea what. That's' a great help.'

'It just means we need to stay alert Brian. We're the only British warship in the area at the moment.'

Chapter 24

Staying fully alert was easier said than done. After their fourth convoy, Prometheus had fallen into a well rehearsed routine. Because the area was deemed to be less dangerous than during the war many commercial ships were now content to sail on their own and unescorted. However, there were enough still with untrusting masters or more likely insurance companies to warrant convoys. The normal number was between five and six and the duty was pretty simple. They would form up at a rendezvous position, normally off Kuwait and take about a day and a half to reach the Straits of Hormuz, the dangerous choke point to leave the Gulf. The straits were actually so narrow at one point that the territorial waters of the countries on either side effectively overlapped. Also, it was so crowded that inbound and out bound separation zones were mandated. However, a United Nations convention allowed for ships to make free passage. Prometheus stayed in Defence Watches for the transit until well clear into the Gulf of Oman where the convoy would disperse, each ship to its individual destination. Prometheus would stay on the more dangerous side of the line of ships although sometimes Jon wondered which side that really was. SNOME's briefing still had him worried.

The first time they went through the straits they were illuminated by several radars from the Iranian shore. Two were identified as 'Starbright' the Silkworm missile tracking system. However, after a few tense hours, they passed clear and by the fourth convoy they were becoming quite used to it. They also regularly picked up an Iranian Frigate, who travelled with them for a few miles before breaking away. Again, the first time he appeared it had raised pulses for a while but now they even exchanged pleasantries over the radio. Once clear of the straits and with their charges gone, there was usually time for a quick break for a swim or on one occasion, a weekend in Muscat before heading back to pick up their next group of charges.

Jon was sitting on his chair on the bridge during the afternoon watch on their latest transit back into to the Gulf. The sea was calm

Bog Hammer

and the weather hot but out to sea the breeze made it pleasant rather than stifling.

The Officer of the Watch was the First Lieutenant. He would not normally be watch keeping in the afternoon but had decided to give the regular officer a break to keep his hand in. The ship was back in Defence Watches as they approached the narrowest part of the straits once more. The area was crowded with ships going both ways but he was not having to concentrate too hard as they were all going in or out in the separation lanes. There was little crossing traffic.

'Did you enjoy the Sod's Opera last night Sir?' Des asked Jon.

'Haven't laughed so much for ages,' Jon replied. 'Although, I thought you came in for a bit of stick, especially from the stoker's mess.'

'Ah well I gave them a bit of a hard time on rounds the other day and it's always a good way for a sailor to get his own back.'

'You know, I do wonder how these naval traditions will fare with the ships that have girls on board. Us Leanders won't have the problem of course. Fleet has decided we're too small to have segregated accommodation. But some of the material last night was pretty near the knuckle.'

'From what I've heard Sir, the women are worse than the men. Maybe we should be worried that things will get even worse.'

Jon snorted a laugh. 'You're probably right. I'm sure you know that my wife is an Officer now and she can certainly give as good as she gets.' He suddenly felt a wave of longing wash over him. He had been too busy recently to miss her but now it all suddenly caught up with him. He was spared the luxury of following up the thought as the bow of the large tanker that had been following them appeared in his peripheral vision. She was travelling at well over twenty five knots and even though she was at least half a mile clear she looked much closer because of her size.

'She's in a hurry, most tankers have the sense not to try and overtake while it's this narrow. In fact, technically she's in breach of the traffic regulations. Luckily, it's not our job to police them. She wouldn't get away with that in the English Channel. What do you reckon Des? She must be at least thirty five thousand tons?' Jon asked as he gave her the once over with his binoculars.

'At least that Sir and Pakistani registered by the looks of her ensign. I wonder where she's off to.'

'Could be any of the Gulf States,' Jon was about to say more when the Operations Room broke in on the bridge speakers.

'Bridge this is Ops, Starbright radar detected on northerly bearings as expected.'

Jon picked up the microphone. 'Ops, this is the Captain, anything unusual?'

'Hang on Sir, yes we have eight fast moving contacts approaching directly towards us from the Iranian shore. Speed over thirty knots and they're in a formation, can only be Bog Hammers Sir.'

'Shit, pipe the ship to Action Stations Number One and also pipe to scramble the Lynx armed with the HMP. I'll be in the Ops room.'

Jon arrived at his position in the Ops room without consciously knowing how he had got there. Brian was also there and they both peered at the command plot where the tracks of the approaching boats could easily be seen.

'Be here in twenty minutes Sir,' Brian observed. 'The Lynx should be able to spot them and keep their heads down with the gun if they try anything funny.'

Just then the Lynx checked in on the radio. 'Fred airborne opening to the north.'

'Bloody hell that was quick,' said Brian. They could briefly hear the growl of the helicopter as it transited away from the side of the ship.

'I told them how we set up the aircraft for the Falklands.' Jon replied. 'Just as long as they haven't broken my record.'

Des's voice came over from the bridge. 'Ship closed up at Action Stations Sir. All upper deck guns are manned and I've got the Flight and some of my team up top with small arms ready as well.'

'Thank you Number One. Let me know what you can identify once they get closer.'

Tense minutes passed and then the helicopter called in. 'Mother this is Fred. We have eight small attack boats approaching. They all have a large machine gun on a mounting and I reckon I can see several crew with shoulder launched missiles.'

'Tell the helicopter to keep well clear for the moment.' Jon told the aircraft controller. 'We don't want to provoke anyone. Not yet anyway.'

Bog Hammer

Suddenly a strongly accented voice came over the VHF radio. 'Unidentified warship, you are in Iranian waters. You will stop at once and be boarded for inspection.'

For a moment there was a stunned silence then Jon looked at Brian. 'We're in the inbound channel aren't we?'

'Yes Sir, as you know it is technically Iranian territorial water but we have the right of free passage under the UN Convention of the Law of the Sea as long as we are not conducting military operations which we aren't.'

'Right this is some sort of game they're playing. Is there any sign of that bloody Frigate that's normally around here?'

The Surface Warfare Controller answered. 'Not within visual range Sir and none of our current tracks are on closing courses except for these eight Bog Hammers.'

'So who the hell is on the radio? It must be one for the Bog Hammers, that's pretty brave of him. Right, pass me the radio.' Jon took the microphone. 'Unidentified contact calling Warship Prometheus, we are in international recognised waters and have the right of free passage you have no right to order us to stop.'

'Prometheus, you will do as ordered or you will be fired upon.'

'This is Prometheus, negative and be advised that if I am fired upon I am authorised to return fire, over.'

There was no reply.

'Sir, they're stopping at about three miles and splitting up, surrounding us,' the Surface Warfare Controller reported. Jon looked at the plot and could immediately see what they were doing. It was a standard Bog Hammer tactic. This didn't look good.

Suddenly the Electronics Warfare Controller broke in, 'Sir, Starbright radar on a bearing of zero zero six has changed mode into fast scan.'

A new track appeared on the plot. '967 radar has detected a fast moving track headed directly towards us Sir, range eighteen miles and closing at close to supersonic speed, classified as hostile.'

'Bridge, this is the Captain come hard right to head north. Fire chaff, Weapons Station, is the Sea Wolf ready?'

'Yes Sir,'

'Very well remove the command override, weapons free.'

'Aye, Aye Sir.'

'What the hell are the Bog Hammers doing?'

'Nothing Sir, they seem to be waiting.'

There was the tell-tale whoosh above their heads as the chaff rockets were fired from their launchers.

'Tell the Lynx they are weapons free, sink the bastards. Also, any upper deck weapons may engage when in range.'

'Silkworm seeker radar detected Sir, estimate range now ten miles.'

Jon acknowledged the EW Controller and silence settled over the Ops room. The blooms of the chaff rockets suddenly appeared on the radar adding more targets for the incoming missile to choose from. There was nothing more they could do. The Sea Wolf 910 radar tracker was waiting for the 967 Doppler radar to track the target to the engagement zone when it would take over and once the weapon was fired, guide it onto the target.

'Missile heading unchanged, the chaff hasn't worked Sir.'

Suddenly, there was a loud bang from the front of the ship which made everyone jump. It was a Sea Wolf missile leaving the launcher. It would accelerate to over Mach 2 in seconds before its motor burned out and it coasted at supersonic speeds to its target.

'Sea Wolf has engaged,' the Weapons Controller called unnecessarily. However, he was watching the television screen that relayed a picture from a camera bore sighted to the tracking radar. 'Target splashed Sir,' he reported in a mixture of elation relief.

'Any more of the bloody things being fired?' Jon asked.

'No more detected Sir and the Starbright radar has reverted to full scan,' the EW director reported.

'Right, what are those surface contacts doing?'

Brian replied. 'They're withdrawing Sir. However, two appear stationary. I suspect that the Lynx has been busy.'

The helicopter came on the radio. 'Mother this is Fred, I've fired on two of the speed boats and they're stopped in the water, one is on fire. Do you wish me to pursue the others over?'

Brian looked at Jon who shook his head. 'Negative Fred. They will be in real Iranian waters in minutes. Stay on station and keep an eye on the two you nailed. We will close and try to recover survivors.'

Jon returned to the bridge. It didn't take long to come up to the two immobilised boats. The smoke from the one on fire could be

Bog Hammer

seen for miles. Just before they arrived there was a sudden gout of flame and the burning boat slipped under the surface. Looking at the other one, Jon could see the crew hauling two bodies up from the sea. The remaining boat was the classic shape Jon had seen from the pre-deployment briefings. Basically it was just a green fibre glass shell with two massive outboards and a large calibre machine gun mounted in the middle. It was clear that the Lynx had done its job. There now seemed to be two people bailing furiously while two others, presumably the survivors from the other boat, were simply staring up at the grey walls of the Frigate as it drew alongside.

Jon looked down at Des who was now supervising the recovery of the four men. A ladder had been let down and one of the ship's crew had clambered down to help the survivors up. Several rifles were also being held clearly in sight and pointing at the men in case they had any idea of offering resistance. There didn't seem to be any.

'Des,' Jon shouted. 'Any chance we can recover that boat?'

'Not really Sir and if we tow it our wake will almost certainly sink it.'

'Right, when the survivors are on board I want you to go down and search it carefully. See if there is any paperwork, charts anything like that. After that, we'll cast it loose and let the helicopter finish its work.'

Des looked up and gave Jon a thumbs up. All the time Jon was dreading the Ops room calling and telling him that the Silkworm battery was gearing up again for another shot but thankfully nothing more happened. It wasn't long before the Lynx flew in and shot the boat to pieces before returning to land. Jon made a note to congratulate the crew when things settled down.

As the ship settled back on course and out of the straits, Jon relaxed the ship back to Defence Watches and joined Brian back in the Ops room to compose the initial signal back to SNOME and Fleet. He could tell them the bald facts but his head was whirling. What the hell was that all about? He had a deep suspicion that it was something to do with the warning SNOME had given him. Once the signal was out, he would go aft and see the survivors maybe he could get some sense out of them.

Chapter 25

Jon looked morosely out of the window of the RAF Hawker Siddeley 125 jet as it banked over the M25 motorway to make its final approach to RAF Northolt. Captain Merryweather was seated in the other single seat in the aisle opposite. They had spent most of the trip back from Dubai, where Prometheus was currently berthed, going over the events of the previous days. Jon's briefcase bulged with the ship's records of the day which he knew would be poured over by CinC Fleet staff as soon as they arrived at Northwood. Despite all their deliberations, neither of them could work out an obvious reason why the Iranians had behaved as they did. Maybe the powers that be would have more intelligence. However, Jon had the glimmerings of an idea which they both agreed needed to be pursued once they arrived.

The four survivors had remained adamantly silent and anyway Jon suspected that no one on the ship actually spoke their language. He had tried out some of the Arabic he had gained during his trip to the Lebanon but either he wasn't understood or more likely the men were determined not to speak. None had been seriously hurt. Jon wasn't too happy to turn them over to the local police but in the end he had no choice. Des hadn't found anything in his search of the boat. Not even any evidence of its nationality which was strange and searches of the men had not revealed any identification either.

The aircraft landed with a thump and they were soon being ushered directly from the aircraft's steps into a waiting staff car. The brief blast of rain in Jon's face made him realise how far they had come in just a few hours and it wasn't just geographically. He wasn't worried that his actions were the wrong ones. His rules of engagement were quite clear but he also knew things always looked different when viewed through a telescope from thousands of miles away.

As if reading his thoughts Captain Merryweather smiled at him. 'Don't worry Jon, you have my full backing. I would have done exactly the same thing if I had been there.'

Jon thanked him and the rest of the journey passed in silence. He suddenly realised that he was only a few hundred miles away from

Helen. He strongly suspected that getting to see her was not going to be on the agenda.

In what seemed like minutes they were through the gates of the naval headquarters, past the Marine sentries and down towards the low building that housed the massive bunker known as 'The Hole' to all who worked there. They were met by a Commander who didn't introduce himself but took them straight to the security window where passes were waiting for them and then through the massive open set of blast doors and into a lift. They descended at least four floors and exited the lift into a quiet, narrow, carpeted corridor. The only sound was the whistle of air from the overhead vents. Along the corridor was a double set of doors and they were ushered inside into a large conference room.

The room was already full. Two dark suited men, two naval Captains and an Admiral who Jon immediately recognised as the Chief of Staff to CinC Fleet.

Everyone stood as they entered. The Admiral spoke first. 'Welcome Captain Merryweather, Commander Hunt. We're glad you could get here so quickly. You must be quite tired, my secretary will get you coffee. Let me introduce you to everyone here.'

Introductions were brief. The two Captains were Fleet staff officers, the civilians represented MI6 and the Foreign Office. Jon managed to forget their names within seconds of being introduced.

Coffee was served, at the same time Jon was relieved of the contents of his briefcase which were taken away by a rather pretty young Wren, who he realised was actually now an Able Seaman. The Admiral then asked him to go through the day's events as they occurred in detail.

He spoke for about an hour, with the occasional interjection from SNOME using a chart provided to show exact locations and times. He was listened to in silence and then the questions began.

The civilian from the Foreign Office seemed to want to query everything Jon had to say until after one particularly pointed question, Jon had had enough. He turned to the Admiral. 'Sir, with respect, I did everything to safeguard my people and my ship and at no time did I exceed my rules of engagement. If there is any criticism of my actions I would be grateful to know about them now.'

The Admiral looked hard at Jon for a few seconds. 'I'm sorry Jon, this whole incident has us totally confused. The potential for a major international incident is extremely high as I'm sure you can understand. There is a great deal of pressure from the highest levels to get to the bottom of this. That said, as far as your actions are concerned you have my full support.' He looked pointedly at the civilians as he said it. 'You had no choice but to defend the ship and as you said you acted completely in accordance with your instructions. You didn't fire until fired upon and as far as I'm concerned the matter is closed.'

Jon breathed a quiet sigh of relief. The Admiral's words were what he had hoped for but you never knew once politics got in the way.

'However, what neither of you probably don't know is what has been happening in the wider world since you were attacked.'

Jon had been dreading this. There had been nothing on the television before they left but the press were sure to have got their hands on the story by now. Unfortunately, his face was well known to them and he was expecting all sorts of unwanted attention. So it was with great surprise that the Admiral's next words filtered through.

'Absolutely nothing. We haven't heard a word from Tehran, no diplomatic protestations whatsoever. When we summoned the Iranian Ambassador in London he flatly denied any incident had taken place. When we protested to him he demanded proof. Not only that but there's been nothing in the press either here or abroad.'

'Sorry Sir but surely we have proof? There are the prisoners in Bahrain, as well as my records and surely there must be some satellite data?'

The Admiral grimaced. 'The police station that held the four prisoners was attacked just as you were taking off, a massive suicide bomb in a lorry. There were no survivors. Your records and testimony are fine for us but with no other corroborating evidence no one else is likely to believe us. The missile was totally destroyed and all the other evidence, such as it was, is at the bottom of the Straits of Hormuz. As no one was paying attention there was no directed satellite data either.'

Bog Hammer

One of the civilians broke in. It was the man from MI6. 'And if no one else is up in arms about this, it may be best to keep it under our hats, at least for the moment.'

The penny dropped. 'This has got something to do with the intelligence that Iran may be up to something hasn't it?' Jon asked.

'Yes Jon we think so and that's what we need to talk about now,' the Admiral responded. 'We now know what happened but do you or SNOME have the slightest idea why?'

Jon considered the question. It wasn't as if he hadn't been asking himself the same thing ever since the missile was fired. 'The whole thing stinks Sir, for several reasons. For a start why fire only one missile? If they were trying to really sink us they should have fired more than one.'

'Maybe it's all they had, we know their serviceability is poor,' one of the Fleet Captains suggested.

'If that's true, why risk it at all? And why the Bog Hammers? The obvious logic would be that they expected to hit us and the small boats would then be able to attempt an attack. But they must know that most navies have decent anti-missile systems these days. The chances were that one missile wouldn't get through. From the way the Bog Hammers reacted when we shot the missile down it was almost as though they expected it, they reacted so fast. However, I don't think they expected our Lynx to be there with a weapon.'

'I'm sorry Jon, are you suggesting something other than a rather botched attack?' The Admiral asked.

'It's only a theory Sir but it took all our attention for over an hour. During that time we weren't in a position to be looking at anything else. I'll also bet that afterwards most of the other naval forces in the Gulf had their eyes off the ball once they heard what had happened.'

'A diversion then but for what?' the MI6 man asked.

'Before I answer that can I ask a general question please?'

'Go on,' said the Admiral.

'What are relations like between Pakistan and Iran these days?' As Jon asked the question he couldn't help but see the startled exchange of looks between the two civilians.

The man from the Foreign Office answered although he didn't look too happy in doing so. 'Surprisingly good. Until 1922, when the Ottoman Empire was broken up, much of Iran and Pakistan were effectively the same country. During Pakistan's war with India in

1971, Iran fully supported Pakistan in many ways and when the Shah was deposed Pakistan was the first country to recognise the legitimacy of the new regime. With the Soviets in Afghanistan both countries have supported the Mujahedeen. So as you can imagine, there is a great deal of sympathy in the populations for each other and that translates up the political and military chain. The problem the Pakistani government has is that they want to be western facing. It's been quite a balancing act for them to keep America happy and not alienate Iran at the same time. Of course, it's far more complicated than that but that's a very brief summary. Does that answer your question?'

Jon looked thoughtful. 'The only merchantman nearby when the incident happened was a Pakistani registered ship. Her name was Firoza. I remember the name because although we don't have a policing role with regards to traffic violations in the shipping lanes, she was travelling far faster than anyone else. I noted it in the ship's log. She overtook us minutes before the attack. I didn't think much of it at the time. Some of the merchantmen are a law unto themselves in that part of the world. However, I do remember something odd about her. It only came to me as we were flying back here. You see nearly all ships going into the Gulf are in ballast and she wasn't.' He saw the blank looks on the faces of the two civilians. 'By that I mean they're empty. It's easy to see. There are laden signs on the hull and anyway with most modern ships you see the top of the propeller out of the water at the stern and the big bulbous bow at the front. This ship was well laden.'

'So why should you consider that odd?' the Admiral asked.

'Well Sir, let's suppose she has some urgent cargo that she doesn't want discovered. She's travelling fast when in the distance she spots a warship. At that stage, she won't know which country it's from but realises that because she's been breaking the shipping rules it may be inclined to stop and have a word with her, even if she slows down straight away. If her cargo was something to do with Iran then maybe we were simply diverted from interfering with her. Sorry I know it sounds a bit far fetched but it's the only thing I can see that fits the facts.'

There was silence around the table while they digested the idea. It was clear to Jon that his suggestion was being met with a great deal of scepticism by most of the attendees.

It was the man from MI6 who surprised them all. He spoke before anyone else could. 'Admiral, gentlemen, I'm sorry but I am going to have to ask anyone without full Top Secret clearance to leave.'

The Admiral confirmed that all present were cleared.

The man continued. 'As you will appreciate I cannot go into detail. However, for some time we have been concerned about a faction in the Pakistani military which seems to be very close to the government in Tehran. Unfortunately, the faction in question, amongst other things, have control over the Pakistani nuclear arsenal.'

'Good God,' the Admiral exploded. 'Are you suggesting what I think you are?'

'Sorry Admiral. Some weeks ago we got a hint that there might be an attempt to give or sell several warheads to Iran. We assumed it would be done by road, after all they share a long mutual border. However, our technical experts have advised that they might try to do it by sea because of the large amount of support and safety equipment that would need to be shipped with the warheads. Also, we have an idea where they might be stored and it's on an offshore island. Indeed there might even be missiles involved as well. So Commander Hunt's idea may well be right. I'll be honest, we weren't expecting anything to happen for months yet but this all seems just too suspicious.'

'Jesus,' the Admiral exclaimed. 'Imagine the damage to the region if Iran became a nuclear power. I hate to think of the consequences.'

'Don't think for a moment we haven't thought long and hard about that Admiral.' the MI6 man answered. 'Commander Hunt's idea, no matter how far fetched, must be followed up as soon as possible.'

Chapter 26

The next day Jon was asked to go to London to brief MI6 at their famous building on the south bank of the Thames. Because of the continuing IRA threat, travel in uniform was strictly banned. All his civilian clothes were on the ship or down in Cornwall so he had to make an emergency trip into Northwood to buy a suit and other clothes.

Once again his story was poured over by a team of experts. By now he was getting rather fed up with repeating himself. Jon was glad to see Rupert Thomas amongst the debriefing team, although initially they hadn't had much time to speak.

During a break for coffee they got together. Rupert looked appraisingly at Jon. 'Jesus Jon, don't you ever stop. We get you out of London so you can keep your head down for a while and look what happens next.' His words were accompanied by an almost conspiratorial grin.

'And you can sod off as well Rupert.' Jon replied in a similar tone. 'Anyway, I thought you'd been retired to a desk. What's your connection with this situation? Everyone seems very reticent to admit to what they do around here.'

'Well as you know, my last field job was the Lebanon and when I returned I was promoted. The spy thing was just a filler for a few months. 'I'm now one of three desk officers covering the whole Middle East. But look, this could be a complete can of worms. All I can say is thank goodness you weren't clobbered by that missile.'

'Thanks for that, you're one of the few people who've even mentioned it. A Silkworm warhead is almost three times the size of an Exocet. We would have lost a lot of people and quite probably the ship. But is this for real? Surely Pakistan wouldn't be that stupid?'

'If we're talking about their government then the answer is almost certainly no. But like many countries in the region, there are factions within factions and I'm afraid it's quite possible. And talking of other countries, we're going to have to share this with the Yanks you realise that?'

'Well you know my view on that lot but to be fair, they seem to have been pretty effective militarily speaking in the Gulf, although I can't get my head around some of their politics.'

'You and me both but this is much bigger than just a British problem. A nuclear Iran poses a threat to the whole world. Don't forget the Israel issue. Many of the Middle East countries hate each other but they all hate the Israelis.'

'Thank God I'm just a simple naval officer. This is all way above my pay grade.'

'It may be but someone has to do the dirty work as well don't forget.'

'Thanks for that Rupert. And on that subject, do you have any idea how long you'll want me here? I really need to get back to my ship.'

'I'm sure you can head back to Northwood this afternoon. How is the lovely Helen by the way?'

'Oh, I managed a phone call last night. She's fine and seems to be really enjoying herself down at Culdrose. It was a bit difficult because there was very little I could say about why I'm back at home but at least it was nice to talk.'

The meeting reconvened but soon reached a point where Jon's input was over. He was politely asked to leave and did so with a degree of relief. Maybe he could now get back to Prometheus.

The Admiral sent for him as soon as he reported back to Northwood that afternoon,

'Jon, how did the MI6 meeting go?' He was asked with no preamble as soon as he walked in the door.

'Fine Sir as far as I can ascertain although basically all I did was repeat what I said yesterday and then they booted me out.'

'As far as I'm concerned you did an excellent job. It's a shame in some ways we can't go public on you shooting down that missile but I'm sure you understand why we can't. That's what I want to talk to you about. When you get back to your ship you must impress on your crew how important it is that this is not discussed anywhere. We asked you to restrict shore leave when you got to Dubai because we were worried something like this would happen and it seems we were right. Your first job is to convince everyone on the need for discretion. I realise it won't be easy and hopefully, at some stage we can be a bit more open.'

'Of course Sir, does that mean I'm going back soon?'

'Yes, you and SNOME are booked on a commercial flight out of Heathrow tomorrow morning. It should be more comfortable than an RAF jet. Now look, there's going to be a big planning meeting in London tomorrow to decide on what to do about this. I suspect it will be hijacked by the Americans to some degree but I know that people on high want us to continue to be involved. We've got two more ships taken off normal operations to come and augment you but it will take at least a month before the first can arrive. I'm afraid that until then you're on your own.'

'What about the Americans, Sir? Is there talk of a joint operation of some sort?'

'Not at this stage but I wouldn't rule it out. Just resume your normal duties and wait and see.'

Jon went back to his cabin in the mess. It was mid-afternoon and he was still tired from all the travel. He was just lying back on his bed and considering testing the inside of his eye lids for light leaks when there was a knock at the door.

'Yes who is it?' he called wearily.

There was no answer even when he called again so he reluctantly got up and opened the door with a rude remark on his lips which immediately died when he saw the naval Lieutenant there. His weariness vanished. There was no need for words.

Half an hour later, in a tangle of sweaty sheets, they got around to talking.

'How on earth did you manage to get time off to come up here Helen?'

'Oh that was easy. I just fluttered my eyes at the Boss. It usually works you know.'

'Hah, why don't I believe that?'

'Oh alright, I'm owed some leave and when I explained that you were here for a couple of days the Boss actually told me to go.'

'Good for him. I'll buy him a big pint when I see him next. So how's the squadron?'

Helen told him all about her first few months, including the rescue of the two people off the yacht.'

'Bloody hell, that sounds as though it was a bit hairy,' Jon observed. 'I hope you all got a big chuck up for it.'

Bog Hammer

'Not so you'd notice. The Boss said well done and that was about it. It was difficult but not that unusual.'

'I suppose you're right but even so it sounds like it was very well done.'

Helen rolled over onto an elbow and looked down on Jon. 'And what about you? You were very cagey on the phone last night. How long are you back for?'

Jon looked at the ceiling. 'Well, the bad news is that we are on a ten o'clock flight from Heathrow tomorrow I'm afraid. So we've only got tonight.'

'And the good news?'

'There's not any of that really. I'm sorry but I really can't tell you why I'm home. You'll have guessed that something's happened but this time it really must be kept under wraps, at least for the present.' And then he looked down to where Helen's hand was creeping. 'Oh I was wrong. There is some good news after all.'

On the flight back which was just as comfortable as the Admiral had predicted Jon was reflecting on the last two days. He was relieved that the publicity seemed to have been non-existent and that his actions had been approved but was worried about what could happen next. He also felt slightly guilty about having been able to spend the night with Helen. It hadn't helped that the bed was a single and they had had to sleep very close to each other which had resulted in little sleep for either of them for more than one reason.

Captain Merryweather saw that Jon was wilting. 'I must say that your wife makes a very attractive naval officer Jon. Thank you for introducing us in the bar last night.'

'Any time Sir, I was just thinking I was feeling a little guilty as all my ship's company have been cooped up on board these last few days and there I was getting some time off with my wife.'

'I wouldn't worry about that. You did a damned fine job with that missile and those Bog Hammers. You deserve some reward.'

'Thank you for that Sir. My real worry, of course, is what the hell could happen now. It seems like we might just have opened a massive can of worms.'

'I'm afraid you may well be right. Just between the two of us, the Admiral called me early this morning. Apparently this has gone right up the chain and COBRA met last night. That's the Cabinet security team chaired by the Prime Minister in case you didn't know. He wouldn't tell me any details but there is apparently a high level debate going on now between us and the White House. I think you can expect a busy time when you get back to the ship.'

Chapter 27

When Jon returned to the ship he could immediately sense that the atmosphere had changed. When he left there was the euphoria of a job well done. The ship's company had survived a very dangerous attack and had acquitted themselves with credit. The adrenalin high was still there. Three days of being confined to a small steel box tied up alongside a jetty had blunted everyone's enthusiasm. It was obvious in many subtle ways, from the attitude of the Quartermaster when he climbed up the gangway, to the strained smile on the First Lieutenant as he saluted him on board.

Never one to let things lie, his first words to Des were simple. 'Number One, clear lower deck on the flight deck as soon as possible please and I want every member of the crew, whatever they're doing.'

Within minutes the flight deck started to fill with expectant faces. Jon waited until the Master at Arms had confirmed that everyone was present. He also went to the side of the ship and looked up and down to see whether there was anyone on the shore who could overhear what he was about to say. They were in a quiet area of a commercial dock and there didn't seem to be a soul about.

He went back to the front of the mustered men. 'Good afternoon gentlemen. I will break the golden rule and start with an apology, actually two. Firstly for dragging you up here in this heat but there is nowhere else on the ship I can talk to you all and secondly for you being cooped up on board for so long. Before I tell you why this was necessary, I want to thank you all again for your performance the other day when we were attacked. You may think it was the job of the guys in the Ops room and the Flight but you'd be wrong. You all played your part, from the stokers who allowed us to manoeuvre to the chefs who made sure we were well fed and alert when we needed it. Not only that, you will all be pleased to know that the First Lieutenant is also happy for a change.'

There was a ripple of laughter at Jon's remark and Des put on a wry smile.

Jon continued. 'When it was all over, we checked and it took only nine and half minutes for the ship to be closed up to Action Stations. However, be warned he will expect no less in the future.'

A wry chuckle went through the crowd. They now all knew the difference between exercises and the real thing.

'Now I am going to have to ask you to trust me. I'm sorry but I can't tell you why we were attacked, in fact, to be honest, no one is totally sure. On top of that, the Iranians are denying that it even ever happened. For various reasons our government haven't made it public either. However, there is a strong possibility that it was part of something far, far larger. I suspect at some time in the future everything will become clear but until then and until I give you permission, no one talks about the incident. Do I make myself absolutely clear? That means when you are ashore, when you are writing to your family, when you telephone home. The incident of four days ago never happened. It's a shame that you won't get the recognition you deserve for a bloody good piece of work but that's the way it is, at least for now. I'm sorry to repeat myself but no one outside this ship talks about it. If or when things change, I will let you know. Moving on, I'm sure you will want to know what happens now. Well, it's back to normal operations for the moment. I've arranged for two more days alongside so you can all get ashore and stretch your legs. Two more ships are being sent out in case things ramp up but they won't be here for several weeks. So until or when we are told otherwise, it's back to normal Armilla operations. Thank you for your forbearance and I hope you all get a decent run ashore before we sail.'

As the men all went below in uncharacteristic silence. Jon turned to Des. 'All Heads of Department in my cabin in half an hour please Des.'

When all the HODs were seated and the door was closed, Jon addressed them all. 'Sorry chaps but there's not a great deal more that I can tell you than I've already told the troops. However, there are two things I will cover. Firstly the incident was part of something that has potentially grave international consequences for the whole region. I can't emphasise enough how important and timely our actions were. The second point is based on my own guesswork. As you may have already worked out, it is no longer a national issue and this means in this part of the world the Americans will be involved big time. I know that our government will want to stay involved in whatever comes next and until the other ships arrive that means us.'

'Any idea when or what will be required of us Sir?' Brian asked.

'Nope, I do know that very high level meetings are taking place as we talk and that something will almost certainly have to be done if and I repeat if what people are worried about has actually taken place. Look, I'm going to be a bit more candid, there is a theory that the attack on us was a short term diversion to allow something else to happen. I know it sounds farfetched but people are taking it very seriously.'

Des interrupted Jon's flow. 'That merchantman, the one that was belting past us, the Pakistani one.'

Jon was surprised by his First Lieutenant's insight but there again he had been with him on the bridge at the time. 'Des, I can't answer that and the rest of you do not discuss this further. Now, we need to be prepared for anything. There is a convoy getting ready off Kuwait in four days time. I want the lads to have a good run ashore but we will sail on time and then I want this ship ready for absolutely anything. Number One and Ops please work up an exercise programme for when we're at sea that doesn't clash with our escort duties. Engineering, I want everything top line, any stores we need let me know as a matter of urgency. Fleet have promised us top priority for anything we need, so don't hold back and that goes for the supply department as well. Any questions gentlemen?'

There were none. 'Oh and one other thing, make damn sure you all get a run ashore as well.'

Three days later Prometheus quietly proceeded to sea. Despite being a Muslim country, there were some bars for the European oil workers and the British sailors all seemed to be welcome. Jon had made it clear that he expected some letting off of steam and it appeared that his crew hadn't let him down. Even so, they had sailed on time with no absentees even if there were plenty of thick heads in evidence that morning.

Nevertheless, he breathed a sigh of relief as the harbour breakwater slipped past and they headed back out into the blue of the open sea. Life out here was much simpler. The incredibly complicated politics of the region and all the hatred, suspicion and religious issues could be left behind. Out here he had a simple job to do and one that was in his complete control. Sitting in his chair on the bridge, he let the routine chatter of the Officer of the Watch and Navigating Officer wash over him while he wondered what would happen next.

For the next ten days very little happened. They met up with their convoy of only three ships this time and took them out into the Gulf of Oman. As a precaution, Jon ordered the ship to Action Stations as they approached the Straits of Hormuz and sure enough, the shore side radars were there as usual. However, none changed their mode and Prometheus was left unmolested. The Iranian Frigate appeared and came to give them a look over. He wished them a friendly 'good day' on the radio but that was all. When they returned, the same happened. The only difference this time was that their next tasking signal came in as expected but with a totally unexpected content. Jon was reading it carefully in his cabin when Brian knocked and came in.

Looking up, Jon motioned to a chair. 'New tasking Brian, have you seen it yet?'

'Yes Sir, I got my own copy. We are to go to a position which is just outside Iranian waters and do a covert pick up. We are to rendezvous with this American Destroyer first for a final briefing. What do you make of it?'

'Well, if I was a betting man I would say that it's the result of our little incident the other week. Kharg Island is a key part of the Iranian infrastructure, both of their oil industry and their military. I suspect that someone is about to do an incursion there to get intelligence and we're going to pull them out.'

'That's how I see it too. I wonder why the Americans aren't doing it themselves though.'

'Probably for several reasons. Because of the other week, we've proved successful against one of the Iranian's most dangerous weapon systems. Also, it was our discovery so maybe they feel we should continue to be involved.'

'Well as you won't tell me what that discovery was Sir, I will have to bow to your judgement on that one.'

'Hah, good point and it won't help you to get me to tell you either. Anyway go and talk to the Navigating Officer and sort out a route to the rendezvous. We need to be there tomorrow night but I would like to be in the vicinity as quickly as possible just in case we're needed earlier.'

'Fine Sir, I'll get on it but there's something else I need to show you down on the radar plot. While we were kicking our heels in Jebel Ali, I spent some time analysing the encounter with those speed boats. Something odd happened but I couldn't put my finger on it. I was looking at it again this morning and I suddenly realised what it was. You really need to see.'

Mystified, Jon went down to the Ops room with Brian, who set up the main plot to replay the events of that day. 'Right, here are the contacts approaching and as you can see they start to split up to encircle us,' Brian explained. 'It's a tactic they've used a great deal but mainly with unarmed merchantmen.'

'Hmm, I thought about that and wondered if it was because they thought we would soon be dead meat after the missile had hit us.'

'I agree, that's what I think too but now watch. Here is the missile track appearing and the first thing we do is fire chaff.' The blooms of chaff appeared on the radar screen. 'Now the chaff is fired either side of us to try and get the missile to lock on to it rather than us and we don't want it flying through the chaff cloud and then re-acquiring us afterwards. As you can see, it blanks out the radar contacts of the boats on either side. Once the missile is taken out, all the boats turn and head away to the north. Our Lynx engages the two to the east but look at the western ones.'

Jon studied the plot. 'What am I looking for Brian?'

'The two western most boats, the ones that were under the chaff cloud, when we re-acquire them, they're much further north than all the others.'

'OK, I can see that but so what?'

'So they turned away before the missile impacted. Why would they do that? The ones in the middle didn't and the two to the east were dodging cannon shells by then.'

'Nope, still not got it Brian.'

'Do you remember the trials we did some years ago when we were on our Lynx Flight? When we were despatching chaff by hand out of the cockpit windows using those horrible little cardboard packages and one burst open too early and blew back into the aircraft.'

'God yes, it made a terrible mess and all those tiny little slivers of foil got everywhere. We were even warned by the medics that inhaling any could be really dangerous. Hang on, I've got it. Those Bog Hammers got physically caught up in our chaff cloud and it made them turn around.'

'Got it in one Sir.'

'Go on Brian I can see you've got more.'

'Well I've spoken to the WEO and MEO and with a bit of modification to the launcher tubes we should be able to launch the rockets on a different lower trajectory, one that would give us another line of defence well outside of the range of any of the guns we have on board.'

'What about if we need to put chaff up for its real purpose?'

'They assure me it shouldn't reduce its primary effectiveness.'

'Do it.'

Chapter 28

The holiday season in Cornwall was getting into full swing. The weather had at last turned fine and the beaches were starting to get crowded. For 771 Squadron this was the start of a busy period. Not the dangers of rain, fog and gales anymore. Now it was little Jonny washed out to sea on a lilo or someone who had fallen down one of the many cliffs. It wasn't even that unusual to rescue the odd cow who had been equally unobservant of all the warning signs.

Helen had been awarded full Captaincy status only the previous week but for the moment was flying in the same crew with Bruce. Today she was sitting in the right hand seat. They weren't on a call out, merely patrolling the coast and keeping their eyes open. The weather was wonderful, with hardly a cloud in the sky and only the barest whisper of a breeze. What was even better was that the sea temperature was over fifteen degrees which meant they could dispense with uncomfortable and sweaty goon suits and fly in light cotton overalls for a change.

Helen looked down at Praa sands as they flew slowly past just offshore. Memories of Jon flooded in. There was the little cove they had swum around to last summer. The tide was higher today and the cove was almost completely awash. She smiled to herself as she remembered their brief night together last week. She just wished she had found out what had been going on. She knew Jon enough now to know that something serious had happened, not the least because of his reticence. He normally confided in her and for him not to do so was solid evidence of the seriousness of whatever it was that had happened.

The sudden bang and lurch caught her completely unawares. The shock travelled up her spine as the cyclic control was almost wrenched out of her hand. Looking around in panic she tried desperately to work out what had happened. Looking over at Bruce she immediately saw that instead of looking worried he was struggling to hold back his laughter. She realised what the bastard had done.

'You idiot Bruce, you almost gave me a heart attack.'

'Whoa, what's going on up front?' Dick called over the intercom in a worried tone.

'The stupid bugger in the left hand seat just pulled my seat adjustment handle, the one that raises and lowers the seat, so the seat just dropped. It scared the hell out of me.' Helen was definitely not seeing the funny side as she readjusted her seat upwards to get it back in the right position.

'Count yourself lucky Helen,' a clearly unrepentant Bruce replied. 'When it was done to me it was at night and we were in the hover.'

Helen realised she had two choices, either she could continue to be angry or she could bide her time until she could get her own back.

'Fine, you big Ozzie bastard but your card is marked. Remember that revenge is a dish best served cold.'

'Fine I'll be watching my six o'clock.' He didn't sound concerned.

He was about to say more when the radio burst into life. 'Five Zero this is approach, we have a call from a merchantman, position two zero five the Lizard, fifty miles. They have a female member of crew in premature labour. Request you close to offer assistance, over.'

Helen immediately turned the aircraft towards the south as Bruce took the radio. 'This is Five Zero, we're on our way, any more information over?'

'Roger, the ship is the Alliance Atlantic, a bulk carrier of twenty eight thousand tons, outward bound to the States. The woman is the wife of the Captain and is not due for another four weeks. They would keep her on board but with a premature birth they have been advised to get her to hospital.'

'This is Five Zero, understood, if we pick her up where do we take her, over?'

'Truro, Five Zero.'

'Roger, estimate we will arrive in twenty minutes, we'll give them a call now, out.'

Dick had come up with an intercept heading and it didn't take long for them to identify the ship. She was painted a rusty red with a massive rear superstructure and cluttered deck. Bruce made contact on the maritime VHF and asked them to alter course to give a

Bog Hammer

relative wind from their port bow. Meanwhile, Helen scanned the ship's deck for somewhere clear enough for her to approach.

'If she's already in labour we daren't put her on the winch and even in a stretcher it could be tricky. I reckon there's room to get on the deck just ahead of the bridge. What do you think Bruce?'

'You're the one in the right hand seat but yes there should be room as long as you keep some of the weight off the wheels, we don't know how strong that deck is.'

After telling the ship what they intended, Helen started her approach. It was only once they were close that she was able to appreciate just how high the bridge structure was. Although the sea was calm there was still a gentle Atlantic swell that was making the stern area of the ship rise and fall at least ten feet. She approached from starboard towards the area of clear deck. As she closed the side of the ship there was a moment of turbulence and then they were through and over the deck.

'Keep a sharp lookout for any flying debris,' she called. 'And Bruce let me know if we look to be getting too close to that bridge screen.'

With no normal flight deck team to help her she had to judge the deck movement for herself and once over the deck there was very little to see. Almost before she could anticipate it, the deck rose and gently touched the wheels. She lowered the collective lever a little and allowed the weight to settle.

'Off you go guys,' she called over the intercom and the two rear crew ran out under the rotor disc just as a screen door in the superstructure opened and three people appeared. One was doubled up and being supported by the other two. Dick and Tiny took the woman from her helpers and placed some ear protectors on her head and a life jacket over her shoulders. They also took over a large suitcase that one of the men had been carrying and then escorted her into the aircraft. Because Helen was keeping some power applied in case the nine tons of helicopter was too heavy for the deck, the downwash was much stronger than normal and the three struggled past the cockpit and out of sight.

What seemed like ages passed and then Dick came on the intercom. 'All secure down aft here, clear to go Helen.'

She grunted an acknowledgment, gently pulled up the collective and transited clear of the massive ship.

The ship came on the radio. 'Thank you Rescue Five Zero. Please keep us informed of any developments over.'

'Of course Alliance Atlantic, any news will be passed straight away, out.'

They set course back to land. Helen checked the fuel gauges. They would have just about enough to get to the hospital at Truro and then back to Culdrose but it was going to be tight.

'How's it going in the back?' Bruce asked.

'She's stable and looks OK. We've got her lying on a partially deflated salvage bag.'

They flew for a few minutes in silence then Dick came back on the intercom.

'Guys, we might just have a little problem here. So either of you know anything about midwifery and where did we stow all the towels and hot water?'

'Oh shit, is she about to produce?' Bruce asked.

'Well you're guess is as good as mine Bruce but if was a gambling man I would bet there will be one more of us before we make it to Truro.'

Helen pulled more power and wound the helicopter up to the fastest it would go.

'Oi, you lot in the front, slow down. All that vibration is making it worse.'

Helen looked at Bruce as she slowed back to normal cruise speed. She gave him an innocent smile as she spoke over the intercom. 'Hey guys are you coping alright in the back there? We don't need two of us up front at the moment.'

Bruce gave her a dirty look as she continued. 'I can't move because I'm in the right hand seat but I'm sure Bruce can be spared.'

'Actually, that's a bloody good idea,' Dick responded. 'The more help back here the better. I know they always say that you should let the mother do the work and nature take its course but we're pretty maxed out here and someone still needs to do some navigating for a while.'

Helen looked at Bruce with one eye raised. He said nothing as he undid his straps.

As he climbed out she smiled at him again and said one word. 'Revenge.'

Two hours later they landed back at Culdrose with the fuel gauges on their minimums. They had indeed arrived at Truro hospital with one more person on board than they had started out with. A little boy, who although he looked small, seemed healthy enough. The hospital staff had whisked mother and baby away but it seemed that everything had gone well.

As Helen walked back into the squadron with the rest of the crew she couldn't help feel yet another glow of satisfaction at a job well done.

She turned to her comrade. 'So Bruce did you enjoy getting your hands dirty?'

'Actually Mrs Hunt, you may not believe this but I did. I'm not sure I'd want to do it again but it was strangely satisfying, especially what the mother said to me afterwards.'

'Oh what was that?'

'She wanted to know my name so she could name her son after me.'

Helen couldn't help but laugh.

Chapter 29

The inside of the C130 Hercules looked like a cavern from hell. The massive cargo cabin was relatively empty except for six people. The red lighting was being used so that their eyesight was acclimatised to the dark. They were all breathing from bottles of pure oxygen for a similar reason. When the time came to open the rear ramp to exit the aircraft the air pressure was so low that if there was any nitrogen in anyone's blood, the pressure drop could easily induce the bends, as well as being too thin to breathe. Breathing pure oxygen purged the blood of the dangerous gas and would keep them alive until they had descended sufficiently. The bends was a problem normally associated with divers ascending too fast from underwater but experience had shown that it could happen here as well. Parachuting into enemy territory with a nitrogen bubble in a joint was definitely a bad idea.

Four men would be jumping tonight, two from the British Special Boat Service and two from the American, Sea, Air and Land team, commonly known as SEALs. The technique was called High Altitude High Opening or HAHO for short and had been perfected by the British SAS. However as this mission would involve significant time in the water, the SBS and SEALs had been selected. As anyone in the SBS would tell you they could do the same as the SAS only wearing flippers.

The four men had trained together extensively over the last ten days and were totally confident in each other's abilities.

Suddenly a voice came over the loudspeakers. 'Ten minutes to target, ramp opening in two minutes, get ready.'

All six men stood. The two load masters started gathering the additional equipment the men would be taking and attaching it to them as they got themselves prepared. Each man was dressed in a bulky black thermal suit. It was minus forty centigrade outside. Each also had a full face helmet and mask which was attached to an oxygen tank secured at their waist. Sticking from the top of each helmet were the binocular lenses of night vision goggles. Unusually, no one was carrying any serious weapons except for a pistol each. Fighting on this mission was the last thing they needed or wanted. Suddenly a warning blared and the ramp at the rear of the cargo bay started to open. The internal pressure had already been bled down when the initial warning was given, so there was only a small blast of air.

The four jumpers completed their final checks almost doubled over with the weight of the equipment they were carrying. Despite their incredible fitness and strength, they would not be able to stay standing for long. With the ramp now fully open, they shuffled towards it, helped by the load masters and stood abreast of each other. Once at the jump point they stopped and stared at the light above their heads. It turned green. In a heartbeat the cargo bay was empty.

The four men dropped in free fall for fifteen seconds and then deployed their chutes. The night had no moon and the canopies were black. However, there was enough starlight for the men to be able to see each other through the NVGs. Their leader assumed the lowest position and the other three steered to be behind and slightly higher. Once in loose formation, they released their heavy loads which dropped on ten foot long lines to dangle below them. The canopies were larger than normal parachutes which was necessary because they now had almost forty miles to fly to get to their destination.

The leader consulted his compass, adjusted their heading and in total silence they slowly descended. At ten thousand feet there was a thin layer of cloud as had been forecast. When they slipped out of the bottom, the lights of Kharg Island oil refinery stood out like beacons. The leader made another small heading adjustment and they continued down towards the beach at the north east of the island.

The lights of the airfield slipped past to their right as they descended through two thousand feet and then the beach was approaching. Intelligence had reported that it had been mined during the war with Iraq but satellite imagery now showed that it was used in the daytime by civilians, presumably refinery workers and their families, so it must have been made safe. The leader prayed that the intelligence was correct just as he flared hard and landed on the soft sand. Within minutes the three others had landed. They removed their parachutes which they took with them to bury in the dunes further up along with the special containers they had all carried with them.

Bog Hammer

Fifteen miles out to the west HMS Prometheus patrolled along a line just clear of Iranian national waters. The night was dark with no moon and a thin layer of broken high cloud. Jon was in his cabin, dressed in his action rig but sitting in his chair trying to doze. He knew a long night beckoned. He also knew his men didn't need him breathing down their necks the whole time. They would call him when he was needed.

That afternoon they had rendezvoused with the American Ticonderoga class, Aegis Destroyer, the Sacagawea. It had been almost surreal in many ways. Jon had transferred over in the Lynx and was immediately struck by the size of the ship. With her massive slab sided, fixed phase array radars all around her superstructure she looked like a floating castle and made his Prometheus look like a toy. The flight deck was in a similar proportion as they landed on and Jon left the aircrew to talk to their opposite numbers as he was escorted along a seemingly endless series of corridors and ladders until they came to the Captain's cabin. He was greeted by a short and rather unassuming, dark haired man with flecks of grey in his hair. He had a powerful handshake that belied his appearance but a slightly haunted look in his eyes.

'Commander Hunt, I'm Captain Jim Morrison, welcome on board the Sacagawea. I've been appraised of your recent good work and it looks like you'll have the opportunity to do some more for me tonight.'

'Thank you Sir, yes I've had several signals about what's needed but also been told that you have the final brief.' Jon answered but the American Captain's remark about doing the task for him immediately put him on guard.

'That's correct, now just so we're both on the same wavelength, I take it you are aware of what we think has been transported into Iraq in the Pakistani merchantmen?'

'Yes Sir, nuclear weapons, number and size unknown. Also, that the merchantman docked at the freight port at Kharg and has been there ever since.'

'That's correct but I can now update some of that. We are pretty sure it's only one warhead that they've managed to acquire at least that's what the intelligence services are saying. Satellite imagery has been hard to get with this overcast of the last few days and SR71 overflights were hard to justify in a peacetime environment.

However, we're pretty sure some of the cargo was taken to a large hangar that has just been built on the junction between edge of the main runway and the freight port. That's why we are putting our team in tonight to try and get confirmation.'

'Any idea what the Iranians are planning Sir?'

'No one is sure, if we can see what's inside that building it will help. Most people think they will either keep it in reserve to generate political leverage or if they're really stupid, use it to attack Iraq. Thank goodness they have no missiles with range enough to go further afield.'

'Would they need a missile to deliver it? These things can be quite small can't they?'

'Maybe one of ours would be but with the level of technology that the Pakistani's have it is almost certainly too big to be anything other than air launched. They could of course be putting it in a free fall bomb for one of their remaining F14s but again that's what we hope to find out. Now your job tonight is to do the pick up. It's a joint US, UK four man team and when they've finished, they will come out to you. I take it you've been briefed on how they intend to do it?'

Jon simply nodded. He was still having trouble getting his head around that.

'Now you've been selected for this job and that's fine by me. You did well with that Silkworm by all accounts but let me stress that I don't want you getting into any firefights this time. I expect you to simply do the pick up and then bug out, is that clear?'

Jon's hackles, which had settled down, started to rise again. 'I think there may be a misunderstanding here Sir. Do you consider that I'm under your command for this operation?'

'Damn right I do. I'm the senior naval officer in this theatre so I have the responsibility of making sure that all goes according to the rules.'

Jon fought back an angry retort. 'Sorry Sir, what rules?'

The Captain looked taken aback by the question. 'Are you questioning me young man?'

Jon decided he needed to draw a line and quickly. 'Yes Sir I am. I have tasking for this operation directly from the Commander in Chief Fleet of the Royal Navy. At no point does it make any reference to the United States Navy being in my chain of command.

I have been instructed to offer full cooperation with you but that is all. I certainly have rules I have to follow but I have no idea how they might align with any that apply to you. Oh and for the record Sir I may be junior to you in rank but I am the Commanding Officer of a British warship and would request that you do not refer to me as 'young man'.'

Captain Morrison looked fit to explode for a second and then clearly reigned in what he was about to say. He looked hard at Jon before he finally spoke. 'They warned me you were a no nonsense kind of guy, I guess they were right. And yes, you're technically correct but we need to make sure we are acting together on this. You may need me to back you up some time.'

'That's alright Sir, you might need me to back you up at some other time.'

The Captain barked out a laugh. 'OK Commander, let's do business.'

An hour later, Jon left his new best friend to go back to the flight deck. They had compared notes on their respective capabilities and also the difference between their national rules of engagement. Jon quickly realised that this would probably be his last chance to get involved as a whole US task force including a carrier were on the way and would arrive within two days. Somehow he didn't expect his little Frigate would be given much to do once they arrived.

As the Lynx launched for the short trip back to Prometheus he leaned forward from the cabin bench seat to talk to the aircrew.

'What did you think of the big brute guys?'

Tom chuckled. 'Well Sir, we didn't see much of the ship but the Flight weren't that impressive. They've got a Seahawk and it's not bad at anti-submarine work but when we showed them our gun and then mentioned that we carry air to surface missiles as well, they looked pig sick. Seems they rely on the ship far more than we do.'

'Oh and when I told them about Sea Wolf, they flatly refused to believe me,' Jerry added. 'I tried to explain how we use another ship's gun so we can track the shell and how it can pick up the leading edge of our rotor blades but they were convinced I was taking the piss.'

Jon wasn't surprised, the Americans always seemed sure of their own superiority. He was more worried about the ship's Captain.

Despite his eventual bonhomie, there was something about him that rang warning bells.

He said the same to Brian when they were back in his cabin. 'He tried to strong arm me into accepting that I was under his command.'

Brian knew from past experience that Jon didn't take well to that kind of tactic. 'And I bet you gave as good you got.'

'Something like that. However, he did update me on the intelligence which I'm authorised to tell you about but only you for the moment Brian. You can tell Des if for some reason he has to take over command.'

That was hours ago. The ship was stood to but at reduced readiness, so that everyone could at least get some sleep. Despite the anticipation, Jon soon found his eyelids drooping. It wasn't long before he was asleep as well.

Chapter 29

The four men crept forward over the dunes. The NVGs were no longer needed. Indeed there was so much light from the lights surrounding the compound they were just about useless. The leader signalled with his hand and two of them split off to either side. Within minutes reports were coming in over the earpieces of the secure radios they all carried.

'This is C, the fence goes all around the back, no sign of sentries at the moment but I don't like the look of that dead ground between the wire and the building. There are video cameras on the poles inside the wire all the way around but they are fixed and looking inwards, just as intelligence reported, silly buggers.'

'This is A acknowledged. D come in.'

'This is D, same here, the road approaches the main compound gate just as the satellite imagery showed. There is a guard house and I've seen at least four, I repeat four armed men inside. However, none are taking any interest in anything other than the road and its approaches. I can see TV monitors through one of the windows.'

'Roger, everyone return now.'

When all four men had regrouped, the team leader briefed them on what to do. They then went around the back of the building to get out of direct sight of the entrance.

One of the men crawled the ten feet to the base of the wire. He didn't touch it but took a small device from a pocket and pushed a wire from it into the ground before touching it to the wire.

'Not electrified,' he said quietly over the radio.

He put the device away and took out some wire cutters and snipped the bottom few strands of chicken wire until there was just enough to crawl through. He crept up to the TV pole in front of him and threw a special rope around it which he then attached to the webbing on his chest. He climbed the pole leaning back on the rope and using his feet until directly behind the camera and then withdrew another device. He pointed it along the same line as the camera and pushed the shutter of the special low light Polaroid camera. As soon as the picture was developed he looked at it carefully before swiftly placing it in front of the camera lens and taping it in place. He also tied a light line to a hole in the edge of the picture and let it drop all

Bog Hammer

the way to the ground. He didn't wait to climb down the pole, simply releasing the rope and jumping down using an experienced parachutist's landing to break his fall before scurrying back through the wire.

All four men waited quietly for ten minutes. If the ruse was going to be discovered, then they didn't want to be on the wrong side of the wire when it was. Eventually satisfied, the leader nodded to one of the other men and the two of them crept back to the wire and crawled through. They would be doing the job, the other two would keep lookout and aid in extracting them if needed.

One of the men took out a small metal detector and a long knife and lying on his stomach slowly crawled forward testing the ground. Each time the detector needle moved or he detected the slightest disturbance to the soil he probed the ground with the knife. Modern mines were often made of plastic and although they needed some metal components they were tiny and wouldn't necessarily be detected. Each time his knife felt resistance he placed a small marker in the ground and continued around the obstruction. All the markers were tied loosely together with a light line. It seemed to take forever to cross the fifteen feet of the minefield safely but in reality, it was less than ten minutes before both men could stand up and sprint to the side of the building. They knew they couldn't move too far in case the next camera picked them up but one of the reasons for going in where they had was the presence of a door set into the wall. To their amazement, it wasn't locked. Slipping in, they disappeared from sight.

Inside, the building was dark and silent as the grave. The two men exchanged puzzled glances. With NVGs back in place they could also see that it was almost completely empty. The only occupant was a large six wheeled vehicle sitting forlornly in the middle of the echoing space. The wheels were massive. It had a large armoured cab which was separated into two with a large square trough in the middle and a long flatbed to the rear. Welding gear and a few tools were lying near the back. That was all.

A quick search confirmed that there was nothing else to find. One of the men took several photographs with a low light camera and then they left as silently as they came. Once clear of the minefield, the string attached to all the stakes was used to pull them all clear, as was the string attached to the photograph taped to the camera. The last man out carefully rearranged the cut wires so that they would be very difficult to see and then all four disappeared into the night.

Reaching the dunes by the beach they stopped quickly to talk. 'There was no one inside and nothing to see apart from a large vehicle, six wheeled with a long flat bed. There was welding gear next to it.' One of the men said quietly.

'Cutting gear actually,' the leader said. 'They had definitely cut something off the bed of the vehicle. I've got photographs but now we all know the basics. No time to speculate what the fuck is going on. It's certainly not what we expected. Time to bug out now.'

Silently the four men dug out their equipment containers and took out the contents. They stripped off all their clothes to reveal the wetsuits they were wearing underneath. The clothes and the parachutes were bundled into the empty containers and carefully reburied. Carrying their last pieces of equipment into the surf, there was no evidence that they had even been there except for a few footprints. Suddenly, there was the hiss of escaping compressed gas and shortly afterwards the loud high pitched whining of two gas turbines and then the beach was empty.

'*You could be as professional as expected on these sort of missions,*' the leader thought to himself as they headed out to sea. '*But it didn't stop it sometimes being incredible fun.*'

He grinned like a school boy at the American lying next to him and got an answering grin back. The two of them lay side by side on an inflatable hull. Just behind their feet was a metal box. Inside it was a small fuel tank and even smaller gas turbine. Small it might have been but it produced well over a hundred and fifty horse power when running flat out, which was now doing and driving the water jet below it. Gas turbines are most efficient when working hard and even with a small fuel tank they easily had the endurance to make their rendezvous. The two man hydroplane was doing almost thirty knots now and heading out to their rendezvous position. Off to one side, the other two men were keeping station. It had taken weeks of practice to master the tricky devices and in anything other than a relatively flat sea they would not be able to go as fast. However, tonight the conditions were perfect. The only problem was visibility. He had a small compass in front of him to steer by and a clear plastic screen protected them both from the worst of the spray. Even so, regular blasts of high speed sea water still hit him and this close to the surface he couldn't see that far anyway. He knew that out to the west of the island were six large oil rigs which they would have to negotiate. As the rigs all stood well clear of the water on massive legs and all would be have a burning gas plume he wasn't too concerned. The supposition was almost his undoing.

Suddenly without any warning, the stars were blotted out and something reared ahead. With a strangled curse he flung the little hydroplane to port and slammed the throttle shut. The wave behind them almost swamped the little craft but they managed to stop just before slamming into the rust streaked side of an enormous sheet of metal. Looking up he could see that what he had first taken to be the leg of one of the rigs was actually the stern of a ship. He realised that this was why they hadn't seen the lights of the rig it must be secured to. It had been screening everything. If only they had been able to use the NVGs but it was too late to worry about that now. For a second he couldn't work out which way to go then he caught a glimpse of the wake of the other crew out to his left and opened the throttle to follow. Just before he opened the throttle he looked up once again and something caught his eye. There was no time to worry about it now but it would have to be looked into later.

'Captain this is the Ops room. Two high speed surface targets approaching, they've just cleared the area of the oil rigs and should be with us in about fifteen minutes.'

Jon shook himself awake. 'Roger Ops, launch the Lynx. I'll be right down.' He grabbed a quick mouthful of luke warm coffee and looked at his watch. Half past three, dead on time.

In the Ops room, they watched the approaching radar tracks. As soon as the Lynx was airborne it was vectored onto the targets and as soon as they were clear of the Iranian territorial boundary, it went down to shepherd the two contacts back to Prometheus. Jon brought the ship to a stop to launch the ship's sea boat and within minutes the four Special Forces operatives were on board. Jon was fascinated to see the vehicles they had been using. He had been briefed on the strange machines but was disappointed like the rest of the crew. As soon as the sea boat had arrived, they had deflated them and let them sink under the weight of their engines, so there was virtually nothing to see.

Jon watched as the sea boat was hoisted back on board. Having ordered the Officer of the Watch to turn and head back to their rendezvous with Americans, he went to his cabin to greet his new arrivals.

The four men came in drying themselves with towels the ship had provided. The first man through the door had a waterproof bag that he was holding carefully. Jon stopped dead when he saw his face.

'Sergeant McCaul, we meet again.'

'Hello Sir,' he held out his hand and Jon shook it warmly. 'But that's Warrant Officer McCaul now. Let me introduce my team. Their names are Smith, Jones and Brown.'

Jon smiled and shook all their hands, not commenting on the names he had been given.

Just then Brian came in and also recognised the man they had relied on so heavily several years ago in the Arctic and the Falklands before that. Introductions over and with a large pot of coffee delivered, they settled down to talk. Mister McCaul briefly told them of the results of their investigations in the large building while carefully not saying how they had got in or out.

'I was told you have the ability to develop film on board Sir?'

Brian answered. 'Yes we do. The sick bay can be used as a temporary dark room. What have you got?'

McCaul handed over the camera from his bag. 'I think that what's on here will help us work out what the hell they're up to. Any idea how long it will take to develop them?'

'A couple of hours,' Brian replied.

'In that case,' Jon responded. 'Let's not waste time speculating. You chaps should get some sleep or at least some food. We will rendezvous with the American ship mid-morning, then we can have a full debrief.'

As the men got up to leave, Mister McCaul turned to Jon. 'A word in private please Sir?'

Jon nodded and when they were alone he closed the door. 'What is it? I can see there's something on your mind.'

'I'm not sure Sir but on the way out to you, I almost rammed a ship tied up alongside one of the oil rigs. It was blocking the light so I didn't see it until it was almost too late.'

'That's not unusual you know, they often have their support vessels alongside at night.'

'I know Sir, but this was far bigger than any support vessel I've ever seen but what was really weird was that it was registered in Iraq, in Basra.'

Chapter 30

Two hours later the SF team mustered again in the Captain's cabin along with Des and Brian. On the table were a series of black and white photographs.

'We'll be with the Americans within two hours and I've already sent these photos back to CinC Fleet and the Sacagawea by HF Fax but have a look chaps and tell me what you think.' Jon handed the photos out to the men.

The man only identified as Jones spoke first in a deep midwestern American drawl. 'Sir what you are looking at is a theatre ballistic missile launcher vehicle, almost certainly of Soviet manufacture.'

'What? A SCUD launcher?' Brian asked.

The second American, Brown answered. 'Sort of Sir, the term SCUD is kinda used generically in these parts. There are quite a lot of variants including some home grown ones these days. However, this is different. All the SCUD launchers I've seen have four wheels on either side. This one has six so it must carry a much bigger load.'

The last man to speak joined in this time in a broad Geordie accent which came as a rather strange contrast. 'I know what it is Sir. We did some intel on these last year. And I hate to contradict my American colleague but it's not Soviet, its North Korean and a launcher for a HWASONG-6 missile. The North Koreans got their hands on some Egyptian SCUDS some years ago and reverse engineered them. They then improved them a great deal. One thing they concentrated on big time was improving the range. A normal SCUD can fly about three hundred and fifty miles max. The bastard this rig is designed to carry can go over a thousand.'

There was a stunned silence for a second and then Des asked the obvious question. 'So where is the rest of the launcher and the bloody missile itself?'

Warrant Officer McCaul spoke. 'It seems clear to me that the equipment lying around the vehicle was used to remove it. Presumably, it's all been moved somewhere else.' He looked speculatively at Jon who shook his head very slightly.

'Right everyone, I expect they've probably worked it out ashore as well but we need to send this assessment back to Fleet straight away and copy it to the Sacagawea as well. Brian, get the Lynx ready to fly me over as soon as practicable, I'll need to talk to him straight away. Warrant Officer McCaul, I'll want you to come with me. One more question please Mister Smith. What sort of warhead is this missile capable of carrying?'

'That depends on its weight Sir but there's plenty of room. It could be anything, conventional, chemical or even nuclear.'

When the meeting finished Jon told Brian, Smith and Warrant Officer McCaul to stay behind.

'Brian, get down to the Ops room and see if you can find out whether any Iraqi merchantmen have been reported as overdue or even attacked in recent weeks. SNOME will know and you should be able to use the satellite comms to talk to him in real time.'

Brian nodded and left.

'Now Smith, if you were to remove the launcher from the flatbed do you have any idea how difficult it could be to remount it?'

'Probably quite easily Sir. The whole thing is attached to one great big base plate. Cut that out and you could easily weld it to another vehicle.'

'And the control electrics?'

'No idea Sir but with decent engineers it should be relatively straightforward.'

'The Argies did something similar during the Falklands, with those two Exocet on a lorry, don't forget Sir,' Warrant Office McCaul stated.

'No, I hadn't forgotten. Right thank you Smith, that will be all, I suggest that you and your colleagues get some proper sleep now. Oh and if for some reason the Action Station alarm goes off I suggest you muster in the hangar with the flight. Get someone to show you how to get there.'

As Smith left, Brian came back in carrying a very large book. 'Two things Sir, firstly we've just picked up the characteristics of a radar that is almost certainly our Iranian Frigate friend from the straits. It looks like he's come down here for some reason. We've got a radar contact on that bearing at about fifty miles.'

'OK, when the Lynx brings me back from the Sacagawea he can go and take a look just to be sure. What else?'

'I spoke to SNOME, you seem to have pre-empted him. An Iraqi grain carrier has gone missing. She's the Irinda and was reported overdue three days ago but the Iraqi authorities have only just gone public about it. They don't normally report them overdue until they are several days late so he could have been out of circulation for some time. He was going to ask us to keep a look out for her but now he wants to know why we're asking. I've managed to find her in this shipping register.'

He held out the book open at a page that showed a large merchantman with a long raised platform running the length of her main deck and several derricks dotted about. Like most merchantmen, all her superstructure was aft in one big island.

Jon showed the book to Warrant Officer McCaul. 'It could be Sir, I only really saw the stern and most of that was overhanging but it's the same sort of shape and I couldn't make out the name but it was quite short. That could be our girl.'

Jon was thinking furiously. 'Brian, a flash signal to Fleet, copy to the Americans, 'believe Iraqi merchantman Irinda now in hands of Iranians and may be used in offensive operations, request urgent satellite or other reconnaissance assets to check for ship alongside one of the Kharg Island oil rigs or on passage towards Iraq'. Got that?'

'On it now,' Brian replied even as he was going out of the door.

An hour later Jon and the Warrant Officer were in the Captain's cabin on board the Aegis Destroyer. This time, Captain Morrison was accompanied by a US Marine officer. He was almost bald and wore thin wire frame glasses which made him look almost like a schoolmaster. He was introduced as Major Martinez. All four were looking carefully at the photographs.

The Major spoke first. 'I can confirm what your man said Sir, this is definitely a HWASONG launch vehicle and we know that there has been some contact recently between Iran and North Korea.'

Jon looked at Captain Morrison. 'Sir, is the Major cleared to Top Secret?'

'It's alright Jon anything you say to me can be said to Major Martinez.'

'Very well Sir, you will have seen my signal about a merchantman, the Irinda?'

'Yes but it wasn't clear why you made the request.'

'Warrant Officer McCaul here almost collided with a ship moored alongside an oil rig on his way out last night. He didn't see much but what he did see was that she was Iraqi registered. I checked with my shore authorities and found that an Iraqi grain carrier was overdue by at least three days possibly more and that it could easily have been the same ship.'

'But you've no real evidence, hence your signal I assume.'

'Yes Sir but I didn't want to say more in case I was barking up the wrong tree.' Jon was about to go on when there was a knock and Lieutenant's head appeared around the door.

'Signal for your eyes only Sir,' and then seeing Jon. 'Oh and the CO of Prometheus,' he handed a clip board to Captain Morrison and closed the door. The Captain read for a few minutes and passed the signal to Jon.

Jon also read for a moment. 'Looks like I was right. It says here that a ship that is probably the Irinda was seen five miles from the area of the oil rigs heading west towards Basra but inside Iranian waters and only half an hour ago.'

'Jon, come on, you've got an idea, what is it?' Captain Morrison looked pensive.

'Very well Sir this is conjecture but frankly I don't think we can ignore the risk. Firstly, there is a strong suspicion that the Iranians have at least one nuclear warhead which they acquired from Pakistan. If they have, it was almost certainly delivered to Kharg Island. Secondly, they seem to have got hold of a long range ballistic missile with a range of over a thousand miles, except they seem to have removed it from its launcher and taken it somewhere else.'

'Go on.'

'According to the SF experts it wouldn't be too difficult to remount the launching equipment on to another type of platform and the deck of a ship would be a very suitable place. In fact, why remove it from a road vehicle with all the flexibility that that gives you unless you were going to use a ship? It wouldn't make sense and now we have this Iraqi merchantman who seems to have just left Iranian territory. The deck of grain carriers tend to be very cluttered with gantries and the like. Hiding the missile and launcher there would be quite easy.'

'So what's the end game?' The Major asked in a puzzled tone.

'Just suppose a missile was launched from Iraqi territory, with a nuclear warhead, what would be the world's reaction?'

'You know as well as me, it would be terrible but who would be the target?' Captain Morrison looked pensive.

'I'm sure you've already worked that out Sir. Who is the common enemy around here? If we're right, then Iran gets its enemy of the last ten years into disastrous trouble and at the same time there's a damned good chance that the other country they hate, possibly even more than Iraq, is also dealt a devastating blow. It doesn't even have to detonate, a dirty explosion would still have the same international consequences and plutonium is a deadly poison as well as highly being radioactive. It would contaminate a massive area. Imagine the effect on a large city. The missile has the range, even if it's fired from southern Iraq. From alongside in Basra for example.'

Major Martinez looked aghast. 'You mean Israel?'

Jon looked at Captain Morrison. 'It can't be anywhere else.'

Chapter 31

The silence in the Captain's cabin only lasted seconds. 'Jon, I have to agree. We will need to act quickly. How long do you reckon it will it take for the merchantman to reach Iraqi waters?'

'Well it's about a hundred and twenty miles to the entrance of the Shatt al Arab waterway so let's say seven hours and then another 80 miles up the river but they are limited to eight knots so that's another ten hours. We don't have much time. When is your carrier arriving Sir?'

'Not until tomorrow at the earliest. But we can't call in an air strike from there or our allies like the Saudis until we're certain. I will signal my headquarters straight away. You had better do the same.'

Before anyone could speak, an alarm sounded cutting off any chance of further conversation.

'General Quarters, General Quarters, the Captain is requested to come to the CIC.'

There was more but Jon ignored it. 'I need to get back to my ship Sir,' he said with urgency.

Captain Morrison nodded. 'Major, take the Commander and his man down to the flight deck as quickly as you can.'

By the time Jon arrived at the flight deck the Lynx had its rotors running. Jon and the Warrant Officer jumped in and in seconds they were airborne. Prometheus was now only half a mile away and the transfer only took a few minutes. However, Jerry was able to update Jon on what was going on. 'Apparently, there are a large number of fast contacts heading our way Sir. They're in the same area that the Iranian Frigate was loitering about. They're about forty miles away and the Frigate seems to be coming towards as well but a little slower.'

'As soon as we jump out you get airborne again and go and have a look. You've got two Skua loaded and I assume the gun is as well but keep well clear. Just try and work out what they're up to. We're right in the middle of the Gulf here so they can't try that trick of saying we are in their waters.'

'Roger Sir, oh and we took a suck while we were waiting on the Yank's deck so we've got full fuel. We should be good for at least two and half hours now.'

Jon was impressed by Jerry's forethought and said so and then left him to land the helicopter on his much smaller deck.

As he jumped out of the helicopter, he turned to Warrant Officer McCaul. 'Stay here and get you guys up here as well. You never know, you might get to take a few pot shots at someone.'

Without waiting for a reply he sprinted to the front of the hangar and down the small escape hatch that led into the ship. Within minutes he was putting on his headset in the Ops room and Brian was briefing him.

'The ship is fully closed up at Action Stations Sir. All weapons and sensors are on line. About fifteen minutes ago the Sacagawea warned us about a number of small contacts closing. That's one hell of a radar they've got. We've picked them up on 968 now as well. There are at least fifteen and the Frigate is following. The Lynx has checked in and will be there in a few minutes.'

'Very good Ops. We need to get an urgent signal to Fleet. Hand me the signal pad please.' Jon started to write out his suspicions about the Iraqi merchantman and was then going to request permission to pursue it when the Lynx came on the radio.

'Golf Mike Charlie Three this is Mike Echo, we are in visual contact and can confirm they are Bog Hammers although none are flying national ensigns. The Frigate is about five miles behind.'

'Range to the Frigate?' Jon asked.

'Thirty miles Sir,' the Surface Controller answered. 'Hold on she seems to be slowing.'

'Mike Echo this is Charlie Three, what's the Frigate doing now?' Jon asked on the radio.

'She's turning, looks like she's heading north. Hold on, something is happening. Shit, she's launched a missile from her stern.'

Just then the Air Warfare Controller called. 'Missile launch detected bearing zero one five. Fast moving assessed as probably an Exocet.'

The helicopter called again. 'Second launch, looks like she's firing the lot, I am descending to Sea Skua launch height request permission to engage?'

'Sink the bastard as soon as you can,' Jon responded realising that it was hardly the language he should be using but that Frigate had four Exocet on her stern and this time it looked like a serious attempt to sink his ship. He was angry, seriously angry.

In the Lynx, Jerry had flung the aircraft down towards the sea. The Frigate hadn't fired on them yet but that didn't mean that they wouldn't be their next target. However, at two hundred feet and five miles away they would be hard pressed to do anything to the helicopter.

While he was getting into position, Tom was powering up the two Sea Skua missiles on the port weapon station. As soon as they were at the right height, he put the radar's cursor over the target of the Frigate and pressed the LOCK button. The radar aerial immediately stopped sweeping and stayed pointing at its target producing a radar beam that the missiles would now be able to follow. A series of lights came lit up on the Sea Skua control panel.

Tom looked at Jerry. 'Target locked, weapons ready.'

'Launch,' was all Jerry said.

Tom lifted the safety flap and pressed the large red button on the weapon controller. The first Skua dropped free. As it cleared the aircraft its rocket motor ignited with a bang that could be heard inside the aircraft and it accelerated away, a blast of orange flame behinds its white pencil shaped body. A few seconds later the next launch light lit up and without asking Tom pressed the release button again. The second missile dropped free.

Jerry slowed the aircraft down to a crawl and turned away sixty degrees. They had to keep the radar pointing at its target and as it only had a one hundred and eighty degree sweep that meant they would still have to close the target as the missiles flew but there was no need to do it at speed.

'Shit they've fired another Exocet' Jerry exclaimed as he saw the pencil plume of smoke at the stern of their target. Suddenly there was another pillar of smoke but this time it was accompanied by a bright orange flash as the first Sea Skua warhead detonated. Travelling at over Mach point eight, the sea skimming missile had blasted in through the side of the Iranian Frigate just below the bridge. The warhead armed on impact but the three hundred pounds of explosives didn't detonate for a few milliseconds by which time the missile was almost in the middle of the ship. The explosion blew out bulkheads and shredded almost half the ship's company in an instant. Fires started in dozens of compartments and all internal communications were lost. A few seconds later, the second weapon arrived. This one had been set with a lower skim height and impacted a few feet above the waterline and entered the engine room. The blast killed all the engineering staff, knocked out the ship.s propulsion and blew a five metre hole in the side of the ship which immediately allowed the sea to start pouring in.

The Frigate was in actuality a large corvette about half the size of Prometheus and only displaced just over seventeen hundred tons. The Sea Skua missiles were originally designed to take out fast patrol boats but the effect of two of them on the small warship had been completely devastating.

In the Lynx, they could see that the ship had come to a stop and was already listing. Smoke was pouring out of her side.

Jerry turned to Tom. 'Fucking hell, that was just like being in the simulator. I never thought I'd get to fire a Skua for real. Bloody hell, they really work. You'd better call mother and tell them that the Frigate is out of it. In fact you can tell them she's about to sink and I'll get us after the Bog Hammers.'

Tom pressed his floor radio transmit button as Jerry accelerated the helicopter back up to its maximum speed. 'Charlie Three this is Mike Echo, we have successfully engaged the Frigate and she is out of it over.'

There was no reply but suddenly there was another explosion from the sinking wreck. A massive gout of flame and smoke rose from the stern area which was sticking high out of the water.

'Shit if I didn't know better I would say something else hit her. I suspect mum or the Yank have had a pop at her as well.' Jerry said. 'Try mother again Tom.'

Tom tried repeatedly but no matter how many calls he made on the UHF or HF radio he was met by silence.

As the Lynx was descending to its attack position the Air Warfare Controller in Prometheus kept calling launches until it was clear there were four Exocet in the air coming towards the two ships. Jon had taken control of his anger and was now icy calm.

Bog Hammer

Brian looked at him. 'Should we engage the Frigate with Exocet Jon? We can't guarantee that two Skua will do the job.'

He was interrupted by the Electronic Warfare Controller calling. 'Eyewater bearing zero one five, steady bearing.'

'Fire chaff and yes Brian engage the Frigate with one Exocet only. Weapons free on Sea Wolf.' Jon didn't want to say it to the ship but he might just need some Exocet later in the day.

It soon became clear that the first missile was locked onto Prometheus but the other three had decided that the American was their target. Once again having fired their chaff there was little more that could be done until the Sea Wolf system decided that it was ready and the target was in range.

'I hope the Yank's close-in weapons work. They've got three of the bastards going for them,' Brian muttered just as there was a terrific whoosh from forward as the Exocet blasted out of its launcher towards its target to the north.

'Exocet launched successfully, on track.' The Surface Weapon Controller reported.

Jon didn't know it but Captain Morrison wasn't convinced that a little helicopter was actually capable of dealing with a Frigate and had also launched two Harpoon missiles of his own. It became a hot matter of debate some time later between the two ship's companies over who had actually hit the target although they all accepted the Lynx got there first. The other thing Jon didn't know was that the decision to fire the Exocet was probably the worst one of his life.

Prometheus was now heading directly towards the incoming missile bows on for two reasons. Firstly it opened up the 'A Arcs' of the Sea Wolf weapon system or in layman's terms made sure the weapon launcher had the best field of fire Secondly it presented the smallest possible target for the incoming missile. The 967, speed sensitive Doppler radar, had a good solid lock on the missile which was travelling close to the speed of sound and so presenting a massive target for the Sea Wolf to respond to. Unfortunately, despite being given a plethora of alternative targets in the form of chaff blooms around the ship, the 'eyewater' in the nose of the incoming Exocet was resolutely locked onto the first target it had acquired, HMS Prometheus.

In the Ops room they watched as the 910 radar tracker of the Sea Wolf slewed around onto the correct heading and then the Sea Wolf operator called positive lock and target acquisition. Then it all went wrong. The outgoing Exocet was flying the inertial course that had been given to it by the targeting computer in Prometheus. It wouldn't turn on its own radar for some time until it was at a pre-set range from its target. However, that course was an exact reciprocal of the one the incoming missile was following. Both missiles passed each other at less than one hundred yards at about five miles from the ship at a combined speed of over fourteen hundred miles an hour. For an instant the 967 radar which had been tracking both weapons saw them merge and also their Doppler returns merge, effectively giving a zero reading. Momentarily it lost lock and the computer dropped the target's designation as hostile. The 910 tracker slewed away and the whole Sea Wolf system was suddenly useless.

In the Ops room, all they knew was that the Sea Wolf Controller called loss of lock and then it was too late. A weapon travelling at Mach point nine takes very little time to travel a few miles and they had lost their one chance at taking it out.

Jon grabbed the main broadcast and yelled, 'Brace, Brace standby for missile impact.' There was a mind shattering bang and he was flung out of his chair hitting his head on the console in front of him, just as the whole Ops room was plunged into darkness.

Things weren't much better on the Sacagawea. The ships incredibly sophisticated radar and computer system was handling the incoming missiles and had easily acquired all three. The ships Phalanx Close-in Weapons systems were ready. These consisted of two small Gatling guns mounted on the top of the main weather deck. At three and half thousand metres they opened fire with their six barrels, firing twenty millimetre depleted uranium shells at a rate of four and a half thousand a minute. It sounded like a buzz saw going off. The first Exocet was shredded to pieces at about a thousand metres from the ship as were the other two as they approached at almost the speed of sound. Only one detonated, the other two were turned into a cloud of debris or more importantly into shrapnel. The problem was that the shrapnel was still travelling at almost the speed of sound and straight towards the ship. The toughest part of a missile is the warhead. It's designed to penetrate steel at high speed and still function. One of the warheads survived.

The effect on the ship was devastating. Thousands of pieces of red hot metal slammed through radio and radar aerials. The fixed array antennas surrounding the bridge that were pointing towards the missiles were shredded with holes. Several fires were started and six crewmen whose General Quarters stations were above decks were killed instantly. The remaining intact warhead only partly detonated on impact but unfortunately it was close to the waterline. A seven metre hole was blasted in the side of the ship by the engine room. Just like the Iranian Frigate only minutes earlier, the sea started to flood in.

In the ships Combat Information Centre, the impacts could be heard like vicious rain impacting the side of the ship. What was worse was that all the radar screens blacked out, every single one, even the navigation radar was down. When the warhead detonated they felt it through the soles of their feet. Several sailors close to the impact point had their ankles shattered. Captain Morrison called for a damage report and it soon became clear that his sophisticated, modern warship was blind, deaf and dumb.

Chapter 32

Jon pulled himself to his feet. His eyes were swimming and he felt a liquid running into his eyes. He wiped his face and it came away sticky with what he could see in the dim glow of the emergency lighting was blood. Ignoring what must be a cut on his forehead he grabbed the emergency intercom. 'HQ One, damage report.'

For a moment there was silence, then the reassuring voice of the MEO was heard throughout the Ops room. 'Looks like the missile detonated down aft Sir. Damage Control parties are investigating now but we're not taking on water. However, we have a fire in the Junior Rates dining hall. The machinery control room reports that one boiler has lost pressure and currently both engines are stopped.'

'Fuck. Casualties?'

'Not known yet Sir I'll let you know as soon as I can.'

'Listen Andy, our first priority has to be our people but before the missile hit there were up to fifteen fast boats bearing down on us. They'll be here in half an hour at the most. I need electrical power back as soon as you can and I must be able to manoeuvre.'

'Roger Sir, I'm already on it and already getting the gennies back on line. It won't be long.'

'And propulsion and manoeuvring?'

'Hang on Sir.' Jon could hear voices in the background. 'Steering is fine Sir you should have limited propulsion shortly.'

'Right I'll let you get on with it. Report when you can.' Jon leant back in his chair as someone pressed something over his eye.

It was Brian. 'For fuck's sake hold still Jon, I'm trying to put a shell dressing over that gash on your head.'

Jon did as he was told until Brian was finished. 'Forgot to call me Sir then,' he quipped.

'Just for a moment you were a casualty not a Captain,' Brian replied seriously. 'But it doesn't look too deep. Do you feel alright to keep going?'

'Don't be so fucking stupid,' Jon replied just as all the lights came back on. 'Right everyone, I want radar and communications back up as soon as possible. Where's the WEO?'

'Here Sir,' came a voice from Jon's right. 'The 967 is out Sir, I'm not exactly sure why but it looks like the aerial is jammed. The 1006 navigation radar on the bridge roof survived and we've got no long range radio, all our HF aerials are trashed, we've got one UHF working but that's it.'

'Right someone try the helicopter,' Jon said before grabbing the microphone to the bridge. 'Bridge this is the Captain, what state is the American in?'

The Officer of the Watch responded. 'She's in a mess Sir. She seems to have lost steerage and there's a bloody great hole in her starboard side at the waterline. There's smoke pouring out near the stern.'

'Right put out a Mayday call for both us, saying we are under attack, damaged and need immediate assistance. Then try to raise the Sacagawea on channel thirteen.'

'Roger Sir.'

Suddenly, a relieved sounding Flight Commander was heard over the UHF. 'Charlie Three this is Mike Echo. I can confirm the Frigate is sunk but there are thirteen Bog Hammers now twelve miles from you. It was fifteen but two are now full of holes. However, one of them fired what looked like a Stinger at me and I had to evade. I'm not going to be able to stop them all, what is your situation over?'

Jon replied. 'This is Mike Echo, we're still trying to evaluate but we've taken a missile hit aft. Can you raise the Sacagawea? Because they're not answering us on any frequency.'

'Negative, we've tried as well. I can see them on radar near you, so they are still afloat. Suggest I continue to try and dissuade these guys, over.'

'Charlie Three, carry on but be careful.'

The First Lieutenant came into the Ops room. He looked exhausted and his overall were stained with what looked horribly like blood. 'Sitrep Sir. The missile seems to have glanced off the side of the ship as it detonated. 'There's a gash down the port side about fifteen feet long and five high where the warhead went off. It's above the waterline but has penetrated the boiler room. The fire is out. One boiler has been damaged and the other was shut down. MEO says we should have it back up in a few minutes but our speed will be very limited. The upper deck is a shambles, especially on the port side. We've no radio aerials down aft and the main radar is jammed over at an angle.'

'Des, what about casualties?'

Des looked stricken. 'At least seven dead Sir and another six wounded in the sick bay. The breach in the hull is by the Junior Rates galley which was empty otherwise it would have been a lot more.'

Jon was silent for a moment. 'Well done Number One. How are the upper deck Oerlikons and also the chaff launchers?'

'The guns on the starboard side are serviceable Sir but four of the casualties were all the gunners, I'm afraid. The starboard chaff launchers should be fine, they were shielded by the funnel.'

'Right, can you get two of your people to man those two guns please? We might need them soon and then carry on with the cleaning up. We will have to close up again if these bastards get closer. I'll want every single gun we have ready on the upper deck when I call for them.'

'Got it Sir.'

Jon picked up the main broadcast and gave the microphone and experimental click, it seemed to be working. 'D'you hear there, this is the Captain speaking. As you will all be aware we took a small thump a few minutes ago. Well done to everyone, for your prompt actions. As I'm sure you are aware we are still afloat and despite some damage we can still bloody well fight. Now in about fifteen minutes a number of Iranian fast attack boats are going to try to have a go at us and our American friend. They are going to get a shock. We will go to back to Action Stations now except for damage control parties. All designated small arms personnel are to muster in the hangar or the bridge wings as per their normal stations. Let's give these bastards some payback, thank you.'

Just then the MEO's voice came on. 'Captain this is HQ One, we have pressure back and you can manoeuvre, maximum speed eighteen knots.'

Jon then picked up the intercom to the bridge. 'Bridge this is the Captain, take us round to close the American and then ensure that our starboard side is pointing north towards the approaching boats.'

'Roger. Oh hang on Sir I've got the Sacagawea on the bridge VHF do you want to come up?'

'On my way.'

Bog Hammer

'Keep me up to date on the Bog Hammers Brian,' Jon called as he shot out of his chair.

Daylight on the bridge almost blinded Jon after the darkness below. Telling the Officer of the Watch to carry on, he grabbed the small commercial VHF radio mike. 'Sacagawea this is Prometheus over.'

The voice that replied was immediately recognisable. 'This is Captain Morrison what is your status? I'm afraid we've no radios but this one and all my sensors are out. I'm taking on water in my engine room. We got hit real bad by debris from those missiles.'

'Right Sir, this is Jonathon. We have limited manoeuvrability and I've one radar working. The Bog Hammers are about ten minutes away to the north, so if you have any upper deck hardware that works I suggest you get it ready. My Lynx is having some success with its gun but there are too many of them for him to be able to fight them all off.'

'I'm afraid my Sea Hawk took some damage so he won't be able to help.'

'Roger that, I'm closing with you now and will take station ahead as close as I can, so we make one target. Oh and I have one trick up my sleeve which might just even up the odds.'

'Roger Prometheus, we'll get as ready as we can.'

Jon turned to the Officer of the Watch. 'I'll be in the Ops room. Relay anything to me and as I said to their Captain, get as close as you can and don't worry about scratching any paint.'

'Aye, Aye Sir.'

When Jon was back in the dark, he took a good look at the radar. The contacts were all well-defined now and approaching the ten mile point.

'They'll probably start to split up soon,' Brian observed as they poured over the plot.

'So when do you want to try your secret weapon?

'They're doing about thirty knots so by my calculations we fire at six miles. Hopefully they'll still be reasonably together even if they've started to bombburst.

'Good, warn the Lynx to get well clear.'

They watched as the range dropped. The boats had indeed started to split up but were still all within a mile of each other as Jon ordered the chaff rockets fired. He immediately ordered a reload and within seconds another set of rockets were on their way. On the radar, the small boats disappeared under the larger chaff blooms.

In the ship, the action was limited to a picture on a glass screen. Five miles away it was very different. Very few of the crews of the Bog Hammers even saw the rockets fire. None of them paid them any heed. When the packets of metal foil exploded in the sky ahead of them, more took notice but nobody felt threatened. As they roared into the chaff cloud they saw a sparkling shimmering curtain ahead, which actually looked quite attractive and certainly didn't seem threatening. As soon as they entered the cloud, things changed. The boats were travelling at over thirty knots and the chaff was relatively stationary. It was blasted into the faces, eyes and mouths of the crews with force. The tiny slivers of metal foil clung to everything and before they realised it the men were starting to breathe them in. Fits of coughing broke out. Eyes were blasted at the same time. Anyone with glasses wasn't affected badly but most of the crews didn't have them and within seconds they were blind. Two boats immediately collided and erupted in an inferno of flames and exploding ammunition. The chaff also got into anything electrical and shorted it out. Several boats stopped dead as their outboards coughed into silence. Within half a minute the force had been reduced to a shambles. Only the two boats well out to the west managed to avoid the danger. The skippers of both looked appalled at the carnage but neither turned. With revenge in their hearts for whatever devilish trick had been played on them they kept going towards their hated targets. On both boats, they had several shoulder launched missiles. They needed to get within a mile of their target preferably closer and no one in either crew noticed the helicopter coming up behind them. Long before they were within range of the two warships, half inch cannon shells started tearing them apart. The first boat to be targeted suddenly dropped off the plane and a fire broke out on her stern. The remaining boat spun around but was also taking hits by then. In a last act of defiance a crewman raised his machine gun to the approaching helicopter and held the trigger down even as a cannon shell cut him in half.

The last burst of machine gun fire hit the nose of the Lynx. In the cockpit, there was a loud bang and parts of the dashboard exploded into the faces of the crew. In accordance with the rules, they both had their visors lowered so their eyes were protected. Tom Pinter was lucky, he received a few cuts on his mouth and chin but otherwise was unhurt. For Jerry it was different. One of the bullets that had smashed the dashboard, entered his left shoulder, shattering bone and sinew. The pain was agonising, as though a red hot poker had been jammed through his shoulder. With an effort of will, he reached over with his right hand and managed to stab the barometric height hold button. The aircraft would now stay at whatever height they were at without any further input. Tom could see the pain his friend was in but with no flying controls, he knew there was little he could do.

'Mayday, Mayday, this is Charlie Three, we've been fired on and taken damage. Pilot has taken a hit, we will attempt to return on board.'

The ship acknowledged the call and broke clear of the American ship to give the best relative wind possible for the damaged helicopter.

Tom talked to Jerry as they headed back. He was losing a lot of blood but there was little Tom could do except keep talking and try to keep his pilot conscious.

Jerry manoeuvred the stricken machine onto a final approach. 'Listen mate, in a minute you will have to release the height hold and lucky you, you get to do some pilot shit. You're going to have to operate the collective for me, OK?'

Tom nodded and loosened his straps so he could lean over and pull the collective lever up and down as directed.

Two minutes later the aircraft landed very hard but safely on the flight deck. As they hit, Jerry's head dropped on his chest as he blacked out. Tom reached up and slammed the engine levers into the shut-off position and then as soon as he could he applied the rotor brake. He didn't dare wave the ground crew in until the rotors were stopped as there was no one holding the cyclic. As soon as they had ground to a halt the Flight team ran in and started to manhandle the unconscious pilot out and down to sick bay.

Tom was surprised to see the Captain emerge from the hangar. Jon came up to him.

'Bloody well done, both for taking out the bad guys and getting that wreck back to the ship. That was an impressive bit of flying. By the way, you're bleeding.'

Bog Hammer

For a second Tom was surprised by the Captains words but when he turned back and looked at the front of the aircraft they had just got back to the deck he realised what the Captain meant. Virtually the whole of the fibreglass radome, which was effectively the nose of the aircraft, was gone. The radar scanner behind it had several holes in it and there were large cracks radiating up the windscreen. Tom realised he hadn't even noticed them when they were flying back. He turned towards the Captain and looked at the stripped away paint, the smoke still issuing from the side of the ship and the edge of the flight deck that had buckled up as the Exocet warhead had exploded.

'Than you Sir, Fred looks almost as fucked up as the ship.'

Chapter 34

Once again Jon's cabin was crowded with his Heads of Department. As soon as they were all there, he singled out the Navigating Officer.

'Navigator, first task, I want the ship headed towards Basra as fast as she can go. MEO how fast is that?'

The MEO looked pensive. 'On one boiler Sir, eighteen knots at the best and frankly I'd rather we didn't even try that.'

'Sorry Engines we haven't finished yet, just give me six hours more. After that, it won't matter anymore one way or the other. What are the chances of repairing the second boiler?'

'Slim Sir, there is a leak in a pipe to the steam drum at the top of the boiler. We may be able to fix it in a few hours but I wouldn't want to make any guarantees.'

'I'm not asking for any. Just for you and your chaps to do your best. I'll explain what's going on to everyone soon but we need to get going now. Nav, I want a course and ETA for the mouth of the Shatt al Arab as soon as you have it. Your only constraint is to avoid any Iranian territorial waters and tell the Officer of the Watch to get going.'

'Aye, Aye Sir,' the Navigating Officer replied and slipped out of the cabin, closely followed by the MEO.

'WEO?'

'Yes Sir.'

Your priority is to get me some communications. HF preferably but even a UHF link to shore would do. What is the state of the satellite?'

'Completely shot I'm afraid Sir. The antennas are trashed and I can't fix them with a bit of wire like the HF aerials which my chaps are rigging as we speak. But I've no idea if we can get even get that to work because of the damage to the electronics in the aerial units themselves.'

'And what else do I have left?'

'967/968 is completely shot Sir. The antenna is de-seated and jammed. The 1006 navigation radar is fine. 910 tracker is jammed on ship's head, although the Sea Wolf launcher is operational and before you ask we're still not sure why the Sea Wolf failed. As soon as we work it out I'll let you know. Sonars are fine and so are the starboard torpedo tubes although the ports side ones are damaged. The same goes for the Oerlikons, the starboard ones are fine but the port ones are beyond repair. The three remaining Exocet are useless because the targeting link is down. However, I have my team working on that and may be able to get them serviceable to fire on manual data fairly soon. On the plus side, the ESM seems to be working so we can see other radars and transmissions.'

'Jesus, OK just do your best but I need some weapons and maybe soon. Ops, draft me a signal summarising the attack and our state. God knows whether we'll ever be able to send it in time.'

'Number One?'

'Sir.'

'As you can gather we are not stopping. What's the state of our casualties?'

'None life threatening Sir but the Doc would like to get them into decent facilities as soon as possible.'

'Noted. Is the galley completely fucked?'

'It's not even there any more Sir. The two casualties from below decks were the chefs. I've got the wardroom galley working on producing food for everyone and that should suffice for the moment.'

'Well done. Now, I know you all want to know what the hell this all about and I'm going to tell you. Not only you but the ship's company as well. As we can't talk to anyone outside the ship I can't ask permission but at the same time I can't be told not to. But I need to talk to our American friend first. So let's have all officers in the wardroom in fifteen minutes. Are there any other pressing issues?'

No one answered so Jon excused himself and made his way quickly up the starboard bridge ladder. Waving to the Officer of the Watch and Navigating Officer to continue, he went to the Marine VHF and switched it to low power and channel thirteen.

'Sacagawea, this is Prometheus over.'

He was answered in seconds.

'Captain to Captain please.'

It didn't take long for Captain Morrison to come on air. 'Jon what can I do for you? I see you are leaving me.'

'Yes Sir, I intend to go after the person we were talking about earlier. If we needed confirmation that we were on the right track then I think I can safely say we just got it.' Jon knew he was on a simple unencrypted channel and had to choose his words with care. 'I hope to have long range comms at some time but can't wait to talk to home.'

'Understood, I'm sorry we've got our fires and flooding under control but we're not going anywhere without a tug.'

'Is there any chance your Sea Hawk will be serviceable any time soon? I have casualties that need evacuation if possible and one of them is my helicopter pilot and anyway my Lynx is completely trashed.'

'We should have her airborne to you within half an hour. They're changing a rotor blade that took a hit. We have a full sick bay and doctor over here so we can look after them.'

Jon breathed a sigh of relief. The medical facilities on Prometheus were basic and not really designed to cope with long term wounded.

'So what was the trick you pulled with the Bog Hammers Jon? I didn't think you had any medium range weapons.'

Jon laughed and told him. There was a stunned silence from the other end for a few seconds and then a barked laugh. 'You crazy Limey, why didn't anyone else think of that? The few that are still afloat seem to be heading off. I guess we just let them go.'

'Yes, I've got bigger fish to fry. We put out a Mayday on sixteen and included you in it. I would appreciate it if you maintain the fiction that we are still with you. I don't want our friends to know if at all possible.'

'Understood, good luck Jon.'

As Jon made his way down the ladder into the Burma Way to go to the wardroom he saw a long queue of his sailors at the door to the wardroom galley and smelled the wonderful smell of bacon permeating the air. He went to talk to his men.

'Morning Chaps,' he called to the queue. 'I hope none of you are getting bored with the sunshine cruise so far.'

Laughter greeted his remark but with nothing like the enthusiasm his men normally offered. He realised they were all as tired as he felt.

'Sir, can we keep the picture window in the Junior Rates dining hall please? The view is really good.'

Jon didn't see the speaker but immediately knew who it was. 'I'll ask the dockyard to double glaze it for you Johnson.'

Another chuckle, slightly more relaxed this time.

'Now listen chaps, I know you all want to know what this is all about and why we're not simply staying for help to come and help us to sort ourselves out. I'm sure you can all make a guess that it has something to do with the Silkworm attack the other day as well. Give me ten minutes with the officers and I'll make a broadcast to you all. Its time everyone knows why we were attacked and why this is all so terribly important. Just give me a few minutes.'

He was about to turn around when a massive bun loaded with bacon and a scruffy mug of tea was handed to him by one of the sailors.

'Thanks Dickinson, you've no idea how much I need that.'

The assembled officers all stood as he entered the wardroom. He waved them back to their seats and took a position with his back to the bar. In simple terms, he told them the whole story. The suspicions about the Pakistani ship. The result of the Special Forces reconnaissance and the conclusions that they had reached. He was listened to in stunned silence. Finally, he covered the attack by the Iranian Frigate and Bog Hammers.

'It's quite clear they're totally determined to carry on with this and won't take the risk of anyone stopping them. Before anyone asks I've no idea whether this is sanctioned by the Iranian government or just some faction. If I had to guess I would say the latter. The Ayatollahs may be pretty extreme in some of their views but they're not that stupid. This has the potential to drag the whole area into a war that no one can win.'

'That's alright Sir, they didn't count on Prometheus being here,' someone muttered.

'Too bloody right DWEO. And it doesn't stop here. We are going after that ship. She's got a head start but we can catch her up and dish out some revenge.'

'What with Sir?' The Navigator asked. 'We've no real guns, our upper deck is a shambles and the Lynx is toast.'

Jon knew that he was only echoing what everyone was thinking, including himself if it came to that. 'Now listen, we've got close in weapons. It will be several hours before we are likely to catch them and we may get the Exocet workable by then as well. Sod it, I'll ram

Bog Hammer

them before letting them fire that missile. Hopefully, it won't come to that. So let's all get to work and put this ship as back together as well as we can.'

There were determined nods all round and Jon took his leave, asking Des to join him on the way out. As he did so he realised his bacon sandwich and tea had gone cold. It didn't stop him eating them.

An hour later he was sitting in his chair on the bridge. He had talked to the ship's company over the main broadcast and also told them the full story. He toyed with the idea of not telling them about the possible nuclear warhead but in the end he decided they deserved the full truth. Seven of their comrades were dead because of it after all. He had then gone around the ship with the First Lieutenant and talked to as many men as he could while inspecting the damage. The blast hole in the side of the ship was quite spectacular. Had they been in the Atlantic it would have been a show stopper but with the calm weather of the Gulf it shouldn't be a problem and certainly not for the next few hours. The upper deck was a mess, especially on the port side. The screen under the bridge was also burned badly but this time because of the exhaust from the departing Exocet. His last visit was to the sick bay. He spoke to all the men. Jerry was out of it due to the effect of the wound and the morphine he had been given. He mentally vowed to ensure that both aircrew were awarded some recognition of their actions whatever the outcome of the next few hours. Then the American Sea Hawk had arrived and taken off all the wounded which was another weight of his mind. Finally, he consoled himself with the fact that it could all have been a great deal worse.

Brian appeared by his elbow. 'Its four hours to Basra, we've got half a tank of gas, a full pack of cigarettes, its dark and we're wearing sunglasses,' he stated, as he looked out of the cracked bridge window at the clear sea and sky.

Jon turned and looked at his friend, realising how exhausted Brian looked. He wondered if he looked the same. 'How about we've got one boiler, hardly any weapons or sensors it will be dark soon and we haven't caught up with the bastards yet?'

'That's about right me old mate. So what the fuck are we going to do when we catch her?'

'That's twice in one day you've forgotten to call me Sir.' Jon smiled sadly. 'You know, I remember the last time we made that joke.' He sighed and was silent for a moment. 'Well to answer your question. When we catch the bastard, we give her one chance and one chance only. That will be more than enough to tell us if we're right about her intentions.'

'What if we get comms back and Fleet tell us to back off?'

'We won't get comms back. I've changed my mind about that, just not told WEO yet,' Jon smiled grimly. 'There are seven of my men down aft in body bags Brian. I'm not going to risk some fucking politician telling me that they died in vain because he didn't have the balls to make a decision. Brian, in case you haven't noticed, I'm angry, I'm fucking angry. This bloody part of the world is completely fucked up. If it's not the lunatic religious zealots, its western politicians more interested in oil than people. Well now its personal and this ship is going to fucking well stop this happening.'

'So tell me Sir, what happens when her one chance has been used up?'

Jon told him.

Chapter 35

Prometheus was lucky. She caught up with her quarry when she was still several miles offshore and in international waters.

Jon had suspected that she would take her time on the transit from Kharg to the waterway in order to enter in darkness and it seemed he had been proved right. Had the quarry gone fast for the entrance then he would be forced to take Prometheus up the narrow channel as well. Despite his stated desire not to talk to the outside world until he'd taken action, entering such a disputed piece of water in a warship could cause all sorts of international problems. However, it was a moot point as despite the efforts of the engineers they still had no communications. As a contingency, he had drafted a plain language signal and if necessary would approach one of the merchantmen nearby and transfer one of his officers over to use their systems, probably a phone patch through Portishead radio to Northwood. Choosing a form of words that would explain his quandary but that could be sent over unsecure communications hadn't been easy but he was fairly sure he had managed it.

As the afternoon progressed, the repairs to the ship had continued and the WEO finally reported that the three Exocet were useable. At one point the UAA1 Electronic surveillance equipment had alerted them to a sector radar which was identified as that of an early F14 Tomcat fighter. It could only be an Iranian aircraft and the bearing was steady towards them. With no effective anti-aircraft weapons left except two World War Two Oerlikons, Jon had nevertheless stood the ship to, at Action Stations and waited.

Once again the Ops room had been silent as events played out. The tension was much higher. This time just about everything was out of their control.

'Any idea of range?' Jon asked the Electronic Warfare Controller.

'Not really Sir, signal strength is low. Must still be over a hundred miles away.'

Jon knew that a supersonic aircraft like the Tomcat could cover that distance in minutes but he was probably cruising on a general surface search and there would be dozens surface contacts for the aircraft crew to sort through.

Bog Hammer

Suddenly everything changed. 'Second F14 radar to the east Sir. It's an American.' The EW Controller called. 'The original one is turning, lost contact with him. The American has changed mode.' And then seconds later, 'All contact lost now Sir.'

Brian looked at Jon. 'Have our American buddies got the message from Sacagawea do you think? If that wasn't a Yank taking out the Iranian, then I'm a banana.'

'Looks that way but as we can't talk to anyone, then we will just have to keep going. But if that's what it was then someone appears to want to protect us and let us get on with it.'

The bridge intercom broke into life. 'Fast jet approaching from starboard.' There was a sudden roar as the aircraft sped past, easily heard in the Ops room. 'That was an American Tomcat Sir. He waved his wings and has shot off to the east.'

'Looks like you're right Sir,' Brian responded.

They waited fifteen minutes and then Jon stood the ship down again.

And now ten miles ahead, plodding along at eight knots, was the ship that Jon was now sure was the root cause of all their woes. He and Des were staring at her through binoculars but it was her behaviour on radar that first alerted them. All the ships heading into the waterway were doing between fifteen and twenty knots. This one had been doing a steady eight knots and allowing everyone to overtake her. Apart from the Frigate coming up from astern there were no more merchantmen around. Obviously, everyone else was keen to be docked before darkness.

'Can't make out the name yet but the superstructure looks the right shape from the photos. What a shame we don't have the Lynx available they could just go and look.' Des remarked without taking the binoculars from his eyes.

'And put a couple of Skua into her for good measure.' Jon replied grimly. 'Of course we don't know whether the original crew are still on board which could be a problem. In fact, we're not totally sure she's up to what we suspect she is.'

'So what now Sir? If we can see her she can see us.'

'Which is why I've slowed down to drop back a little. If they are in radio contact with their lords and masters they will hopefully still think we are still with the Sacagawea and not looking behind them too much.' Jon picked up the microphone for the machinery control room. 'MEO it's the Captain, what's the story on the second boiler now please?'

There was a moment's pause. 'It's been repaired Sir and my guy is a good welder but it really ought to be tested before its put into use.'

'But if we flashed the boiler that would be the test. There's no danger to personnel I assume as the boiler room runs unmanned.'

'No Sir but I would hate to promise something and then find it fails straight away.'

'Understood, it's a risk we might have to take. How long before you can raise pressure?'

There was a slight chuckle in the MEO's voice. 'Actually, we lit the boiler half an hour ago and its slowly coming up. I sort of expected you'd want it straight away. Fifteen minutes and then if the pressure holds she's all yours.'

'And what speed can I hope for?'

'Honestly Sir, if you ask for more than twenty five, something will definitely break again.'

'Noted, Engines. Just call me as soon as you're ready.'

Jon turned to Des. 'Action Stations yet again Des, in five minutes please. I won't be going down to the Ops room for this. I want you to take my place. I will fight the ship from here and ask Ops to come and join me. You know the plan.'

'Aye, Aye Sir,' Des left and a few minutes later as the Action Station alarm was once again blaring Brian came onto the bridge.

Jon turned to him. 'All set Brian?'

'Yes Sir, let's just hope we can get close enough. The book says her top speed is eighteen knots. She's quite old, so I'd be surprised if she can do anything like that. What do you think they will do?'

'Fucked if I know old friend. If it was me and I was such a fanatic that I was on the ship in the first place then I would fight as hard as I could but I've no idea what other weapons they may have on board. The satellite imagery didn't show anything but it's pretty easy to cover up things on a large ship's deck, especially with all the clutter that's already there. You know I can't help but feel that none of them expect to get off. Once they fire they will become the target for God knows how much retribution.'

'The world's biggest suicide bomb?'

'Which means this isn't going to be easy. We've got to get quite close to challenge them. If they're innocent then no problem but if they react aggressively we will probably have to counter whatever they've got very fast. At least the gloves will be off and I can follow the rules of engagement with a clear conscience.' He laughed tiredly. 'There's poor old WEO struggling all afternoon to make the Exocet available and we will almost certainly be too close to use them. God, I wish I had a bloody gun, a nice old fashioned four point five inch simple fucking gun.'

'Well we've got something else haven't we?'

'If it works.'

Suddenly the MEOs voice came over the intercom. 'Bridge machinery control officer here, you have two boilers ready and the dilithium crystals are also warmed up.'

'Good man Scottie, let's go.'

Chapter 36

Prometheus increased speed. The vibrations of her twin shafts could be felt through the soles of the crew's feet as she steadied at just over twenty five knots.

'Bridge, this is the MEO, pressure's holding.'

'Thanks Engines.' Jon transferred his hand to the main broadcast. 'D'you hear there, this is the Captain speaking. Our target is about eight miles ahead now and as I'm sure you all know we're going to go and have a polite chat which will be followed by a much less polite one if he wants it. You are all now aware of the stakes we are playing for so please stand by for just about anything.'

Jon called to the Ops room. 'She must have seen us by now. What's she doing?'

'Nothing Sir, just maintaining course and speed.'

Jon pursed his lips. It was only a few miles to Iraqi waters. He was surprised they hadn't sped up and made an attempt to get there first.

'Anyone see any activity?' He asked the bridge staff in general, all who were looking at their quarry through binoculars. No one could.

Then the Officer of the Watch reported. 'I can see her name now Sir. It's definitely the Irinda, registered in Basra.'

Jon wondered if everyone felt as tired as he did. He suddenly realised he had hardly slept for almost two days. One way or another this would be over soon. Within what seemed like minutes but was actually close on a quarter of an hour they were closing the stern of their target ship. He had been expecting some sort of reaction by now. *'Was he wrong? Was the ship on innocent passage after all?'* He wondered.

Telling the Officer of the Watch to draw alongside at two cables distance Jon took the microphone of the maritime VHF. He made sure it was on channel 16 and set to low power. He didn't want this conversation blasting out all over the area.

'Motor Vessel Irinda, this is Royal Naval Warship Prometheus, please stop your engines and prepare to be boarded.'

There was no response. Jon tried again but no one even appeared on the bridge wing to acknowledge their presence. This was crazy.

'Ops, this is the Captain get one of the starboard Oerlikons to fire a burst across their bows please.'

Jon waited a minute and then there was the familiar clatter of the gun and a series of white splashes in front of the Irinda.

Jon repeated his radio call and this time he was answered. The voice had a strong accent and sounded annoyed. 'British warship, why you fire at me? What you want?'

'This is Warship Prometheus, stop your engines and prepare to be boarded for inspection.'

'What you do if I not stop eh? You have no big guns I can see.'

'No but I have plenty of little ones and some missiles. At the moment they are all trained on your bridge. Now stop your engines and prepare to be boarded.'

Nothing happened for a second and then it was clear that the Irinda was slowing down even though no one came back on the radio. Prometheus slowed with them. Suddenly a rope and wood slatted ladder was thrown almost contemptuously over the side near the stern.

'The boarding party to the bridge please Officer of the Watch,' Jon ordered as he continued to study the Irinda through his binoculars. Although the Irinda's reaction had not been what he expected they had briefed for this contingency. Within minutes the First Lieutenant, the four Special Forces soldiers and two more of the ship's seamen were mustered on the bridge. Wearing life jackets and tin helmets, they were armed to the teeth with pistols and sub machine guns. The SF soldiers also had several other lethal looking guns which Jon couldn't identify.

'Chaps, I didn't expect this but we have no choice. It seems that they are either completely innocent or are playing some other game. I want a thorough search of that ship but be very, very careful, understand? Keep in radio contact with us the whole time. If it all goes wrong you may have to jump for it so make sure the RIB stays close. Warrant Officer McCaul, you are responsible for the inspection team's security. Des, you take your chaps and make damn sure there's nothing hidden over there. If you find anything or are attacked in any way you are authorised to return fire, is that clear.'

Des nodded but looked worried. 'You have to think that if he's prepared to stop and be inspected then there can't be anything on board. Hiding something as big as that missile would be just about impossible.'

'I agree,' Jon said. 'But be careful and thorough. Off you go.'

As they departed Jon had a feeling of helplessness. He hated the idea of putting his men in harm's way but there was no choice and he was starting to have serious doubts about his earlier suspicions.

The boarding team were soon in the RIB and speeding across to the waiting ship only a few hundred yards away. As they approached they could see a brown face peering down at them. The helmsman skilfully brought them alongside the ladder and then Warrant Officer McCaul was swarming up it with astonishing speed closely followed by his three comrades. A thumbs up quickly followed and Des grabbed the rope sides of the ladder. Never one for heights, he was careful not to look down. It was over twenty feet to the deck above. The ladder was awkward to climb but he had noted how the soldiers had done it and surprisingly quickly found himself being hauled up the last few feet by the strong arm of one of the soldiers. Once his other two seamen had joined him he turned to the crewman who was patiently waiting and asked to be taken to the bridge. The man didn't seem to understand but Des pointed up a ladder that clearly led there.

'One man stays here and the rest come with me,' he ordered and followed the crewman up the ladder.

The bridge was massive compared to that on the Leander and almost deserted. There was just a rather fat man in a white shirt with faded gold bars on the shoulders who came up to Des and a sailor on the helm.

The fat man didn't seem to be too happy to see armed men on his bridge. 'Why you stop me heh? I do nothing wrong.'

Des had done this sort of boarding before and wasn't going to be put off by bluster. 'May I see your ship's papers including the bill of lading from your last port please?'

The Captain muttered under his breath but produced the papers. Clearly, he had been expecting the request. Des studied them carefully. The ship's last port of call was in India where she had filled up with grain. There was no mention of stopping anywhere else.

Des turned to the Captain. 'You ship's log please.'

There was a slightly shifty look in the man's eyes as he handed over the document. Again Des studied it carefully. There was no mention of any stopover in Iranian waters. Des studied the speeds and time and realised they didn't add up.

'This has been tampered with Captain,' he stated flatly looking carefully at the man as he said it. 'You left Mumbai over three weeks ago and it says you had some trouble with your engine but we know differently.'

The Captain started to look defiant but Des kept going before he could speak. 'We know that this ship was in Iranian waters for several days and at one time was tied up to an oil rig. Would you like to explain that to me please?'

The Captain seemed to deflate like a balloon. 'OK, OK, we do stop at oil rig. I do a little extra trade with some of my family who live in Iran. Now the war is over we are friends now. That is all.'

'So why isn't it in your log?'

'The owners would not like it but there are shortages of many things in Iran and good money to be made. Please, we do not break any laws. You do not have to report this.'

The man looked desperate and if there was any truth in what he said then any contraband would have already been offloaded. There would be no evidence left.

Des made a decision. 'Very well, how you conduct your business is not a matter for me unless you are carrying weapons or drugs. We will now search your ship. You will come with me.'

Suddenly eager to please the man readily agreed. The more Des saw of the ship, the less it seemed likely that it was hiding a thirty foot long nuclear missile but he wasn't going to leave until he was totally sure. They started with the crew's quarters which all looked in order if rather scruffy. There didn't seem to be that many crew around but Des knew that a ship of this size could easily be managed with about twenty five people. Most of the systems on board were automated. He took a cursory glance in the engine room and apart from the one massive diesel engine there was nothing untoward. Satisfied that the stern area was in order they went onto the upper deck. Once again he couldn't see anything amiss. There was no sign of any unusual deck equipment covered or uncovered and no sign of any work having been carried out. Paint was flaking in places and it all looked dreadfully normal. Des walked the length of the deck and it all looked the same.

'I will want to see in your holds please Captain,' he said pointing to one of the massive double hatches.

'No Sir, we have to use the cranes to open them and I cannot use them when we are at sea.'

Des knew when he was being deceived. 'Yes but you have safety inspection hatches don't you?'

The Captain shrugged. 'Of course Sir, follow me.'

It took another hour and it was just starting to get dark by the time they had finished. The ship had four massive holds and each one was full of grain. It could be seen through the small hatches set into the massive doors that covered each hold. Des checked every one feeling more and more frustrated as he did so.

Finally, they stopped and he turned to the Captain who had faithfully followed him around during the inspection. 'Thank you Sir we will not detain you any longer. You have been most helpful.'

Just for a second, Des saw what looked like a gleam of triumph in the man's eyes that didn't fit with his manner but there again why shouldn't he be pleased? One thing was certain there was no hidden missile or the people necessary to fire it in the ship and no reason for Des to detain them any longer. As they returned to Prometheus in the RIB he continued to puzzle over what they had or in this case had not discovered. Something was wrong but what?

Chapter 37

The Irinda was already underway by the time Des made it back on to the bridge along with the rest of his team. He could hear the thump, thump of her propeller as it started to slowly accelerate the big ship back up to speed. Jon looked at them all.

'Nothing? For fuck's sake nothing? You're absolutely sure?'

Des answered for them. 'We searched the whole bloody ship Sir from stem to stern. There were crew around but hardly enough to run the ship let alone man and launch a weapon. The only space for the missile and the launcher itself was on deck and there was nothing there and no sign that anything had been there. All the holds were completely full of grain. I checked each one individually. I even stuck my arm in, it was just grain.'

'Sorry Sir, I agree with the First Lieutenant.' Warrant Officer McCaul offered. 'There was something odd about the ship which I can't put my finger on but the story about contraband with the Iranians was probably what it was. The skipper was definitely a shifty character. I'm sorry, I feel that I might have started off this wild goose chase when I saw her last night.'

'Good God, was it only last night?' Jon exclaimed. 'It seems like weeks ago. Well thank you gentlemen for a job well done. WEO tells me he should have some comms up soon, so we can report this whole sorry mess back to Fleet. Meanwhile, we can keep the MEO happy and creep back to Jebel nice and slowly or wherever they tell us to go with our tail between our legs. I wonder where that bloody missile and launcher is though. It's got to be somewhere.'

A voice broke in on his thoughts. Midshipman Rogers was the Second Officer of the Watch and one of the ship's officers under training. As such it went against all his instincts to interrupt his Captain. However, he had just seen something and it wouldn't wait.

'Sir, sorry Sir but I used to be in the Merchant Navy and if that ship has full holds then it's not with wheat.'

Jon turned sharply to the young man. 'What do you mean Mid?'

'Well Sir, she's designed to carry grain and her displacement would be fully taken up if her holds were completely full. She's heavy but we can still just see the top of her propeller and the loading marks on her stern are about five feet above the waterline.

So her holds can't be full. I would estimate that she's no more than seventy five per cent loaded.'

'But I checked them all Mid.' The First Lieutenant said indignantly. 'Are you questioning my judgement?'

'No Sir, of course not but we can all see she's not as deeply laden as she should be.'

Before Des could respond further Jon interjected with a note of excitement in his voice. 'Des, the lad's right. Everyone hold on a second. Ops room, this is the bridge, how fast is the Irinda going now?'

After a brief pause the answer came back. 'Almost twenty knots Sir.'

'What? Brian, I thought you said she was only capable of eighteen.'

'That's fully laden Sir, in ballast or partially loaded she could go much faster.'

There was silence for a few seconds and then Jon reacted. 'Officer of the Watch, maximum revolutions please and get after her.'

'Aye, Aye Sir.'

The atmosphere on the bridge which had been despondent minutes ago was suddenly highly charged.

'Well done Mister Rogers you saw what we all missed. Des, I'm sorry but they must have something hidden under that grain. Could they have made a false floor in one of the holds do you think?'

Des looked stricken. 'I guess so Sir, why the bloody hell didn't I think of that?'

'Why would you? Look, don't beat yourself up over it. None of us saw what was staring us in the face. It's not as if she looks completely empty after all. Now let's go and sort out the bastard properly. Brian and Des down to the Ops room please, Mister McCaul take your guys down aft and get ready. I think you might just get to use your weapons at last.'

As the bridge cleared, Jon made another broadcast to the ship's company telling them what was going on before picking up the microphone for the VHF. To no one's surprise, there was no reply from the Irinda.

'How long before she gets into Iraqi waters?' Jon asked the Ops room.

Brian came on the intercom. 'She'll be there in about ten minutes Sir and so will we. We're catching her but not that fast.'

'Roger, at this stage of the game I'm going to ignore any imaginary line in the sea.'

He was interrupted by the Officer of the Watch. 'Sir look, something's happening.'

As Jon took up his binoculars he could see the Irinda silhouetted against the setting sun. For a moment he thought she was on fire. A large cloud of smoke seemed to be streaming from her on both sides. Then he realised what he was seeing.

'She's ditching grain from her holds somehow. We were right. Ops room are we far enough away to engage with Exocet?'

'No Sir we're only two miles away. Why what's going on?'

Jon briefly explained and also realised as he spoke, that he would need more evidence than just a cloud of wheat to justify sinking a merchant ship.

'Let's get alongside her but not too close. With those high sides, we won't be able to see what's happening on deck. Half a mile please Officer of the Watch.'

As they got closer they could see activity on her decks. It seemed that two sets of hold doors had been opened despite their Captain saying it couldn't be done at sea. One set of doors near the bow and the other close to the rear superstructure could be clearly seen lying open on the deck. However, because of the respective heights of the two ships it was almost impossible to see what was happening inside the holds.

Jon made one final attempt to talk to the Irinda on the radio. 'Motor Vessel Irinda, this is Warship Prometheus, you are ordered to stop and cease all activity on your decks. Failure to comply will result in me firing upon you.' He repeated the message but there was no response. He wasn't surprised.

'We're now in Iraqi territorial waters Sir.' The Ops room reported.

'Sir, they're doing something up forward on Irinda's deck.' The Officer of the Watch reported in an urgent tone. 'Shit they've got some sort of gun.'

Jon snatched up his binoculars just as there was a flash of orange light from the foredeck of the ship. Suddenly there was a rumbling whistling noise and a gout of white water erupted only ten feet in front of Prometheus's bows.

'I have the ship,' Jon ordered. 'Quartermaster, starboard twenty five, stop starboard engine.'

The Quartermaster repeated the order and the ship started to heel hard as she turned towards the Irinda.

'Ops room, this is the Captain I am turning towards the Irinda. I want the Sea Wolf Controller to tell me when he has her visible. Target the bow area please.' That gun was his first priority now.

'Ops room Aye Sir.'

'Quartermaster, ease your wheel to ten, slow ahead both engines. Steer three five six.'

'Bridge this is the Ops room, target acquired, come left three degrees on three five three.'

Jon realised that the Quartermaster had made the adjustment without having to be told. 'Engage when ready,' he ordered.

In the Ops room the Sea Wolf Controller had the cross hairs of the Sea Wolf television picture steady on the bows of the Irinda. He couldn't alter the tracker system in azimuth as it was jammed but he could change the elevation. As soon as he was ready, he lifted the command override that was stopping the system firing. The speed gate that would not allow the missile to fire at targets below a certain speed had been set to zero. It immediately assessed the target as a threat and fired.

On the bridge, there was a loud bang and streak of flame from the launcher just ahead of the Exocets as the missile motor fired and accelerated it to more than twice the speed of sound in seconds.

At almost the same time the gun on the foredeck of the Irinda fired again. The sudden turn of their target had confused the gunners for a second but as soon as she straightened up they reacquired the ship. Supersonic missile and supersonic shell screamed past each other in flight. On the Irinda, the Sea Wolf slammed into the ship's side just below where the gun was sited. It only had a thirty pound warhead but was designed to produce maximum blast and fragmentation. The explosion was augmented by the shrapnel of the steel hull of the ship as it was blasted apart by the kinetic energy of the disintegrating weapon. The crew of the One Hundred and Five millimetre gun that had been hidden in the forward hold didn't stand a chance. Bodies were shredded, torn apart in the blast and the gun itself hurled off its improvised mounting.

Prometheus fared marginally better. The shell hit the break water on the ship's bows just forward of the Sea Wolf launcher and exploded there. It blew a hole downwards into the ship. Luckily there was no one in the NAAFI canteen at the time as most of it was obliterated. Shards of metal sprayed the Sea Wolf Launcher and the blast flung it around to end up leaning drunkenly to port. Somehow the Exocets survived.

On the bridge, the bang of the missile firing was almost immediately followed by the explosion of the shell arriving. There was a blinding flash and one of the bridge windows on the port that had been previously damaged blew in. Shards of armoured glass sprayed around the bridge. The Officer of the Watch staggered and fell to his knees. The Quartermaster gave a muttered curse and fell backwards off his seat. The Midshipman saw what had happened and ran to help. Seeing that the man didn't appear badly hurt he grabbed the steering yoke and looked to the Captain.

Jon was still shaking off the effects of the blast. He could see that the front of the ship was a mess and that his Sea Wolf wouldn't be firing again but he could also see that the damage wasn't critical. Looking at the Irinda, he could see flames starting to appear around the bow area and what looked like the barrel of the gun pointing skywards.

'Ops this is the bridge, we've taken out their gun but taken a hit of our own on the foredeck. I need a first aid party to the bridge now, the Wolf launcher is beyond repair. Get damage control parties up forward and let's prepare to sink the bastard.'

The Ops room acknowledged and Jon turned to the Midshipman on the helm. 'Port twenty five, make your heading due west, both engines half ahead, revolutions for twenty knots.'

The Mid repeated the order and the ship heeled to starboard, as she accelerated on to her new course. Just then the first aid party arrived. Jon pointed to the two casualties and then turned to concentrate on his quarry. As he looked at her his blood ran cold. Clearly coming into view above the side of rear most hold was the nose of the missile.

The ship steadied up on her new heading alongside the Irinda who was now about a quarter of a mile away. 'Ops room, when will you be ready to fire?' Jon asked while keeping his eyes on the missile as it was clearly being slowly raised into its firing position.

'Stand by. Ready at your order Sir,'

'You have a good sonar bearing?'

'Couldn't be clearer Sir,'

'Fire.'

Jon rushed out to the starboard bridge wing and looked aft. He knew he wouldn't hear anything as the first of three Stingray torpedoes left its launcher down by the hangar. The torpedoes were designed to sink tough Soviet submarines. Unlike their predecessor, the aged American Mark 46, which had a habit of attacking the sea surface if set to run too shallow, the Stingray suffered from no such problems. The torpedoes had therefore been set to run shallow and go out on a search bearing given to them by the ship's sonar. Having seen the first out of the launcher he went back into the bridge and grabbed his binoculars. Unlike wartime films there were no tracks to be seen on the surface but with such a short distance separating the two ships he knew it wouldn't take long at all.

The first explosion was evidenced by a blast of water near the middle of the ship. The torpedo was designed to go for the centre of any sonar echo and that's what all three did, one after the other in quick succession. Their one hundred pound warheads were tiny compared to the massive ones found in a submarine launched torpedo. It was enough to sink a submarine surrounded by crushing pressure of the sea. Jon was praying that three of them would be enough to damage a large merchantman.

'Bridge this is Ops, sonar reports three warhead explosions,' Brian's voice reported.

'This is the Captain, three explosions seen but not a lot else seems to be happening I'm afraid. We can't wait to see what the effect will be that's a very large ship. I want all upper deck guns manned and all small arms ready. We will now close and see if we can do anything about that fucking missile which they still seem hell bent on launching.' Jon could see that despite the explosions of the torpedoes, the missile was now fully raised. He had no idea how long it would take before it was ready to launch and if he had his way they wouldn't be given the opportunity to try.

He turned to the Midshipman, 'come to starboard ten degrees and ease us in closer. She seems to be slowing, so reduce revs to keep us alongside where we are now.'

'Aye, Aye Sir.'

Jon was just about to order all his upper deck guns to fire when the Irinda pre-empted him. Several faces appeared along the side of the ship and the barrels of various weapons could be seen. He suddenly saw several large flashes and then explosions in the water short of the ship.

'Silly bastards are firing RPG's they should have waited. We're too far away. Ops this is the Captain, open fire please. Everything we've got, only one target, the missile.'

The deep chatter of the two starboard side twenty millimetre guns was joined by a cacophony of small arms. The General Purpose Machine Guns were firing tracer and Jon could watch the arc of the bullets as they flew over the scuppers of the Irinda. Jon also realised that they were taking return fire.

What he didn't know was what was happening under water. The three Stingrays had impacted close enough to each other that they had created one single hole in the side of the Irinda. The hole was letting sea water into the hold behind it. Right into a hold that was still full of wheat, which was busily absorbing it and swelling fast. The internal pressure of the expanding cereal grains was enormous and suddenly the weakened side of the ship could take no more. A split started to propagate through the thin skin of the ship. It travelled up from the original hole but also downwards towards the keel. Suddenly, the residual strength of the hull was no longer enough to contain the forces exerted on it by the speed of the ship through the water and continuing pressure from within the hold. The ship literally burst apart. She was still travelling at over twelve knots and that was enough to complete the job.

All weapon fire from the Irinda stopped as the forward half broke at right angles to the rest of the ship and the stern section heeled dangerously towards the Prometheus. Jon could see bodies being thrown into the water. More importantly, as the ship heeled, the whole missile could be seen at last. No one waited and it was peppered with small arms fire. Immediately, one of the Oerlikons found its target and a line of small explosions marched down its body until they reached its rear.

Jon could see what was about to happen. 'Take cover,' he yelled into the main broadcast and then flung himself to the deck waiting for the inevitable explosion as the rocket motor ignited. Nothing happened but all the firing stopped. He waited for what seemed like an age and then carefully lifted his head to look out. He was just in time to see the missile fall from its launcher and over the side of the ship which was now heeling at well over sixty degrees. The rear of the weapon was burning, fire jetting out of a series of holes but that was all. It hit the water in a massive hissing splash and disappeared under the waves. The fires, which needed no oxygen, continued to illuminate its plunge to the bottom. The remains of the ship continued to capsize on top and then with her propeller pointing skywards the whole carcass disappeared under the sea.

'Ops this is the bridge, make damned sure we have an accurate position logged. Cease fire all guns, standby to pick up survivors.'

Epilogue

'Let me get this straight Jon. You used chaff rockets to stop a Bog Hammer attack and almost certainly saved an American Aegis Destroyer into the bargain, having just survived an Exocet attack yourself.'

'Well, my helicopter got four of them.'

SNOME continued as though Jon hadn't interrupted. 'You took out an enemy gun with a partially damaged anti-aircraft missile system. You sank a bloody great big enemy merchantman with anti-submarine torpedoes and finally you destroyed a nuclear tipped ballistic missile with a load of rifles and twenty mill cannon?'

'No Sir I didn't do any of those things. HMS Prometheus did them.' Jon said with pride in his voice and stared back challengingly at the Captain. They were sitting in his cabin with Prometheus safely back alongside in Jebel Ali. A police cordon was keeping any curious onlookers from examining the battered state of the ship.

'All I can say is that I'm amazed you're even afloat. You realise that we knew what you were up to after the Iranian Frigate attacked you?'

'I sort of got an inkling when the American F14 came to our rescue Sir. Look, tell me, are we in the shit over this? I don't care about myself but the ship's company did an outstanding job. If there's any flack it should stop with me.'

SNOME chuckled. 'Don't you worry about that. We tried to talk to you but the Sacagawea managed to get some comms back and let their command and Fleet know what you intended to do. There was no one else in a position to intercept the Irinda and we couldn't have stopped you anyway. Funny how quickly you got your comms back afterwards though.' SNOME raised an eyebrow.

Keeping his expression deadpan Jon replied. 'Yes our WEO had almost lashed something up when we caught up with Irinda but obviously we were then a little busy for a while.'

'And it had nothing to do with the worry that some poxy politician would have told you to back off in case you infringed the health and safety of the crew of Irinda? The original crew, by the way, have been found unharmed in a ship's boat kindly lent to them by the Iranians it would seem.'

'I couldn't possibly comment on that Sir. I simply did my duty as I saw it.'

'And I'm pretty sure just everyone agrees with that assessment. Now look, your actions against the Frigate and Bog Hammers goes on public record and no doubt you and your ship's company will get the recognition you deserve. However, the incident with Irinda never happened. An American recovery ship is already on its way to try to find the warhead which is hopefully still intact. The story that's been put around is that they had a fire on board and the crew abandoned ship. As she was carrying grain, an explosion is possible especially if one hold was empty, grain dust is very explosive as you probably know. In private, the Iranian government have already apologised, they blame a radical faction who have, as they put it, been dealt with. I don't suspect we'll ever get to know the truth. But that's it. No one is going to take it further.'

'And what do I tell the families of my seven dead crewmen Sir? Sorry, it was all a mistake. The Iranians are really sorry they've murdered your husbands, your fathers, your sons?'

SNOME looked grim. 'That's exactly what you say or do you want the world to know what really happened? Can you imagine what the repercussions would be with Israel and the rest of the region? It would be almost as bad as if they had actually fired the bloody thing. Not only that but what would India think if she found out that their nuclear neighbour was dishing out warheads to their unstable friends?'

Jon sighed and lay back in his chair. He knew SNOME was right but that didn't make the taste in his mouth any less bitter. At least he would be able to acknowledge most of his men's contribution publicly.

'And what happens now Sir?'

'You go home. Patch yourselves up here and go home. The two other ships arrive in three days time and I don't expect any trouble from Iran for a while.'

'Then if you'll excuse me Sir, I have seven letters to write and then I'm going to see how far down a bottle of scotch I can get before I fall asleep.'

A week later HMS Prometheus slipped from the jetty in Jebel Ali to make her way home. Most of her system repairs would have to wait until they reached Devonport but a large metal patch now adorned her port side. A few miles out of harbour she was ambushed by a Type 42 Destroyer and a Type 22 Frigate. The ships closed in on either side at high speed and much to Jon's embarrassment lined the sides of their ships with sailors and gave three cheers to him and his surprised crew.

The rest of the journey back was uneventful, even the Straits of Hormuz were quiet. Jon gave his men as much time off as possible. Unlike the trip out, the First Lieutenant didn't ask them to go to Action Stations even once. Through Suez and the Mediterranean, they briefly called into Gibraltar for fuel and then up the coast of Portugal and Spain. As they transited northwards, they were all amazed to hear the announcement on the BBC World Service. Not only had the Poles recently kicked out their communist government but the East German people had simply defied their government and crossed the Berlin Wall, which, even as the announcer was speaking, was being smashed to pieces by the mobs. What was even more surprising was that Russia was sitting and watching it all happen with the stated policy of not interfering. No one was sure what to make of it but despite the ramifications, most of the crew were still really only looking forward to one thing. Going home.

Biscay was gentle on them and then it was around Ushant with Plymouth ahead. They had been asked to ensure their ETA was mid-afternoon and had adjusted their speed accordingly. It was quite a surprise when small boats started to appear when they were several miles out. First a couple of large motor boats, then yachts and even small fishing boats. Everyone in them was smiling and waving including the crew of a small helicopter with a cameraman in the door.

Jon was standing on the bridge conning the ship in past the breakwater and trying to avoid sinking some yacht or other when Brian came up to his side. 'Remember when we were on this ship and returned here in eighty two Sir?'

'How could I forget,' Jon replied. 'It looks like we're going to get the same sort of reception this time.'

Suddenly, there was a loud roar and a grey and red Sea King shot past. Jon caught a glimpse of blonde hair sticking out of a flying helmet in the cockpit window and someone waving. A lump came into his throat. He didn't have time to ponder as yet another small boat seemed intent on getting under his bows and being sunk.

The ship made its way past Plymouth Hoe where more people had gathered to wave at them and then round the corner into the Hamoaze where they tied up at the dockyard wharf and Jon was at last able to ring down 'finished with main engines'. The jetty was packed with families all waving and cheering. Someone had even organised a Royal Marine band to play. He suddenly felt a great weight lift off his shoulders. They were home. He briefly wondered how many other naval ship's Captains had felt the same emotions in this piece of water. Putting the thought aside he made his way down to the flight deck. He would make sure all his men were reunited with their families and then maybe some time later he would be able to sneak away and see Helen.

The First Lieutenant had let the men down the gangway and all sorts of joyous reunions were taking place there. There was even a TV crew interviewing some of them. He wondered how long it would be before they collared him. He wasn't watching as a naval officer climbed up the gangway until he was grabbed in a hug and suddenly Helen's face was there. All thoughts of propriety went out of the window and he kissed her hard. He very briefly thought about all the new rules regarding men and women having contact on board ship before he completely forgot about them.

'Hang on a second. You just flew past me in a Sea King. How the bloody hell did you get here?'

'Oh that wasn't me. That was a big butch Australian who I fly with occasionally. I must tell him to stop wearing that wig.'

Bog Hammer

Author's Notes

So once again let me attempt to explain what is fact and what I blatantly made up to produce what I hope is a good story.

You probably won't be surprised to know that Helen's flying training is a direct crib of my own experiences. I still remember sneaking out with my wife one Sunday before my survival course to hide some food at King's Hat enclosure in the New Forest. Then the terrible fear that I couldn't find the stuff three weeks later – I did and then had the problem of scoffing it with my partner in crime before the rest of the course rumbled us and wanted some. Many years later in my last job in the navy as a Commander on the Fleet Air Arm Admiral's staff it was my job to set policy for this course and no, I never owned up.

I had exactly the same problem Helen had trying to land the Bulldog but in my case, even less of an excuse as I already had a private pilot's licence and over three hundred hours on three types of aircraft. However, as in her case a change of instructor was all that was needed.

When my course left RAF Leeming we did perform 'morning colours' but I have to confess that it was another course who left the little present in the grass.

As for girls not being able to fly jets if they were too light – that is true and I assume that the seats were eventually modified to cope. That said many men have also been turned down for being too big so it's nice to see some equality.......

Helen's desire not to be stuck in the Harrier loop echoes many others. A colleague of mine who went to fly Harriers after his first front line helicopter tour deserted to the RAF once he looked at what he was likely to do for the rest of his career. Lucky chap, he was one of the last pilots to convert to the Lightning.

Helen's Search and Rescue stories are partly based on some of my own. I distinctly remember asking what to do if a woman started to give birth in my aircraft. The answer was nothing – nature would take its course. There has been more than one occasion when this happened for real and to my knowledge at least one baby named after a member of the crew.

Bog Hammer

Flying low level from Looe Bar up to Culdrose happens. One year, my squadron were waiting on deck in HMS Bulwark in Mounts Bay. We had been in the States for several months and were very, very keen to get home. Unfortunately, although we were in the clear, the air station a hundred feet higher was fogged in and Commander (Air) had just made the decision to close the airfield for the day, when he heard the sound of eight Sea Kings hopping over the perimeter fence. I heard later that the CO got a bollocking but we all got home.

The Helicopter Machine Gun Pod makes its rightful appearance here. I pinched the idea for my book 'Sea Skimmer' but its real gestation was pretty much as I describe in this book. Its range was short but the theory was that if you are being shot at by a helicopter you probably won't be firing at other people.

Basic Operational Sea Training carried out by Flag Officer Sea Training, ie BOST by FOST goes on to this day and is bloody hard work. We must be fairly good at it though as many other NATO countries send their ships to us. The story about fanning the flames of a fire during DISTEX is exactly true and I did go up to sick bay and apologise to the girls afterwards. They saw the funny side. The story of the Russian submarine is also largely true. The reality was that we found him on the surface while doing a surface search in the Lynx. He was in the south western approaches alongside a support ship but didn't stay on the surface for much longer.

The Henry VIII wine cellar also makes an appearance in my book 'The Guadeloupe Guillotine' but it's probably even more appropriate here as when I worked in MOD we did indeed hold monthly aviators meeting there and have a small glass or seventeen afterwards. If you want to see it, just google it.

'Culture shock' is something most military experience when they have to stop playing with the toys and as I try to explain here some take to it like a duck to water, others hate it. One thing is certain the ambitious officer has plenty of opportunity for brown nosing.

The 'Batch Three' Sea Wolf Leanders were outstanding ships and very heavily armed for their size but their big weakness for general duties was the lack of a decent gun. Very much designed for the

Cold War, they were not so suitable for policing duties. The cover photograph for this book is actually HMS Andromeda my old ship when she was on Armilla patrol. All the weapons and sensors mentioned in the book can be seen. The six barrelled Sea Wolf launcher is just ahead of the 4 Exocet. Just behind the bridge roof is the 910 Sea Wolf tracker radar and on top of the forward mast the 967/968 radar scanner. She only had one Oerlikon on either side and these can just be seen on either side of the main mast. The STWS torpedo tubes are just out of sight at the rear, near the hangar.

One of the great debates when sea skimming missiles became a threat was how to counter them. A missile like Sea Wolf with a fragmentation warhead could intercept them far away and blow them safely to bits. However, there was the risk that the Sea Wolf would miss and then it would all be over. The counter argument was the 'blast lead down the bearing' concept and the Vulcan Phalanx and other systems use this principle. However, because they are much more range limited there is very much the risk of shredding the missile and still being clobbered by a cloud of potentially explosive shrapnel. Both these things happen in this book.

My ship Andromeda was the first of her class and so we got to fire quite a few Sea Wolfs (Wolves?) in proving trials. I remember being told that the missiles themselves were almost like self-powered shells from a gun in that the rocket motor only fired very briefly. Indeed when they went off it sounded very much like a gunshot hence the idea of firing one at a ship. I've no idea whether this could be done for real but don't see why not.

Chaff proved to be very successful at confusing missiles during the Falklands War. At one time we were issued with small cardboard containers of the stuff for use in the helicopter. The Observer would open his cockpit window and throw the packet out. If one burst open too early in the slipstream we were warned to be very careful as it was lethal stuff. It didn't take long for a proper external launcher to be fitted to the aircraft. However, it did give me the idea for Jon's 'secret weapon' but I've no idea if it would have really worked.

As we deployed to the Falklands War we were given the first warshot Stingray torpedoes and the weapon controller was the first to be fitted for actual use to my Lynx. The briefing on its use was surprisingly short. However, we did learn that one of the improvements the weapon had over the older Mark 46 torpedo was its ability to run very shallow. It could also be released a great deal further from the target. I distinctly remember being told not to drop one at its shallow setting if the QE2 or Canberra cruise ships were about as it could sink them. Hence Jon's use of them to sink the Irinda.

Bog Hammers or more rightly Boghammars were a real problem for everyone, military and civilian and posed a threat far in excess of their actual military capability. By the time Prometheus arrives in the Gulf, the Iran Iraq War is over but tensions were still high.

I really wonder what would have happened if the British who seemed to have arbitrarily carved up the region in 1922 had done a better job. Whatever criteria they used to set international boundaries seems to have largely ignored the needs of the poor people who lived there.

Rather like in the previous book in the series (Arapaho) I tried desperately to research the whole situation in the region and the reasons for it. Once again it was like trying knit fog. There were so many factions, political reversals and double dealing that I doubt two people could write the same history. One thing that was clear to me was, in my opinion, the unsavoury political machinations of the west and by that I primarily mean America although Britain and other western countries must take their share of the blame. The Iranian Shah was a despot but because he liked us and spent his oil money with us, we supported him. We didn't like the Ayatollahs, so suddenly when they arrived we immediately supported another bloody despot called Saddam Hussein. There is a strong body of thought that if we had stopped Saddam trying to capitalise on the internal turmoil in Iran by invading so soon after their revolution, then the Iranians themselves would have thrown the Ayatollahs out and a more moderate form of government would have appeared. Once the country united against the Iraqi threat that was never going to happen. And it's absolutely true that Iraq obtained the chemicals needed for chemical weapons from us, which he then used on thousands of Iranians and his own people. Funny isn't it that it was barely reported on at the time but got quite a lot of coverage when we suddenly decided we really didn't like Saddam? No maybe not.

The rest of the story is fiction. Although SCUDs were modified by the Iranians and the North Koreans, none of them would have had the range to reach Israel from southern Iraq. At least as far as I could discover.....................

Jon and Brian will sail again.

GLASNOST

Three days in 1991 that changed the world. Commander Jonathon Hunt has been appointed as Assistant Defence Attaché to the British Embassy in Moscow just as President Gorbachev's reforms are causing a constitutional crisis. That summer, a coup while Gorbachev is on holiday, nearly destabilises the whole world. Jon, together with his colleague Rupert Thomas from MI6 are caught up in a race against time to help end the Cold War forever.

Printed in Great Britain
by Amazon